a&b

The Silver Locomotive Mystery

EDWARD MARSTON

Allison & Busby Limited
13 Charlotte Mews
London W1T 4EJ
www.allisonandbusby.com

A CIP catalogue record for this book is available from
the British Library.

Hardcover published in Great Britain in 2009.
Paperback first published in 2010 (978-0-7490-0778-2).
Reissued in 2011.

10 9 8 7 6 5 4 3 2 1

ISBN 978-0-7490-1034-8

Typeset in Sabon by
Allison & Busby Ltd.

Printed and bound in the UK by
CPI Bookmarque, Croydon, CR0 4TD

EDWARD MARSTON was born and brought up in South Wales. A full-time writer for over thirty years, he has worked in radio, film, television and the theatre and is a former chairman of the Crime Writers' Association. Prolific and highly successful, he is equally at home writing children's books or literary criticism, plays or biographies. *The Silver Locomotive Mystery* is the sixth book in the series featuring Inspector Robert Colbeck and Sergeant Victor Leeming, set in the 1850s.

www.edwardmarston.com

To the people of Cardiff

in the hope that they will forgive any liberties I've taken with their history. Jeremiah Box Stockdale and Wlaetislaw Spiridion lived in Cardiff in 1855 but the events related here are entirely fictitious.

CHAPTER ONE

1855

Nigel Buckmaster knew how to make an entrance. When he swept into the bustling concourse at Paddington Station, the crowd parted before him as for royalty. Those close to the actor-manager gaped and gasped as he strode past. Those farther away craned their necks to see what all the fuss was about. Tall, lean and lithe, Buckmaster wore a black cloak that swished behind him and a wide-brimmed black felt hat out of which long, lustrous, dark locks fell to his shoulders. His face was striking rather than handsome, his most significant features being a pointed chin and two large, smouldering eyes separated by a narrow, tapering nose. It was the face both of a hero and a villain, combining bravado with menace in identical proportions and exuding a sense of unassailable purpose.

Contributing in equal part to their dramatic arrival was the stately leading lady whom Buckmaster led on his arm.

Kate Linnane was approaching thirty but she still had the stunning bloom and beauty of a much younger woman, features glowing, eyes dancing, delicate chin uplifted with regal disdain. Blond curls peeped out from a poke bonnet trimmed with ostrich feathers. Her light blue waistcoat was in subtle contrast to the exquisitely tailored navy jacket. Hidden beneath a decorated navy skirt that ballooned outwards, her feet tripped along so gracefully that she appeared to be gliding in unison with the majestic gait of her companion. Opened the previous year, the London terminus of the Great Western Railway was a spectacular cathedral of wrought iron and glass where thousands of passengers came to worship daily at the altar of steam. Nigel Buckmaster and Kate Linnane had momentarily transformed it into a vast apron stage on which they could perform before an open-mouthed audience.

As befitted such a splendid couple, there was a sizeable retinue in their wake. Where they led, other members of the troupe followed. First was a group of strutting, long-haired actors of varying ages along with some pretty, perfumed, gesticulating young actresses, eager to grab their share of attention. Behind these preening peacocks was a motley stage crew, noticeably less well-dressed and marked by an air of collective resignation. The cavalcade was completed by a line of porters wheeling well-worn trunks on their rumbling trolleys or carrying costume baskets, scenery and stage properties on their rattling carts. Buckmaster's Players were on the move. They surged on to the platform as if commandeering the whole train. A strict order of precedence was observed. While the two luminaries headed for a first class carriage, the other artistes had to travel second class and the remainder of the company was forced to supervise the loading of the luggage and the theatrical paraphernalia before being received into the comfortless embrace of third class.

Buckmaster opened a carriage door with a flourish so that Kitty could step into the compartment. When he climbed in after her, he shut the door, flung off his hat, whisked off his cloak and sat with his back to the engine. Kate lowered herself on to the seat opposite him. Now that there were no spectators to impress, she let her features rearrange themselves into an expression of sheer boredom.

'I hate all this travelling, Nigel,' she said, peevishly.

'Needs must when the devil drives,' he told her. 'If the mountain will not come to Mahomet, then Mahomet must go to the mountain.'

'Why can we not play at Drury Lane or Covent Garden?'

'Because they don't yet deserve us, my love,' he said with a grandiloquent gesture. 'Until they do, we must seek pastures new.'

Kate sighed. 'But why on earth must we do so in *Wales*?' she complained, bitterly. 'It's like being cast into outer darkness.'

Twenty minutes later, just before the train was due to depart, two figures suddenly appeared outside their carriage. Kate was annoyed that their privacy was about to be invaded but Buckmaster took an interest in the touching little scene that was being played out only feet away from him. Though he could hear no words, he found the mime eloquent. A short, whiskery old man with rounded shoulders was giving a set of instructions to the passenger, peering over his glasses and wagging his finger repeatedly. Still in his twenties, his companion had a fresh-faced, boyish look to him, nodding dutifully in obedience and releasing an occasional affectionate smile. He was carrying a large bag, its heavy weight making him shift it from one hand to the other. Judging from his apparel, his bowler hat and the worried glances the young man threw at the train, Buckmaster surmised that he was not a regular traveller in first class. Indeed, when he eventually opened the door, he looked around warily as if unsure if he was entitled to climb aboard.

'Come in, come in, my friend,' said Buckmaster, beckoning him forward. 'We are delighted to have some company.'

Resenting the newcomer, Kate hid her irritation behind a dazzling smile. He gave them both a nod of gratitude then stepped between them and sat by the window on the opposite side of the compartment. Buckmaster pulled the door shut and nodded to the man on the platform. Within a minute, a whistle sounded and the locomotive exploded into life. As the train moved forward, the young man gave a farewell wave to his erstwhile escort. Mouthing some last advice and with one hand holding his top hat in place, the old man scurried solicitously alongside the carriage until he ran out of breath and platform. Buckmaster was intrigued.

'You are a regular Laertes, my friend,' he observed.

The newcomer blinked. 'I beg your pardon, sir.'

'You are clearly not familiar with the greatest play ever written. I refer, of course, to William Shakespeare's *Hamlet*,

12

a role in which I have garnered endless plaudits. In earlier days, however, when I was a juvenile in the company, I often took the role of Laertes and received wise counsel from my father, Polonius, in much the same way as you took advice from your own revered parent just now.'

'Mr Voke is not my father, sir.'

Buckmaster was surprised. 'Really? Did my eyes deceive me?'

'It's true that he has been like a father to me in some ways,' said the other, nervously, 'especially since his own son deserted the business, but we are in no way related. Mr Voke is my employer.'

'Ah, I see. And what form does that employment take?'

'We are silversmiths.'

It took a long time to draw him out. Hugh Kellow had clearly never met any Thespians before. Arresting upon any stage, Buckmaster and Kate were positively overwhelming in the smaller confines of a railway carriage, albeit one on the broader gauge of just over seven feet. The silversmith was uneasy and tongue-tied at first. He sat in the corner with an arm looped protectively around his bag. They slowly won his confidence, eliciting his name and destination from him. It was almost half an hour before he had the courage to look Kate full in the face. Buckmaster resorted to flattery.

'You have never trod the boards, I take it?' he began.

'No, sir,' replied Kellow, modestly. 'I've been to a few Penny Gaffs in London but that is all.'

Kate snorted. 'Contemptible places!'

'They provide a service, my love,' said Buckmaster,

tolerantly. 'What they can never do, of course, is to reach the heights to which we soar. While they offer base amusement for the uneducated, we deal in true art, profound drama that can reach into the very soul of those privileged to watch.' He studied Kellow. 'Unless I am mistaken, you could have the makings of a fine actor.

'Not me, sir,' protested the silversmith. 'I lack any talent.'

'You have a good voice and a handsome face, two necessary attributes of any actor. If you can master the craft of a silversmith, you obviously have the dedication needed to train for the stage.' He looked across at Kate. 'Do you not agree?'

'I was struck by his appearance the moment I set eyes on him,' she said, taking her cue. 'You have *presence*, Mr Kellow, and that is the most important quality of all. Vocal tricks and histrionic gestures can be taught but stage presence is a natural gift. Come now, there must have been times when you felt the urge to perform in public.'

'Never, Miss Linnane,' said Kellow with a self-effacing laugh. 'The truth of it is I'm rather a timid fellow.'

'Timidity is something that can easily be shed.'

'Kate is right,' added Buckmaster, taking a silver case from his pocket and extracting a card. 'Here – take this. If ever you change your mind, there will always be a place for you in my company.' Kellow took the gold-edged card and inspected it. 'You would have to start at the bottom, you understand, with small parts and meagre rewards but think what glories might lie ahead – Hugh Kellow in *Hamlet*!'

The silversmith shrugged. 'I think I will stick to my trade, sir.'

'Keep my card and come to see us perform in Cardiff.'

'Oh, I am not staying in the town, sir.'

'No?'

'I simply have to make a delivery,' said Kellow, slipping the card into his pocket, 'then I catch a return train to London. On that journey, I fear, I will not have such distinguished company in first class. Mr Voke bought me a second class ticket.'

'I fancy that I see why,' said Kate, who had been watching the way his arm never left the bag. 'You must be carrying something of great value if you would not let your luggage be stowed on top of the carriage. May we ask what it is?'

Kellow bit his lip before speaking. 'It's a locomotive,' he said. 'To be more exact, it's a silver coffee pot in the shape of a locomotive.'

'How singular!' cried Buckmaster. 'Pray, let us see it.'

'Mr Voke forbade me to show it to anyone, sir.'

'But we are not anyone, Mr Kellow – we are friends.'

'Trusted friends, I hope,' said Kate, her appetite whetted. 'What harm is there in letting us have a peep at it? We are very discreet and it is not as if your employer will ever know.'

Hugh Kellow wrestled with his conscience for several minutes, unwilling to open the bag yet not wishing to let them down. He did not wish to spend the rest of a long journey in a strained atmosphere. They had offered him friendship and he needed to respond.

'Very well,' he said, capitulating. 'But you must promise not to touch it.' The others nodded their consent. Kellow undid the straps on the bag and took out an object that was wrapped in muslin. He drew back the folds of the material.

'Here it is – a replica of the Firefly class of 1840, exact in every particular.'

Buckmaster and Kate were astounded. What they were looking at was nothing less than a miniature masterpiece, a scale model that was well over a foot long and that had the substance and sheen of high quality silver. The boiler was fitted to a tall, domed, gleaming firebox. Either side of the two large driving wheels were much smaller carrying wheels. While Buckmaster whistled in amazement, Kate's eyes widened covetously. Kellow was pleased at their reaction.

'The framing has been simplified a little,' he explained, 'and we added some boiler mountings. As for this little embellishment,' he went on, indicating a silver crown at the top of the smokestack, 'it is not mere decoration. It has an important function.' He flicked the crown back on its hinge. 'It keeps the coffee warm before it is poured.'

'It's magnificent,' said Buckmaster. 'I've never seen such fine detail. It must have taken an age to make.'

'It did, sir. Mr Voke is a perfectionist. He worked for an eternity on this commission. He even sent me to Swindon to make some drawings of Firefly locomotives.'

Buckmaster's eye twinkled. 'Did you travel first class?'

'I had to make do with third class on that occasion,' admitted Kellow, sadly. 'Mr Voke is very careful with his money. Some call him mean – his son certainly did – but I think he's being sensible. He's taught me to manage my own income with similar caution.'

'I've never seen anything like it,' said Kate, feasting her eyes on the locomotive. 'Your employer has turned an ugly, dirty, noisy, iron contraption into a thing of real beauty. It

16

must be an honour to work for such a superb craftsman.'

'It is, indeed,' returned Kellow, gratefully, 'though the coffee pot is not entirely Mr Voke's handiwork. The truth of it is that his eyesight is not what it was so he asked me to take over some of the more intricate work such as the crown and the insignia on the side of the firebox. I was also responsible for the pistons and for the railings on either side of the footplate.' A note of pride intruded. 'It was because I was so involved in making it that Mr Voke gave me the honour of delivering it to its new owner.'

'And who is that?'

'Mrs Tomkins of Cardiff – her name is on the boiler plate.'

'I envy her!' said Kate with feeling. 'I *adore* silver. No, no,' she went on quickly as Kellow tried to cover the locomotive up again. 'Don't hide it away, I beseech you. Let me gloat!'

Amid clouds of smoke, sulphur and soot, the train roared into Cardiff General Station and slowed to a juddering halt. The passengers alighted and waited for their luggage to be unloaded from the roofs of the carriages. Larger items had travelled in the guard's van. Before he stepped on to the platform, Nigel Buckmaster put on his hat, cloak and imperious expression. He helped Kate Linnane to get out then he shook hands with Hugh Kellow. The silversmith was anxious to deliver the coffee pot but Kate was reluctant to let him go, clutching his arm with one hand while surreptitiously stroking his bag with the other. When he finally pulled away, she let out an involuntary cry of distress.

'What ails you, my love?' asked Buckmaster.

She watched Kellow until he was swallowed up by the crowd.

'It's that silver coffee pot,' she confessed, a palm to her breast. 'It's stolen my heart, Nigel – I'd *kill* to own it!'

The corpse lay on the bed, impervious to the breeze that blew in through the open window to rustle the curtains. When a fly came into the room, it described endless circles in the air before settling on the top of a large, open, empty leather bag.

CHAPTER TWO

'Why do we have to go to Cardiff?' asked Victor Leeming, grumpily.

'Because that's where the murder occurred,' said Colbeck.

'But Cardiff is in Wales.'

'You don't need to lecture me in geography, Victor. I know exactly where it is and how long it will take a train to get us there.'

'Far too long,' moaned Leeming.

'A change of air will do you good.'

'Don't they have their own police force?'

'We were expressly requested by the South Wales Railway.'

'You mean that *you* were, Inspector. Every railway company in the country is after your services. At the first sign of trouble, they send for Robert Colbeck, the Railway Detective.'

'A murder is rather more than a sign of trouble.'

'What exactly happened?'

'The telegraph gave us only the merest details,' said

Colbeck. 'A guest at the Railway Hotel was killed in his room. That's all we need to know at this stage. The summons had me reaching for my *Bradshaw* and that's why we're on our way to Paddington.'

Leeming grimaced. 'I detest boring train journeys.'

'That's a contradiction in terms. To a trained observer – such as a detective sergeant like you – no train journey should ever be boring. It's a delight to the eye and a continual stimulus to the brain. Travel broadens the mind, Victor.'

Leeming grunted mutinously. Colbeck knew why he was being so churlish. The sergeant was a married man with a wife and two children on whom he doted. He hated having to be absent from them at night and an investigation in Cardiff could well mean days away. As soon as the telegraph arrived at Scotland Yard, Colbeck had told Leeming to grab the valise he kept at the office in case of an assignment away from London. It contained a change of clothing. The two men were now ensconced in a cab as it rolled noisily towards the railway station over a cobbled street. They were, in appearance, an ill-assorted pair. Colbeck was tall, slim, debonair, impeccably dressed and with an almost flashy handsomeness while Leeming was stocky, of medium height, inelegant even in a frock coat and top hat, and with the startling ugliness of a fairground bruiser who has come off worst in a brawl. Yet his family loved him deeply and Colbeck admired him for his sterling qualities as a policeman. Leeming had the tenacity of a man who, once set on the right path, would never deviate from it until a case was solved.

Colbeck sought to cheer up his jaded companion.

'There are consolations,' he argued. 'For a start, we'll be out of reach of Superintendent Tallis for a while.'

'That's always a bonus,' agreed Leeming. 'He's been very liverish these past few weeks.'

'It's understandable – there have been far too many crimes and far too few convictions. The superintendent expects us to catch every single law-breaker and put him or her behind bars. We both know that it's an impossible demand.'

'If he wants us patrolling the streets of London, why is he letting us charge off across the Welsh border?'

'I think that vanity comes into it, Victor,' decided Colbeck. 'The fact that we've been sought by name indicates that the reputation of the Detective Department has spread far and wide. That feeds his self-importance. In that uninhabitable waste land known as his heart, I fancy that he rather likes the notion of despatching his men to solve crimes in different parts of the country – as long as we are quick about it, naturally.'

'It can't be quick enough for me this time.'

'There's no call for alarm. Estelle and the children will survive without you for a night or two.'

'That's not what irks me, Inspector,' confided Leeming. 'My worry is that I won't be able to survive without *them*.'

The brisk clip-clop of the horse changed to a slow tap-tap of hooves as the driver pulled on the reins. The cab soon stopped and the two men got out. Colbeck paid the fare then led his companion into the maelstrom that was Paddington Station on a busy afternoon. Over the tumult, he called out to Leeming.

'Then there's the other consolation, Victor.'

'Is there, sir?'

'When we get to Cardiff, we'll meet an old friend.'

'Oh – and who might that be?'

'Jeremiah Stockdale.'

Leeming brightened instantly. 'Now that *is* a consolation.'

And for the first time in his life, he stepped into a railway carriage with something resembling a smile on his face.

Archelaus Pugh had many virtues but he was not a man for a crisis. As the manager of the Railway Hotel in Cardiff, he was unfailingly efficient. Faced with everyday problems – awkward guests, mistakes over reservations, indolence among his staff – he was calm, patient and decisive. Confronted with a dead body in one of his rooms, however, Pugh swiftly deteriorated. Sweat broke out on his corrugated brow, his eyes darted uncontrollably and his clothing was suddenly too tight for him. He was a short, neat man in his forties with a crisp and authoritative voice that had now become a baleful croak.

'You can't leave him there, Superintendent,' he wailed.

'I can do and I will do, Mr Pugh,' said Jeremiah Stockdale.

'Think what it looks like. If a policeman stands outside that room all day, it will frighten my other guests.'

'It's more likely to reassure them, sir. And it also prevents any of them from stumbling into the room by mistake. Think how horrified they'd be if that happened.'

Pugh tried to assert himself. 'I have a hotel to run.'

'And I have a crime to solve,' retorted Stockdale, looming over him. 'That takes precedence over everything.'

'Can't you at least move the corpse out of here?'

'No, Mr Pugh.'

'Why ever not – it's the most dreadful advertisement for us.'

'My sympathies are with the victim. He stays where he is until Inspector Colbeck arrives from London. I want him to see exactly what we found when we went into that room.'

Stockdale was adamant. He was a big, brawny, bluff individual in his forties with a thick, dark moustache and a fringe beard. English by birth, he had had a brief military career as a mercenary in Spain before being invalided home. Recovering from his wounds, he had joined the recently formed Metropolitan Police Force. As a result of the training and experience acquired on the dangerous streets of London, he had secured, when only twenty-four, the post of Superintendent of the Cardiff Borough Police. That made him, in effect, the town's Chief Constable. For almost two decades, he had been a very successful law-enforcement officer in spite of an inadequate budget, limited manpower and the constant criticism of the Watch Committee.

It was pointless to argue with Jeremiah Box Stockdale. He was his own man. He did not suffer fools gladly or bend to the wishes of panic-stricken hotel managers. Archelaus Pugh could bleat at him all day but it was a futile exercise. The corpse would stay where it was and the policeman would remain on guard.

They were in the foyer of the hotel and guests who went past viewed the superintendent with a curiosity liberally tinged with fear. The imposing figure was dressed in a uniform of his own devising – a dark blue tunic and trousers trimmed with red cord, a peaked cap and a sword belt from his army days. Pugh was invisible beside him.

'When will the inspector get here?' asked the manager.

'I'm sure that he will have caught the first available train,' said Stockdale, 'and I'm equally sure that he'll be bringing Sergeant Leeming with him. You should be grateful to have two men of their ability coming here, Mr Pugh.'

'The only time I'll feel the slightest impulse of gratitude is when they carry that dead body out of here and remove the stain of murder.'

'Don't you *want* this crime solved?'

'Of course, I do, but my concern is for the other guests.'

'Suspicion comes before concern,' said the policeman, darkly. 'Did it never occur to you that the killer is likely to be someone who is staying under this roof?' Pugh gulped and took an involuntary step backwards. 'He might be going about his business as if nothing had ever happened. In other words, Mr Pugh, somewhere among those guests about whom you are so concerned may be the self-same villain who committed this foul crime.'

Pugh was aghast. 'The killer is still *here*?'

'It's something I am bound to consider.'

Leaving the manager to digest this devastating possibility, Stockdale broke away from him and marched over to welcome the two men who were coming in through the door. Colbeck and Leeming had walked the short distance from the railway station. They were pleased to see their old friend. There was an exchange of greetings and warm handshakes. The mutual respect between the three men was evident. Stockdale introduced them to the manager but Pugh was less than impressed. Expecting policemen in uniform, he was instead looking at what he perceived as a dandy and a pugilist.

'When will you move the body, Inspector?' demanded Pugh.

'When it is time to do so,' snapped Stockdale, quelling him with a glare. 'Meanwhile, I suggest that you move your own body out of the way so that we can go upstairs. I'm sure that Inspector Colbeck will want to speak to you later.'

'I will, indeed, sir,' said Colbeck, turning politely to Pugh. 'I'm sorry for the disruption this must have caused. I can understand your anxiety. It's possible that Sergeant Leeming and I may have to stay in the town for a while. I take it that you have a room available?'

'It's already booked in your name,' said Stockdale.

'Thank you, Superintendent.'

'Here,' he continued, relieving them of their valises and handing them to the manager. 'Do something useful and have these sent up to their room.' He beamed at the others. 'Follow me, gentlemen.'

As the detectives ascended the carpeted staircase, Stockdale provided them with preliminary details.

'The victim is a young silversmith from London. His name was Hugh Kellow and he worked for a Mr Leonard Voke of Wood Street. He came here to deliver an item – the invoice was in his pocket – and it's been stolen. Robbery was clearly the motive for the murder.'

'What was the item?' asked Leeming.

'It was a silver coffee pot in the shape of a locomotive.'

Colbeck was fascinated. 'Then it must be very valuable.'

'It is,' said Stockdale, enviously. 'It cost far more than any of us lesser mortals could ever afford.' They reached a landing and he led them down a long passageway. 'A guest was passing the room when she heard what sounded like a muffled cry for help. She alerted the manager and, to his credit, he came up here at once. There was no response when he knocked on the door so he used a master key to open it and made the discovery.'

At the end of the passageway, they turned a corner and saw a uniformed policeman standing outside the first room on the left. At the sight of his superior, he immediately straightened up and gave a deferential salute. Producing a key from his pocket, Stockdale flicked a hand to move his colleague aside.

'Almost nothing has been touched, Inspector,' he said. 'I remembered what you once told me about the scene of a crime. Important clues could be lost if people trampled all over it or, in the case of a murder, if the body was moved before it had been properly examined.'

'We're very grateful to you,' said Colbeck.

Stockdale unlocked the door. 'What you're about to see,' he told them with a grim smile, 'is exactly what the manager saw – though unlike Mr Pugh, you will not have an attack of hysteria.'

The door swung open and they stepped into the room. Colbeck and Leeming surveyed the scene. The corpse lay on its back on the rumpled bed. He was wearing a shirt that was partly unbuttoned, an open waistcoat, a pair of trousers and some stockings. His shoes were on the floor beside the bed and his coat and cravat over a chair. His bowler hat stood on a small table in front of which was an empty leather bag.

There was bruising on the victim's face and dried blood on his forehead from a scalp wound. What made Leeming catch his breath was that the man's mouth and chin were disfigured as if they had been badly scalded.

'Some kind of acid was used,' explained Stockdale. 'The killer poured it down his throat. Some of it spilt on his face.'

Colbeck walked around the bed so that he could view the body from a different angle. He bent close to scrutinise it. Then he crossed to the open window and looked out. His gaze shifted to the coat.

'What did you find in that?' he asked.

'Very little,' replied Stockdale. 'It looks to me as if his wallet was stolen along with the coffee pot. All that remained were the things you see on the dressing table – an invoice from his employer, a second class ticket to Paddington and a business card.'

Colbeck went over to pick up the card. 'Nigel Buckmaster,' he read aloud. 'Now there's a name I know well.'

'I've never heard of the man,' said Leeming.

'That's because you never go to the theatre, Victor.'

'How can I on my wage, Inspector? I have a family to feed.'

'Mr Buckmaster is an actor-manager. He has his own company of strolling players. I saw him give a masterly performance as Othello on one occasion.' His eyes moved to the corpse. 'How on earth did his card come to be in the victim's pocket?'

'I can tell you that,' said Stockdale, keen to show that he had not been idle. 'Buckmaster's Players arrived today to spend a week at the Theatre Royal. It appears that Mr

Buckmaster and his leading lady, Miss Linnane, shared a compartment with Mr Kellow on the train. They were horrified to hear what happened to him. It was they who confirmed his name. What surprised them was that he came to the hotel. He told them that he was travelling back to London as soon as he had delivered the coffee pot.'

'Perhaps he was due to hand it over to its new owner right here,' suggested Leeming.

'No, Sergeant. He was supposed to take it to the house.'

'What house?'

'The one belonging to Mr and Mrs Tomkins,' said Stockdale, 'though it's more like a small palace than a house. Only someone like Clifford Tomkins could afford to buy an expensive coffee pot like that. He made his fortune in Merthyr as an ironmaster then had a mansion built in Cardiff. The coffee pot was a gift to his wife.'

'Let's go back to Mr Buckmaster,' said Colbeck. 'If he travelled all the way here in the company of Mr Kellow, he might have picked up some useful intelligence. I'll need to speak to him.'

'Then you won't have far to go. He and Miss Linnane are staying at the hotel.' Stockdale smirked knowingly. 'They have separate rooms but my guess is that only one of the beds will be used.'

'I don't hold with that sort of thing,' said Leeming, bluntly.

'There's no law against it, Sergeant.'

'Sometimes I think there should be.'

Stockdale laughed. 'Then I'd have to lock up half the town.'

'The superintendent is right,' said Colbeck. 'One cannot legislate against certain things. One has to live and let live – even though the consequences may be fatal, as in this case.'

Leeming was puzzled. 'What do you mean?'

'Tell me what you see in here, Victor.'

'I see what we all see. The murder victim was battered then acid was poured down his throat. What surprises me is that Mr Kellow didn't put up more of a fight. He looks like a healthy young man yet there's no real sign of a struggle.'

'That's what troubled me,' admitted Stockdale. 'He must have been surprised. I know that he was supposed to be returning to London today but this room was, in fact, reserved in his name. My theory is that Mr Kellow came in here to rest, took off his hat, coat and shoes then lay down on the bed. Someone caught him off guard. Once he murdered his victim, the killer took everything of value and escaped through the window.'

'Yes,' said Colbeck, 'I noticed how easy it would have been to climb on the roof of that shed below. It could well have been a means of escape. But,' he added, crossing to kneel beside the bed, 'there's another explanation that occurs to me.' He peeled back the cuffs of the dead man's shirt. 'It's just as I thought. He was tied up. You can still see the marks of the rope on his wrists.'

Stockdale was upset. 'I should have noticed that myself.'

'You were only looking for things that fitted your theory.'

Leeming scratched his head. 'The killer must have been a strong man,' he noted, 'if he could overpower and tie up his victim. Why didn't Mr Kellow scream his head off? That's what I'd have done in the circumstances.'

'I very much doubt it, Victor,' observed Colbeck with a smile. 'You would never have been in those circumstances. Your wedding ring would have saved you from illicit sexual contact. What I believe may have happened is this,' he went on, thinking it through. 'Mr Kellow is a young man with a day off in a strange town. He was probably lured in here by a woman who persuaded him to let her tie him up so that she could tease him to heighten his pleasure.' Leeming was shocked. 'Once she had him in that condition, either she or a male accomplice took full advantage of him.'

'That's disgusting!' protested Leeming.

'It happens all the time in Butetown,' said Stockdale, wearily. 'Foreign sailors come streaming off their ships after months at sea and run straight to the arms of the nearest whore. After a drunken night of passion, they wake up to find they've been robbed of every penny. The only difference here is that poor Mr Kellow will never wake up.'

'A trap was set,' concluded Colbeck. 'That's why I incline to the notion that there were two of them. They knew when Mr Kellow was coming to Cardiff and what he would be carrying. He simply had to be enticed away from his errand. This room was booked by a man, giving his name as Hugh Kellow. When his female accomplice had rendered their victim helpless, he committed the murder and they fled.' He turned to Stockdale. 'The body can be moved now, Superintendent. I'll want an autopsy.'

'Of course, Inspector,' said Stockdale.

'I'll need to speak to the manager then I'd like some time with Mr Buckmaster and Miss Linnane. They must have talked at length to Mr Kellow.'

'What about me, Inspector?' asked Leeming.

'You must go straight back to London,' said Colbeck, 'but I'm not sending you there simply to spend the night with your wife. You must call on Leonard Voke as a matter of urgency, acquaint him with the details of this sorry business and find out who else knew that his assistant would be travelling to Cardiff today with an item of great value in his possession. Oh, there's one other thing, Victor.'

'Is there?'

'Warn him.'

'You think that he's in danger?'

'No,' replied Colbeck, 'but his stock may be at risk. Since he was given the important task of delivering that coffee pot, Hugh Kellow was obviously a trusted employee. He would almost certainly have had keys to the silversmith's premises. Tell Mr Voke that they are missing.'

CHAPTER THREE

Madeleine Andrews was so engrossed in studying her sketchbook that she did not even hear the familiar footsteps on the pavement outside the little house in Camden. When her father let himself in, therefore, she looked up in alarm as if an intruder had just burst upon her. She smiled with relief at the sight of Caleb Andrews, back home from another day as a driver on the London and North West Railway.

'You took me by surprise, Father,' she said.

'It's not often I do that, Maddie,' he said, taking off his coat and cap before hanging them on the back of the door. 'In any case, I'm the one who should be surprised. I was expecting to find the place empty. You were going out with Inspector Colbeck this evening.'

'Robert sent a note to cancel the arrangement.'

'Did he give a reason?'

'He had to go to Cardiff at short notice.'

'That means the Great Western Railway,' said Andrews with a sneer, 'and Brunel's Great Big Mistake of installing a broad gauge. If only he'd had the sense to use a standard gauge on his track, life would be so much simpler for all of us.'

'That's one way of looking at it,' she said.

'It's the *only* way, Maddie.'

'Mr Brunel would argue that the LNWR and other companies were at fault when they chose a narrower gauge. If everyone else had fallen into line behind him, there'd be no argument.'

'Stop provoking me.'

'I was trying to see it from his point of view.'

'In this house,' he declared, stamping a foot, 'Isambard Kingdom Brunel doesn't *have* a point of view. I work for a rival company.'

'Then I won't show you this,' she said, closing her sketchbook.

'What was it?'

'A sketch I made of a locomotive in the Firefly class.'

'That's one of Daniel Gooch's designs,' he said with grudging admiration. 'It's a good, reliable engine and it's stayed in service. The train that took Inspector Colbeck to Wales might even have been from the Firefly class. You should be drawing *our* locomotives,' he added with sudden petulance, 'not those of our competitors.'

'I draw what catches my eye, Father.'

Putting her sketchbook aside, she got up and went into the kitchen to set out their supper on the table. She was disappointed that Robert Colbeck was unable to see her that evening but she was accustomed to such last-minute changes of plan. He worked long and uncertain hours at Scotland

Yard. Close friendship with the Railway Detective meant that she had to tolerate his sudden departures and unforeseen commitments. Madeleine had her work to console her. It was Colbeck who had discovered her artistic talent and encouraged her to develop it to the point where it began to have commercial value. Not for her the tranquil landscapes and dainty water colours of other female artists. Her subject was the railway system and in her father, who had spent a whole working life on it, and Robert Colbeck, who was its devotee, she had two continual sources of inspiration.

When he drifted into the kitchen, Andrews was smoking his pipe. He was a short, sinewy man in his fifties with a wispy beard salted with grey. His workmates knew him for his irascibility but he tended to mellow when at home. Since the death of his wife, his daughter had taken care of him, feeding him, nurturing him and keeping him from despair. As he watched her now, bending over the table, he was reminded so vividly of his wife that his eyes moistened. Madeleine had the same quietly attractive features, the same clear complexion and the same auburn hair. He had to remind himself how different they really were in character. Madeleine was far more gifted, more assertive and more self-possessed. She could set her sights on something higher than being the wife of a railwayman.

Halfway through the meal, Andrews broached the topic.

'Has the Inspector said anything?' he asked, gently.

'Robert has said lots of things. He's very talkative.'

'You know what I mean, Maddie.'

'I'm sure that I don't,' she said, briskly, reaching for her teacup. 'What sort of a day have you had?'

'The kind of day that I always have,' he replied. 'It was long and tiring. Now don't try to avoid the question.'

'I'm avoiding nothing, Father.'

'Well?'

'Eat your food.'

'I'm waiting for an answer.'

'Robert and I are good friends.'

'You always say that.'

'Then why don't you believe me?'

'Because you've been saying it for years now, Maddie,' he went on. 'People are beginning to pass remarks about the two of you.'

'Well, they'd better not do so to my face,' she warned with a show of temper worthy of her father, 'or they'll get more than they bargained for! I'm surprised you listen to worthless tittle-tattle.'

'They're bound to wonder – and so am I.'

She took a deep breath. 'Robert and I have an understanding,' she explained, trying to rein in her irritation. 'You need have no fears about him, I promise you. He's a perfect gentleman.'

Andrews gave her time to calm down. There was an obvious bond between Colbeck and his daughter but it vexed him that he did not comprehend its true nature. In the normal course of events, an engine driver's daughter would never have the opportunity to befriend a detective inspector, especially one who had enjoyed a career as a barrister before joining the Metropolitan Police Force. All three of them had been thrown together by a dramatic turn of events. During a daring robbery of a train that Andrews had been driving, he had been badly injured and there had been a string of related crimes. Colbeck had not only solved them, he had rescued Madeleine when she was abducted by the men responsible for the robbery in which her father had almost died. Drawn together by adversity, Colbeck and Madeleine had something far more than a friendship yet somewhat less than a formal betrothal. While she was happy to accept the situation for what it was, her father was not. He waited until the meal was over before he returned to the delicate subject.

'I'm your father, Maddie,' he said, softly. 'It's my duty to look after you. I know that you look after me most of the time,' he went on with a chortle, 'but this is different. I have a responsibility.'

'I've told you before, father. You can rest easy.'

'You don't want to be stuck here with me forever.'

'I'll do what I feel is right.'

Andrews was tentative. 'Is it to do with his job?' he wondered. 'I know that it's dangerous work and that he has to work even longer hours than I do. Perhaps he thinks it would be unfair on you to ask you to be his ——'

'That's enough,' she said, interrupting him. 'I don't wish to end the day with an argument.'

'I'm not arguing, Maddie. I have your best interests at heart.'

She heaved a sighed. 'I know, Father.'

'I'm bound to feel uneasy at the way things are.'

'Well, you have no cause.' She got up and cleared away the dishes before turning to face him. Folding her arms, she weighed her words with care. 'All I can tell you is this – and it's strictly for your ears only. I don't want any more gossip about us.'

'I'll be as silent as the grave,' he promised.

'You must be, Father. If you keep prying, you'll upset Robert as well as me. As I've told you a dozen times,' she went on, 'we're close friends but there's a point beyond which our friendship never goes. He hasn't put it into words but I sense there's some kind of obstruction. It's to do with his past.'

'You mean that he's already *married*?' said Andrews, worriedly. 'I won't have any man trifling with your affections, Maddie, however high and mighty he might be,'

'He's not married and he never has been. And Robert is certainly not leading me astray. But there was someone in his past and, every so often, that person comes into his mind. At least, that's what I think. It's the only way to explain them.'

'Explain what?'

'Those odd moments,' she said, pursing her lips, 'when he seems to be in mourning for someone.'

The passage of time had not served to calm down Archelaus Pugh. When Colbeck spoke to the manager in his office, Pugh was still in a state of shock, body tense, face pallid, his Welsh lilt exploring higher octaves.

'This could be the ruination of us, Inspector,' he said, dabbing at the perspiration on his brow with a handkerchief. 'The hotel has not long been opened. Murder is bound to affect our business.'

'Temporarily perhaps,' said Colbeck. 'The important thing is to solve the crime as soon as possible so that it does not remain at the forefront of the public's mind. You'll be pleased to hear that I've sanctioned the removal of the body.'

'Thank goodness for that!'

'I'd recommend that you keep that room unoccupied for a while.'

Pugh gave a hollow laugh. 'Who'd want to stay there?'

'I think you'd be surprised, sir. Never underestimate the ghoulish curiosity of some people. Now,' he went on, 'I need some details from you. When was that particular room reserved?'

'This very morning, Inspector,' replied the manager. 'Mr Jones, who was on duty at the time, believes that it was around ten o'clock. The room was booked for one night by a Mr Hugh Kellow.'

'Except that it couldn't have been the real Mr Kellow because his train did not arrive in Cardiff until almost an hour later. The man was patently an impostor.'

Pugh was defensive. 'Mr Jones was not to know that.'

'Of course not,' said Colbeck. 'He acted in good faith. What can he tell us about this bogus Mr Kellow?'

'Very little, I fear,' said Pugh. 'He's an observant man – I teach all my staff to be alert – but other guests were arriving at the same time. All that Mr Jones can remember is that he was a personable young man with a ready smile.'

'Did he have a Welsh or an English accent?'

'English.'

'Was it an educated voice?'

'Oh, yes. We don't cater for riffraff here. It's one of the reasons I moved to Cardiff from a hotel in Merthyr. We had to cope with a lower class of person there at times.'

'Did Mr Jones notice if the man was carrying any luggage?'

'He had a large bag with him, Inspector.'

'Then what happened?'

'He signed his name in the register and was shown up to his room. About half an hour later, this so-called Mr Kellow was seen to leave the hotel by the front door.'

'Did anyone see him returning?'

'Not to my knowledge, Inspector,' said Pugh. 'He might have come in through the rear entrance, of course, or even slipped in during the rush. The London train brought in a number of guests so there was a small crowd at the desk for a while.'

'When did you become aware of a problem?' asked Colbeck.

'It must have been a little after noon. A Mrs Anstey, one of the guests, happened to be passing the room in question when she heard clear sounds of distress as if someone was calling for help. She came to report the incident and I went upstairs to investigate.' He gave a low gurgle. 'I think you know the rest.'

'I do, Mr Pugh. What you've told me is very helpful. It's in accord with my early suspicions.' He sat back and studied the manager with interest. 'You come from Merthyr Tydfil then?'

'Yes, Inspector,' Pugh told him, pocketing the handkerchief. 'I was born and brought up there. It's a dirty, brawling, boisterous industrial town with a lot of immigrants – Irish, Spanish and Italian, mostly. Merthyr was always far bigger than Cardiff. Indeed, until recent years, Cardiff couldn't hold a candle to Merthyr, Swansea or Newport. It was a sort of poor relation.'

'Things have certainly changed. It's a thriving coal port now. Superintendent Stockdale was telling me how the population has trebled in the time he's been living here. Inevitably,' said Colbeck with a shrug, 'it's meant a sharp increase in the amount of crime.'

Pugh was rueful. 'The worst excesses occur in Butetown – that's the dockland area. It's a vile place, filled with the dross of humanity who believe they were put on this earth to do nothing but drink, fight, gamble and enjoy carnal pleasures in sordid dens of wickedness. You'll not want to be in Butetown when foreign ships come in,' he warned. 'It's like hell on earth. You'd expect a murder there but not,' he continued, spreading his arms wide, 'in a respectable hotel like this. Oh, Inspector, *please* tell me that you'll be able to catch the villain who inflicted this horror upon us.'

Colbeck was confident. 'I think I can guarantee it, Mr Pugh.'

Jeremiah Stockdale was not looking forward to the visit. Being the bearer of bad news always made him feel uncomfortable. Since the bad news had to be passed on to Clifford Tomkins and his wife, Stockdale had reason to be even more uneasy. He steeled himself to bear the onslaught of anger, bitterness and criticism that was bound to come. Winifred Tomkins, a plump, pampered middle-aged woman, dripping with expensive jewellery, led the attack. No sooner had he given them the salient details of the crime than she pounced.

'My coffee pot has been *stolen*!' she cried, outrage making her already bulbous eyes move even further out of their sockets. 'How on earth could you let this happen, Superintendent?'

'I think it's unfair to blame me, Mrs Tomkins,' said Stockdale, stoutly. 'Neither I nor my men were engaged to guard the item.'

'Well, you should have been.'

'This is most distressing,' said Tomkins, oozing disapproval. 'Do you know how much that coffee pot cost?'

'Yes, sir – I've seen the invoice.'

'Then you'll have noticed that I had already paid fifty pounds deposit. Money does not grow on trees, you know.'

Stockdale was about to point out that, in a sense, it did. The ironmaster had cultivated a small forest out of the blood, sweat and early deaths of the poor wretches who toiled in his ironworks, leaving him to pluck metaphorical banknotes from every branch. The vast neo-Gothic residence that Tomkins had had built on the outskirts of Cardiff bore testimony to his wealth and the drawing room in which they were now standing was awash with Regency furniture, silver ornaments and gilt-framed portraits. Forthright on most occasions, Stockdale held his tongue. There was no virtue in alienating them even more.

'I want that coffee pot back!' insisted Winifred.

'An investigation has already been set in motion,' said the visitor, 'but please bear in mind that the theft was only a secondary crime. Cold-blooded murder was committed in that hotel.'

'That's immaterial.'

'Not in my view.'

'Nor in mine,' said Tomkins, reasonably. 'I know that you're upset, my dear, but the fate of that young man compels attention. It's a dreadful thing to happen to him.'

Winifred was dismissive. 'He's beyond help,' she said, waving a hand, 'so let's not waste time on him. After all, he was only the silversmith's assistant. I shall be writing to Mr Voke to ask him why he didn't take more steps to ensure the safety of my coffee pot.'

She continued to complain loudly and to upbraid Stockdale as if he had been the thief. He weathered the storm and collected an apologetic glance from Tomkins as he did so. Though he disliked the man intensely, Stockdale had compassion for any husband wedded to such a garrulous termagant. Clifford Tomkins was a tall, skinny, straight-backed man in his sixties with a mane of silver hair that reinforced his air of distinction. Callous to the point of brutality as a captain of industry, he was more restrained in a domestic setting. Over the years, his cheeks had been reddened by heavy drinking and hollowed by a dissipation about which his wife knew absolutely nothing. Stockdale, however, had his true measure, having once caught the old man in a compromising position during a raid on one of Cardiff's more exclusive brothels.

'Thank you, Winifred,' said Tomkins when his wife's tirade finally came to an end. 'Now let's hear what the superintendent is doing to solve these appalling crimes.'

'I've done the most sensible thing possible, sir,' explained Stockdale. 'Since the crimes occurred on the property of the South Wales Railway, I advised the managing director to send for Detective Inspector Colbeck of the Metropolitan Police Force.'

'Why on earth did you do that, man?'

'I can see that you're not familiar with his reputation. The inspector has dealt with crimes relating to the railway system all over the country. His record of success is unparalleled. I've worked beside him so I know what a brilliant detective he is.'

'Can he recover my coffee pot?' challenged Winifred, eyes at the extremity of their bulge. 'That's what I wish to know.'

'Inspector Colbeck is certain of it. No pawnbroker would touch an object as distinctive as that and I venture to suggest that there are very few ladies with your abiding interest in locomotives.'

'Years ago,' she announced, grandly, 'my father was a major investor in the Great Western Railway. I inherited his passion for trains. I always preferred to play with my brother's toy engine rather than with my dolls. It was partly in memory of my late father that I wanted that silver coffee pot made and my husband was kind enough to commission it.'

'Mr Voke was highly recommended,' added Tomkins, 'so we put our trust in him. He sent us a series of sketches and my wife chose the one that she wanted. We didn't want to buy a pig in a poke.'

'Do you still have the sketch, sir?' asked Stockdale. 'It would be helpful to know exactly what we're looking for.'

'It's in the library, Superintendent. I'll get it for you.'

As Tomkins went out, Stockdale turned to the still fuming Winifred. Nothing but the instant return of her coffee pot would placate her. The murder did not somehow impinge on her consciousness.

'Mrs Tomkins,' he began, 'Inspector Colbeck pointed out that whoever stole your coffee pot must have been aware of the time of its arrival in the town. They knew exactly when to strike. Is there anyone of your acquaintance in whom you confided such a detail?'

She was enraged. 'Are you suggesting that one of my friends is a thief?' she cried. 'Our social circle is above reproach.'

'I realise that. But if you'd described the item to anyone and told them when it would be delivered, they might accidentally have let slip that information to someone else.'

'That's quite out of the question.'

'Somebody must have known,' he pointed out. 'Think carefully, Mrs Tomkins. Who did you tell? I know, for instance, that you number Sir David and Lady Pryde among your acquaintances.'

'Not any more,' she rejoined with controlled vehemence. 'Lady Pryde has proved herself unworthy of my friendship. She is no longer welcome here. However,' she said as a thought struck her, 'she did see the sketch of the coffee pot and knew when it would be coming. And she has always had an acquisitive streak. Not that I'm accusing her, mind you,' she added, hurriedly, 'but it might be worth bearing her name in mind.'

'Is that the only name you can offer me?'

'It is, Superintendent. Unless, that is…'

'Go on,' he coaxed.

'Well, now that I think of it, someone *was* extremely

45

interested in the sketch when I showed it to her. Like me, she collects silver.'

'Who is the lady?'

'Miss Evans,' she said. 'Miss Carys Evans.'

Before Stockdale could pass a comment, Tomkins came back into the room with sheet of cartridge paper. He handed it to the superintendent who was impressed by the meticulous detail of the sketch, noting the name of Hugh Kellow in a bottom corner. The young silversmith had also been a competent artist.

'Thank you, sir,' said Stockdale. 'May I hold on to this?'

'If you wish,' answered Tomkins.

'It's a highly individual item and very difficult to sell.'

'Heavens!' exclaimed Mrs Tomkins, clutching at her throat. 'Surely, the thief wouldn't destroy my precious coffee pot and have something else made out of the silver?'

'Not according to Inspector Colbeck,' said Stockdale, firmly. 'He believes that the villain has a much better plan.' Pausing for effect, he cleared his throat. 'He intends to let you buy it back from him.'

Winifred emitted a howl of indignation and her husband's jaw dropped. The last time Stockdale had seen such an expression of comprehensive dismay on the old man's face was when he had found him writhing naked between the thighs of a young Welsh prostitute.

As Colbeck walked along St Mary Street, he saw very little of its fine buildings, its plentiful shops, its clean pavements and its gas lamps. He was preoccupied with thoughts of Madeleine Andrews. But for the urgent summons to

Cardiff, he would have taken her out to dine that evening and luxuriated in her company for hours. Instead, he was a hundred and sixty miles away, a distance that only intensified his regret. He knew that she would be sorely disappointed but there was nothing he could do about it. His private life was always subsidiary to professional demands. Victor Leeming frequently talked about his family and Colbeck encouraged him to do so. He was very fond of Estelle Leeming and the two children. Yet he never discussed Madeleine with the sergeant. Leeming wore his heart on his sleeve. Colbeck's heart could beat just as fast even though it was kept discreetly from view.

When he reached the end of High Street, he was jerked out of his reverie by something that sprung up before him to demand his attention. Cardiff Castle was a daunting structure. Beginning as a Roman fortress, it had been rebuilt by the Normans then extended and embroidered by successive owners. Some of its interior had fallen into disrepair but its high walls and massive gatehouse remained. For hundreds of years, it had dominated the town completely. Cardiff was now slowly fighting back, surrounding it with houses, encroaching on its margins, laying siege architecturally. A castle with a town had become a town with a castle. Colbeck took a few minutes to appraise it and to speculate on how much misery its dungeons must have known in the time when they were the home of any local malefactors.

Turning right and with the castle on his left, Colbeck strode in the direction of the Theatre Royal. Stockdale had told him that it was situated in Crockerton but that turned out to be his pronunciation of Crockherbtown. It was only a short walk from the castle. What had once been a leafy suburb of Cardiff was now an integral part, linked to the centre by a series of houses, shops, inns, chapels and other buildings. Colbeck had not gone very far beyond the castle when he was accosted by a young woman whose bonnet framed a face of exceptional loveliness.

'May I give you one of these, sir?' she said, sweetly, offering him a playbill. 'Buckmaster's Players are performing here this week.'

'I know,' he said, taking the handbill and glancing at it. 'As it happens, I'm on my way to the theatre right now to speak to Mr Buckmaster.'

'He's been there all afternoon.'

'I take it that you're a member of the company.'

'Oh, yes,' she replied, showing a perfect set of teeth in a broad smile. 'I have two parts in *Macbeth* – I play one of the witches, then I reappear as Lady Macduff.'

'Then I must question the casting,' he said, gallantly. 'You're far too beautiful to be a witch.' She laughed gaily at the compliment. 'What is not in doubt is your boldness in staging a play that has a reputation of bringing bad luck. Mr Buckmaster is a brave man.'

Her face ignited with ardour. 'I think he's a genius!'

'He's an outstanding actor, to be sure. I marvelled at his Othello and recall his Romeo with fondness.'

'Every part he touches, he makes his own.'

'I daresay that's also true of you – may I know your name?'

'Of course, sir – it's Laura Tremaine.'

'I hope I have the chance to see you perform, Miss

Tremaine. But let me give you a warning,' he went on, looking around. 'Light will start to fade before too long. It's not wise for an unaccompanied young lady to be on the streets. Cardiff is not short of public houses, as you can see. I'd hate to think of your being harassed by drunkards.'

'There's no danger of that,' she said, chirpily. 'I'm called for a rehearsal quite soon. Besides, I'm not alone. Duncan and the Porter are keeping watch on me.' She indicated the figure of a stout, stooping, middle-aged man some thirty yards away. 'That's Sydney Hobbs. He plays both parts. In a small company like ours, we have a lot of doubling. Mr Buckmaster says that it's good experience for us.'

Laura Tremaine had the burning conviction of a true Thespian. Colbeck felt a pang of sympathy for her. Not for the first time, he thought how gruelling the life of a touring actress must be. Laura would be constantly on the move, going from place to place in search of an audience, travelling cheaply, eating poorly, staying in drab accommodation, living on a pittance and paying for her brief moments of glory on stage by doing such mundane chores as handing out playbills to passing strangers and running the risk of molestation.

She seemed to read his mind. 'Do not worry about me, sir,' she said, happily. 'I would gladly suffer all the indignities that the world can subject me to for the privilege of working with Mr Buckmaster.'

Colbeck was touched by her blazing sincerity. 'He is evidently a remarkable man,' he said. 'I look forward to meeting him.'

CHAPTER FOUR

The Theatre Royal had been opened almost thirty years earlier by interested parties who formed a joint-stock company. What they got for their investment was a neat, rectangular structure with a Gothic façade whose plethora of arched windows gave it an inappropriately ecclesiastical air. Striking in appearance, it was not, however, known for its comfort and its interior lacked the sheer scope, luxury and embellishment of London theatres. Nigel Buckmaster made light of its deficiencies, confident that the brilliance of his performance would divert the minds of any audience from the hardness of the seats. He was reeling off some instructions to his stage manager when he was interrupted by Robert Colbeck. Hearing why the inspector had come, he immediately conducted him to the main dressing room at the rear of the stage.

Gas lighting gave the room a garish glow and created shifting patterns in the mirrors. Colbeck noticed that the actor's costume for Macbeth was already hanging up. A dirk and claymore lay on the table beside a large make-up box. Buckmaster waved him to a seat but remained standing in a position where the best of the light fell upon his face.

'I'd hoped to speak to Miss Linnane as well,' said Colbeck, 'but I was told that she was indisposed.'

'This hideous business at the hotel unnerved her,' explained Buckmaster, 'so she took to her bed. Kate – Miss Linnane – is a sensitive creature. It's ironic. Tomorrow, as Lady Macbeth, she'll urge me to slaughter the King of Scotland and she'll be utterly merciless in doing so. Yet when a real murder takes place so close to her, she is quite unable to cope with it. I, on the other hand,' he said, thrusting out his chin, 'am made of sterner stuff.'

'So I see, Mr Buckmaster.'

'I had the courage to identify the body when Superintendent Stockdale requested me to do so. It was a hideous sight but I didn't flinch. An actor must have complete self-control. Not that I didn't shed a tear for him,' he went on, inhaling deeply through his nose. 'Mr Kellow was a pleasant young man with a patent love of what he was doing. Apparently, he helped to make that silver coffee pot. It showed exceptional talent.'

'How would you describe him?'

'He struck me as an intelligent, well-spoken, responsible chap. He was somewhat unworldly, though, and felt uneasy at travelling in a first class railway carriage. It was obviously a rare treat for him. Miss Linanne and I are used to people being cowed by our presence – that's part of an actor's stock-in-trade, after all – but Mr Kellow was completely over-awed.'

'Did he tell you anything about his work?' probed Colbeck.

'Not at first,' replied Buckmaster. 'We found it hard to get more than two words out of him – and he kept hugging his leather bag as it if contained the Crown Jewels. We had great difficulty persuading him to let us see the coffee pot and we were not allowed to touch it.'

'What was your first reaction when you saw it?'

Buckmaster hunched his shoulders. 'I knew that I was looking at a work of art, Inspector.'

'Was it really that good, sir?'

'Don't take my word for it. Miss Linnane is something of an expert on silver – perhaps because her admirers have showered her with gifts made of silver over the years – and she was entranced by it. I'm sure that she'll tell you that when you speak to her. At the moment, alas,' he said with a sigh, 'she has this foolish notion that that murder only happened because we are staging a play that has a history of disasters associated with it.'

'*Macbeth* is steeped in superstition.'

'Superstition is the sign of a weak mind, Inspector. I have no truck with it. When this theatre opened in 1826, the first play presented was *Macbeth* with the great William Macready in the title role. I seek to emulate him.'

'I have no doubt that you will, Mr Buckmaster,' said Colbeck, admiringly. 'I've always enjoyed your performances.'

The actor beamed. 'Thank you, Inspector.'

'As for the choice of play, I'm inclined to agree with you. I fear that Mr Kellow would have met the same fate had you been staging *A Midsummer Night's Dream*.'

'That's well beyond our capabilities,' admitted Buckmaster. 'Even with strenuous doubling, it has far too many characters for a touring company. Actors need to be paid and our income is very restricted. That's why we have to rely on patronage.'

'Yes,' said Colbeck, 'I noticed from your playbill that the first night is being sponsored by the mayor.'

'There are three other bespoke performances so we can rely on an audience for those. The challenge is to fill the theatre on the other nights as well as at the matinee.'

'Word of mouth will surely do that for you, sir. And there is no shame in patronage. Elizabethan theatre was built on it. Shakespeare and his ilk all needed patrons. However,' he said, noting how satanic the actor looked in the flickering gaslight, 'let's return to Mr Kellow. Did he tell you anything about his private life?'

'He didn't seem to *have* much of a private life, Inspector,' said Buckmaster. 'His employer, Mr Voke, made him work long hours and the poor man could not afford much in the way of entertainment. Mr Kellow rented a room near the shop. I gather that his parents had both died years ago. He spoke of a sister who lived in London but they saw very little of each other.'

'What did he tell you of Mr Voke?'

'Oh, he spoke very fondly of him but I'd already observed the deep affection between the two of them. Mr Voke waved him off at the station. They seemed so close that I took them for father and son. As it turned out,' he recalled, 'Mr Kellow has been more of son to the old man than his own flesh and blood.'

Colbeck's ears pricked up. 'In what way, sir?'

'Well, it transpires that the young Mr Voke, also a silversmith, expected to take over the business in time and resented the fact that his father gave some of the best commissions to Mr Kellow because he deemed him the superior craftsman. There were also constant rows between father and son about money. In the end, there was a serious rift in the lute and the son stalked off to work elsewhere.'

'So he might bear a grudge against Mr Kellow.'

'I think it unlikely that anyone would do that, Inspector.'

'Why?'

'He was so shy and self-effacing. He was the sort of person who would run a mile from an argument. At least,' said Buckmaster, 'that's my estimate of him. Miss Linnane's will be the same. The only way to get at the truth, of course, is to talk to Mr Voke himself.'

'Precisely,' agreed Colbeck, getting up from the chair. 'I expect that my colleague, Sergeant Leeming, will be doing that very soon.'

It was late evening when Victor Leeming finally reached the little shop in Wood Street. His first duty on returning to London had been to call in at Scotland Yard in order to apprise Superintendent Tallis of the latest developments. Thanks to a message transmitted by telegraph, the superintendent was in possession of news that the sergeant had not heard. The South Wales Railway Company was offering a large reward for information leading to the capture of the person or persons responsible for the murder of Hugh Kellow. Notice of the reward would be carried the following morning in London newspapers as well as in more local periodicals. Leeming and Colbeck would not be working in the relative anonymity of Wales. The metropolitan press would now be watching them as well.

Chastened by this intelligence, Leeming went off in a hansom cab to visit Leonard Voke. It was now dark and the silversmith had retired early to bed. Roused from his sleep, Voke put on a dressing gown and spoke to the sergeant through an open upstairs window. Leeming removed his hat to address the man. Viewed from above in the half-dark, he was an unprepossessing visitor, his upturned face, illumined by the moon, looking more like that of a desperate criminal than of an officer of the law. It took the sergeant minutes to convince the old man of his identity. Only the mention of important news relating to Hugh Kellow persuaded Voke to come to the front door.

When he opened it a few inches, he peered through the crack to appraise Leeming. Holding an oil lamp in one hand, he eventually opened the door with the other. Once his visitor was inside the premises, Voke locked the door and pushed home three large bolts. He then took Leeming into a room at the rear of the shop and set the lamp down on the table. The silversmith's bleary eyes blinked behind his spectacles.

'What's this about my assistant?' he asked.

'Perhaps you'd better sit down before I tell you, sir,' advised Leeming. 'I bring bad tidings.'

Voke lowered himself into a chair. 'What sort of bad tidings?' he said, worriedly. 'Hugh hasn't been involved in an accident, has he?'

'It's worse than that, Mr Voke. Prepare yourself for a shock. It's my sad duty to tell you that Mr Kellow was murdered early today in a hotel room in Cardiff.'

Recoiling as if from a blow, Voke seemed about to fall off his chair. He put a steadying hand on the table. Tears streamed down his face and he removed his spectacles to brush them away with the back of his hand. During his years in the police force, Leeming had often been called upon to pass on dire news to grieving parents. It was always a distressing duty for him because there was no way to soften the pain. Voke was thunderstruck, reacting like a father whose favourite son had just been killed. Leeming gave him time to recover.

'You have my deepest sympathy, sir,' he said at length.

Voke was still stunned. 'Who could possibly wish to harm Hugh?' he said, helplessly. 'A more likeable and blameless young man doesn't exist upon this earth. Hugh Kellow was much more than an assistant to me, sergeant. He was my mainstay. I put absolute trust in him. That's why I let him deliver a silver coffee pot to a client in Cardiff.' Realisation suddenly hit him. 'Dear God! Someone stole it, didn't they? *That* was the reason Hugh was murdered!'

'Yes, sir – the coffee pot has disappeared.'

'Then it's my fault,' confessed the old man, beating his chest with a palm. 'This is all my doing. I should have paid someone to act as an escort for him. I exposed him to unnecessary danger.'

'You weren't to know that someone had designs on the item. I gather that it was concealed in a leather bag.'

'It was, Sergeant Leeming, and I told Hugh that he must

57

not take it out for any reason whatsoever. I even went with him to Paddington Station to select a first class carriage in which he could travel safely. All that Hugh had to do,' Voke went on, 'was to deliver the coffee pot to Mrs Tomkins at the address I gave him.'

'And, presumably, collect some money,' noted Leeming.

'Of course – fifty pounds had already been paid on deposit. The balance was to be collected by Hugh. That's how much I trusted my assistant, you see. I let him collect a substantial amount of money on my behalf. I have to tell you,' he said, replacing his spectacles, 'that I couldn't have entrusted my own son with such an errand. Stephen would have been liable to temptation.'

The detective was shaken. 'He would surely not have stolen from his own father?'

'It would not have been the first time, Sergeant. But enough of Stephen,' he said, bitterly. 'I've disowned him. He's no longer welcome here and has no claim on the business. Unlike Hugh, he would never *apply* himself. That's the secret of the silversmith's trade in one simple word – application.'

'I can't imagine ever disowning either of my children. I love them too dearly. In any case,' said Leeming, earnestly, 'my wife would never allow such a thing to happen. I'm surprised that Mrs Voke was ready to renounce her own child.'

Voke stifled a sob. 'My wife died a couple of years ago,' he said. 'While she was alive, Stephen was far less trouble. Alice knew how to handle him. Once she had gone, he became surly and disobedient.'

'When did you and he come to the parting of the ways?'

'It must have been two or three months ago.'

'Would you have started work on that coffee pot by then?'

'Oh, yes,' replied Voke, 'that was a bone of contention. Because my eyesight is fading a little, I needed someone else to do the more intricate work on that locomotive. Stephen expected that I'd turn to him but Hugh was always my first choice.'

'So your son was aware of the details of the commission?'

'Naturally – why do you ask?'

'Someone lay in wait for Mr Kellow,' said Leeming, 'so they must have known that he was carrying something of great value. Apart from your son, can you suggest anyone else who might have known what your assistant's movements would be?'

'No,' said Voke, 'I would never disclose such details. Hugh has delivered expensive items before without mishap, largely, I suspect, because nobody realised what he was carrying.'

'Could Mr Kellow have confided to anybody that he was going to Cardiff today?'

'I warned him against doing so, Sergeant. Besides, in whom could he confide? He had few friends and he never talked to his sister about his work here.'

'Does his sister live in London?'

'Yes – she's in service at a house in Mayfair.'

'Do you have an address for her, Mr Voke? She needs to be informed of what's happened – and so do his parents.'

'Hugh and Effie are orphans, I'm afraid. They lost their parents. As to her address, I can't help you. I only met Effie Kellow a couple of times. She was a pretty girl. This horrible news will destroy her,' said Voke, sorrowfully. 'She looked up to her brother and Hugh was very kind to her. I know that he gave her money from time to time.'

'Is there any way of finding her address?'

'You might ask Mrs Jennings. She was Hugh's landlady and has a house not far away from here. But don't call on her this late,' he cautioned. 'Mrs Jennings would never open the door to a stranger after dark even if he is a detective.' Voke reached across to open a drawer in a sideboard and took out a pencil and some paper. Closing the drawer again, he scribbled an address and handed it to Leeming. 'That's where Hugh lived,' he said. 'His landlady will be terribly upset at what happened. I know how fond she was of him.'

'I'll speak to her tomorrow,' decided Leeming. 'I'll also need to have a word with your son.'

Voke was peremptory. 'I no longer have a son,' he snapped. 'But the person you're after works for a silversmith in Hatton Garden. Look for Solomon Stern.'

'Thank you, sir.'

'What will happen to the body?'

'I assume that it will be reclaimed by his sister.'

'Effie Kellow is in no position to pay for the funeral,' said Voke with a surge of affection. 'I'll bear any costs involved.'

'That's very generous of you, Mr Voke.'

'Hugh was the best apprentice I ever had. When he stayed on as my assistant, he was loyal and hard-working. It's the least I can do for him, Sergeant.'

'I'll pass on that information,' said Leeming. 'I'm sorry to have disturbed you, sir, but I didn't only come to tell you what happened to Mr Kellow. There's another troubling matter.'

'My assistant is murdered and a silver coffee pot is stolen – what can be more troubling than that?'

'We believe that Mr Kellow may have had keys to the shop.'

'He did,' confirmed Voke. 'He had to let himself in.'

'Those keys have vanished. Inspector Colbeck, who is leading the investigation, sent me specifically to give you a warning. Look to your property, sir. It may be in danger.'

Robert Colbeck and Jeremiah Stockdale ended the day in the lounge of the Railway Hotel with a glass of malt whisky apiece. Before they compared notes about what they had learnt, Stockdale banged the arm of his chair with a fist and made his declaration.

'I want this man caught and caught quickly, Inspector,' he said. 'I won't tolerate murder in my town. I police Cardiff with a firm hand and villains fear me for that reason.'

'Your reputation is well-earned, Superintendent, but why do you think the killer must be a man?'

'It's what you suggested. You felt that a woman was involved to lure Mr Kellow here but that she needed a male accomplice to do the deed itself. How else could it have happened?'

'I've been mulling that over. The young woman could have been acting alone.'

Stockdale shook his head. 'No, I refuse to believe that.'

'Look at the way he was killed,' said Colbeck. 'He was struck on the head to daze him then acid was poured down his throat. Why choose that method? Remember that Mr Kellow was defenceless. A man would either have strangled him or battered him to death. A woman, on the other hand, would be less likely to turn to violence.'

'She could have stabbed him.'

'Most women would draw back from that. No, I think that she deliberately selected acid and I'll be interested to find out why. In doing so, of course, she does give us a definite line of enquiry.'

'How did she get hold of it?'

'Exactly,' said Colbeck.

'According to medical evidence, it was sulphuric acid.'

'Do you have many chemists and druggists in Cardiff?'

'Well over a dozen,' replied Stockdale, 'and many of them are in Butetown. There are people there who don't ask questions of their customers. They just give them what they want. It's the reason we had three poisonings in the district last year.'

'Mr Pugh was warning me about the perils of Butetown.'

'It can get lively,' conceded Stockdale with a grin, 'but that's part of its charm. Archelaus Pugh wouldn't venture anywhere near the docks without an armed guard but I know my way around. It was also the sight of one of my early triumphs. It must be almost fifteen years ago now,' he recalled with a nostalgic smile. 'A number of sea captains had been assaulted and robbed near the West Dock. So I dressed up as a sailor one night and acted as bait.'

'That was a bold thing to do, Superintendent.'

'Luckily, it worked. When I saw that three men were following me, I broke into a run and they gave chase. One of them was much faster than the others and got well clear of them. I stopped, punched him on the nose and knocked him to the floor. Seeing what I'd done, his friends turned tail.'

'What happened to the man himself?'

'I arrested him, charged him with robbery and sent him for trial. He was transported for seven years.' He gave a throaty chuckle. 'I was in court to savour the moment.'

'I hope that we'll both be able to savour the verdict that's passed on the killer.'

'Whether it's a man *or* a woman,' remarked Stockdale.

'Or, indeed, both,' said Colbeck. 'If two people were involved, they are both culpable and will end up side by side on the gallows.'

'It's where they deserve to be, Inspector.'

Colbeck took another sip of his drink then told his friend about the conversation with Nigel Buckmaster. Stockdale listened intently. He was amused by what the actor had told him about identifying the dead body.

'So he didn't flinch, did he?' he said. 'Mr Buckmaster took one look at the body, nodded his head to signal that it was indeed Mr Kellow then rushed off to be sick somewhere. He'd never make a policeman.'

'Murder victims are never pretty.'

'The ones hauled out of the River Taff are the worst. If they've been in there long enough, they're bloated. I doubt if Mr Buckmaster would even dare to look at such horrors.'

'The most useful thing he told me was that Mr Voke and his son had parted company.'

'It sounds to me as if the son needs more than a passing glance,' said Stockdale. 'There must have been bad blood between him and Hugh Kellow. That gives us a motive.'

'We'll certainly bear him in mind,' agreed Colbeck,

'though, in my experience, obvious suspects are often proved innocent.'

Stockdale guffawed. 'Not if they live in Butetown!'

'What did *you* find out, Superintendent?'

'Well, at least I discovered what was stolen,' said the other, taking out the sketch and handing it over. 'Mr Tomkins showed me this.'

Colbeck unfolded the paper. 'It's a locomotive based on the Great Western Railway's Firefly class,' he said after only a glance. 'It was designed by Daniel Gooch in 1840 and has proved a reliable workhorse. There are, however, some modifications. In some respects, it's been simplified but there are also refinements that never existed on the original engine – that crown on the smokestack, for example.'

'You seem very well-informed, Inspector.'

'I've always loved trains.'

'I thought I'd show this to every pawnbroker and silversmith in town just in case the killer is tempted to try and sell it.'

Colbeck handed the sketch back. 'I think that's highly unlikely,' he opined. 'How did Mrs Tomkins respond to the news that her coffee pot has gone astray?'

'She was livid,' replied Stockdale with a scowl. 'Nobody had told her that she ought to separate the message from the messenger. She more or less accused me of betraying her.'

'Did she give you any names?'

'Not at first – she refused to believe that anybody in her circle could be implicated in any way. It was only when I put it to her that one of them might inadvertently have passed on details of the coffee pot to someone else that she deigned to think again. Mrs Tomkins eventually provided the names of two people with a particular interest in that silver coffee pot.'

'Who are they?'

'The first one is Martha Pryde – she's the wife of Sir David Pryde, who owns the largest shipping line in Wales. Lady Pryde and Winifred Tomkins used to be very close but the frost seems to have got into that friendship. Heaven knows why,' he went on. 'I'd be interested to find out why the two of them fell out.'

'Would it be relevant to the investigation?'

'It could be, Inspector. Mrs Tomkins described Lady Pryde as acquisitive. I could add several other adjectives to that and none of them is very complimentary. Mrs Tomkins is only a well-bred harridan,' he said, 'whereas Lady Pryde is a venomous snake.'

'What about Sir David?'

'That's the curious thing. When I was leaving, Mr Tomkins mentioned something that might have a bearing on the case.'

Colbeck raised an eyebrow. 'Well?'

'Leonard Voke, the silversmith, was recommended to them by no less a person than Sir David Pryde.'

'Links of the chain are starting to join up,' said Colbeck, tasting more whisky. 'It must have been very galling for Lady Pryde if her former friend was boasting about a coffee pot locomotive made by someone suggested to her by Lady Pryde's own husband.'

Stockdale chuckled. 'Yes,' he said, 'I can imagine that Sir David got a flea in his ear for making that recommendation. Of course, that was at a time when they were friendly with

Mr and Mrs Tomkins. Now they seem to be at daggers drawn. But,' he added, 'that's not the only link in the chain. Another name was mentioned.'

'Who was that?'

'Miss Carys Evans.'

'Do you know the lady?'

'Every red-blooded man in Cardiff knows Miss Evans.'

'An attractive young woman, then,' guessed Colbeck.

'She's rich, unmarried and obscenely beautiful,' said Stockdale, rolling a tongue around his lips. 'Carys Evans is the sort of woman who turns heads wherever she goes and who puts naughty thoughts into the purest minds.'

'And you say that she's another link in the chain?'

'She could be, Inspector.'

'Why is that?'

'One of the few compensations of this otherwise joyless life in uniform is that you get to know what happens beneath the surface of a town. That's how I come to know that the two names given to me by Mrs Tomkins are intimately connected. In short,' he said, leaning over to speak in a whisper, 'Carys Evans is Sir David Pryde's mistress.'

Leonard Voke was so heartbroken at the horrific news about his young assistant that he hardly slept a wink. When he was not recalling happier memories of Hugh Kellow, he was listening for the sound of any disturbance below. A silversmith's shop was always likely to be a target for burglars so he had taken care to secure his property. The most valuable items were locked away in a safe but there was nothing on display in the shop itself that was inexpensive.

Voke produced quality work and expected to be paid for it. What continued to bore into his brain like a red hot drill was the thought that his own son might, in some way, be connected with the crime. They had parted after an acrimonious row and the father had let his tongue run away with him. Had his harsh words provoked a lust for revenge? Was he indirectly responsible for Kellow's murder? Such fears made any sustained slumber impossible.

Propped up on the pillows, he had an old musket across his lap, a relic of the days when his father had run the shop and kept the weapon in good working condition. The only time it had ever been discharged was when Voke Senior mistook the passing shadow of a policeman for a burglar about to enter the premises at night. Firing by instinct, he had shot out the shop window and sent glass in all directions. It was one of the many reasons why Leonard Voke prayed that he would not have to use the musket. Simply holding it, however, was a comfort and, if his silverware was being stolen, he would not hesitate to use the musket.

Fortunately, his proficiency with the weapon was never put to the test. A false alarm sent him creeping downstairs in the dark and he was mightily relieved to find the shop empty. It was half an hour before his heart stopped thudding. Dawn found him dozing fitfully. As soon as light penetrated the gap in the curtains, he came fully awake. Putting the musket aside, he got up, reached for his glasses, slipped on his dressing gown and opened the curtains. London was already wide awake, Carts, cabs and pedestrians were flashing noisily past. People were going to work or hurrying to the markets to get early bargains. The daily cacophony from yowling dogs, hissing cats and clattering hooves was set up. Leonard Voke yawned.

Grabbing a bunch of keys from a drawer, he put on his slippers and padded downstairs. He unlocked the door to the shop and saw, to his intense joy, everything safely in its place. It was the same in his workroom. Nobody had come, nothing had been touched. The sense of relief flooded through him and he chided himself for his anxieties. Just because someone had stolen Hugh Kellow's keys, it did not mean that his silverware was in danger of being stolen. The killer might have no idea what locks the keys would open. Voke had had an almost sleepless night for nothing. It was only later, when he went to the safe to collect some items to put on display in the shop, that he discovered his relief was premature. Inserting two keys into their respective locks, he turned each in turn then pulled the heavy door back on its hinges.

Calamity awaited him. The safe had been full of cherished objects, made over the years with an amalgam of skill, patience and a craftsman's love of his work. Every single one of them had vanished. While Voke had been lying in bed with his loaded musket, someone had entered the premises and robbed him of his most irreplaceable silverware. Brain swimming, he slumped to the floor in a dead faint.

CHAPTER FIVE

After an early breakfast, Victor Leeming bestowed a farewell kiss on his wife and two children and gave each of them a warm hug. He set off for another day's work, uncertain if he would be returning home that night. His first port of call was the house in which Hugh Kellow had rented a room. When he found the address given him by Leonard Voke, he realised why the landlady would not have admitted him after dark. Mrs Jennings was embarrassingly nervous. She was a short, flat-faced, bosomy woman in her fifties with badly dyed hair and a look of permanent suspicion in her eyes. She questioned him on the doorstep for a long time before she agreed to let him into the house.

'My husband is at home,' she said, vibrating with tension, 'and so are two of my lodgers.'

What she did not mention was the fact that her husband was a bedridden invalid or that the lodgers were elderly females. Leeming could see how edgy she was. Telling him that she was not alone was a means of warning him that help could be summoned in the event of any physical threat to her. His unbecoming features clearly worried the landlady. It was a three-storeyed terraced house in urgent need of repair and there was a prevailing mustiness. Mrs Jennings showed him into a cluttered room with fading wallpaper and a threadbare carpet. She invited him to sit down and he perched on a chair beside an enormous aspidistra. She sat opposite him.

'What's this about Mr Kellow?' she asked, hands clasped tightly.

'Perhaps your husband ought to be here as well,' he suggested. 'You may need his support.'

'He's busy at the moment, Sergeant Leeming.'

'Is there someone else you'd like to be present?'

She began to tremble. 'It's bad news, isn't it?'

'I'm afraid that it is.'

'Something has happened to Mr Kellow – I knew it. He went off to Cardiff yesterday and never came back. I had supper waiting for him as usual but...'

Her voice trailed off and she brought out a handkerchief to stem the tears that were already forming. Leeming knew that he could not tell her the full truth because Mrs Jennings was not strong enough to cope with it. From the way that she mentioned her lodger's name, it was clear that she was fond of Hugh Kellow. The sergeant had to be tactful.

'He met with an accident, Mrs Jennings.'

'Was he badly hurt?'

'I'm afraid that he was killed.'

She gave a shudder and used the handkerchief to smother the cry that came from her lips. Swaying to and fro, she went

70

off into a kind of trance, gazing at the ceiling and talking silently to herself. It was minutes before she remembered that she had company.

'I'm sorry, Sergeant,' she said. 'That was very rude of me.'

'No apology is required, Mrs Jennings,'

'I just can't believe it. Mr Kellow was such a nice young man. He's been with us for almost two years. He always paid the rent on time. We appreciated that, sir. He was so quiet,' she went on, 'and I can't say that about all the lodgers we've had. He spent most of his time reading those books.'

'What books would they be?'

'Books about silver,' she explained. 'He showed them to me one day. They had wonderful drawings of things that we could never afford to buy – silver tableware and such like. It's another world, Sergeant.'

'I know,' said the detective with feeling. 'Only the rich can buy such things. I certainly can't.'

'It was strange, really – Mr Kellow said so himself. He was living here in a rented room yet he was making silver ornaments that might end up in the homes of the aristocracy.'

'Did he talk much about his work?'

'Not really, sir – he kept to himself most of the time. I always looked in Mr Voke's window as I went past the shop in the hope of seeing him there. Mr Kellow waved to me once.'

'What about Mr Voke's son, Stephen? Was he mentioned at all?'

She brooded for a while. 'I don't think so.'

'But he must have talked about his sister.'

'Oh, he did. Effie was all he had in the world. They were close.'

'Did you ever meet her?'

'No, Sergeant,' she said. 'The girl was in service and that meant she had very little spare time. Mr Kellow used to walk all the way to Mayfair to get a glimpse of her. They sometimes went to church together on a Sunday. He had hopes that one day he'd own a shop of his own and be able to employ his sister in it.'

'Did he ever give you her address?'

She looked blank. 'He had no need to.'

'No, I suppose not. But, as you'll understand, I'm anxious to find her. Effie Kellow is his next of kin. She needs to be told that he's been...' He stopped to rephrase what he was going to say. '...that he met with an unfortunate accident.'

'My husband will be distraught when he hears,' she said, blowing her nose into the handkerchief. 'He's not in the best of health. I don't really know how to break it to him.'

'I'd wait until you get used to the idea yourself, Mrs Jennings,' advised Leeming. 'I can see that it's been a terrible shock for you.'

'It has, Sergeant. It's almost like losing a son.'

Tears which had threatened throughout suddenly came in a waterfall and Leeming could do nothing until she had cried her fill. He sat and watched helplessly. When she finally regained a modicum of composure, he rose from his seat and glanced upwards.

'Could I possibly see Mr Kellow's room?' he enquired.

Mrs Jennings stiffened. 'Why?'

'It would be interesting to see where he lived.'

'The room is cleaned regularly,' she said, striking a defensive note. 'I look after my lodgers, Sergeant. It's the reason they stay with me for so long. I'm not like some landladies.'

'Mr Kellow was obviously very happy here.'

Mollified by his comment, she got up, wiped away the last of her tears then led the way upstairs. Kellow's room was on the top floor. It was surprisingly large and its window gave him a clear view of the street below. Unlike the room downstairs, it was sparsely furnished. Apart from the bed and a sagging wardrobe, there was only a table and an upright chair. On the table were a couple of well-thumbed books on the art of the silversmith and a notebook with a few sketches in it. When Leeming tried to open the door of the wardrobe, Mrs Jennings was affronted.

'You can't look in there,' she chided. 'It's private.'

'Then perhaps you'll do so on my behalf, Mrs Jennings. I just wondered if there might be some letters from his sister that bore her address. Could you take a look, please?'

She rummaged reluctantly through every item in the wardrobe but there were no letters. Nor was there anything else to indicate where Effie Kellow lived. It troubled Leeming that she was still unaware of her brother's fate. As he took a last look around the room, a wave of sadness splashed over him. The young silversmith had lived modestly yet been murdered in possession of a highly expensive coffee pot that he had helped to make. His talent had been his undoing. Now he would never be able to fulfil his ambition of owning his own premises and rescuing his sister from the drudgery of service.

'Thank you, Mrs Jennings,' he said. 'I'll let myself out.'

But she did not even hear him. The landlady had gone off into another trance, lost in happy memories of her former lodger and pressing one of his beloved books against her ample breasts as if it was imparting warmth and reassurance.

Robert Colbeck was pleased to see that the manager was in a less hysterical state that morning. Now that the corpse had been removed, Archelaus Pugh felt that he was in charge again and could devote all his energies to the smooth running of the hotel. It was he who told the inspector that Kate Linnane was now able to see him at last. Colbeck went up to her room at once. He did not expect her to add much to what Nigel Buckmaster had already told him but he wanted to hear a woman's appraisal of the silversmith.

In response to his knock, he was invited into the room. He opened the door to find the actress reclining on the chaise longue with a book in her hands. Wearing a silk robe with a floral pattern on it, she looked up with an inquiring smile. Colbeck closed the door then introduced himself.

'I'm pleased to meet you, Inspector,' she said, smile remaining in place as she looked him up and down. 'I do apologise for not being able to see you yesterday but I was profoundly upset by what happened here yesterday. The murder was only three doors away.'

'I'm glad to see that you've recovered now, Miss Linnane.'

She put her book aside. 'You've spoken to Nigel, I gather.'

'Mr Buckmaster was very helpful.'

'I hope that I can be equally helpful,' she told him. 'But do please sit down.'

'Thank you,' said Colbeck, taking a seat and noting that she had been studying the text of *Macbeth*. 'I understand that you think this tragedy is in some way connected with the play you've chosen to perform in Cardiff.'

'I'm convinced of it, Inspector Colbeck.'

'Have you had bad experiences with *Macbeth* before?'

'More than once,' she replied with a slight grimace. 'The worst occasion was in Abergavenny last year. I was in the middle of the sleep-walking scene when a balcony at the rear of the hall collapsed. There was the most appalling amount of noise and dust so I simply raised my voice over it. Miraculously, nobody was badly injured but I was so grateful to get offstage at the end of the scene.'

'I don't think you'll have that problem in Cardiff, Miss Linnane.'

She rolled her eyes dramatically. 'I *always* have a problem in Wales,' she moaned. 'That's why I hate coming here. On our last visit, we performed *The Merchant of Venice* in Swansea.'

'Then you doubtless took the role of Portia.'

'I tried to, Inspector. During my speech in the trial scene one night, a dog suddenly scampered up on to the stage and bit Bassanio on the ankle. Laughter drowned out every subsequent line.'

'I'm sure you overcame the interruption like the consummate artiste you are,' he said, nobly. 'I had the good fortune to see your Desdemona and your Ophelia. Both were truly memorable.'

'Thank you!' she said with a delighted titter. 'I had a feeling that you might be a theatregoer though, judging by your appearance, you should be on the stage rather than in the audience. You have the look of a born actor, Inspector.'

'I did toil in an allied profession,' he admitted. 'For some years, I was a barrister and there's a histrionic element in every court case. To that extent, I was something of an actor though I could never aspire to the standard set by you and by Mr Buckmaster. However,' he went on, 'diverting as it would be, I haven't come to discuss the world of theatre. A more pressing business has brought me here.'

'Mr Kellow!' she sighed. 'It's terrifying to think that such a thing could happen to him. I was amazed to hear that he was in this hotel. When he left us at the station, he was going to deliver the coffee pot to a house on the outskirts of the town.'

'Someone clearly deflected him from that purpose.'

'How?'

'That's a matter for conjecture at this stage. Perhaps you could begin by telling me what impression Mr Kellow made on you.'

'To be quite frank,' she said, 'he made very little impression at first. He was out of his depth, Inspector. When he stepped into a first class carriage, he was floundering. We managed to bring him out of his shell eventually and he had a simple integrity that was rather touching. Nigel and I both had the feeling that he was being exploited by his employer, who under-paid and over-worked him, but Mr Kellow nevertheless spoke highly of him. And when he showed us that coffee pot,' she continued, eyebrows arching in unison, 'we were astonished. It was nothing short of magnificent.'

'Mr Buckmaster says that you have a *penchant* for silver.'

'I *crave* it, Inspector,' she confessed, using sensual fingers to caress her silver necklace. 'I love the sight, the feel, the gleam of it. I've been an avid collector for years. Fortunately, most of the pieces have come from admirers in whom I took the trouble to confide my life-long yearning for silver.' Getting up, she crossed the room to open a portmanteau, taking out a velvet-covered jewellery box. 'These are some of the gifts that Desdemona garnered for me.'

Opening the lid of the box, she showed him an array of rings, brooches and earrings, all superbly fashioned in silver. The most striking object was a small statue with arms outstretched. Colbeck was quick to identify it.

'That's you as Desdemona,' he said. 'I remember that gesture vividly as you pleaded with Othello.'

'Nigel presented it to me at the end of that season,' she said, taking the statue out to admire it. 'You can imagine how much the contents of this box cost, Inspector, and I travel with larger objects as well. It's the other reason I went to ground in here yesterday,' she told him, replacing the statue and closing the lid. 'If someone was prepared to kill for a silver coffee pot, I felt that my own collection might be in danger – not to mention my life.'

'The hotel has a safe, Miss Linnane.'

'That's where everything will go when I leave for the theatre.'

'A wise decision,' he said.

Admiring her as an actress, Colbeck found her less appealing as a woman, her self-absorption masking any finer qualities she might have. Her towering vanity matched that of Nigel Buckmaster. He waited until she had put the jewellery box away in the portmanteau and resumed her seat. She beamed at him with the confidence of a woman who could rely on her beauty to enchant any man.

'How would you describe Mr Kellow?' asked Colbeck.

'He was very reserved, Inspector,' she replied, 'and ill at ease in our company. As a rule, when I find myself travelling in public, men have a tendency to steal at least a glance at me. Some just stare blatantly. Mr Kellow barely raised his eyes. I felt that he was rather immature for his age – or perhaps naïve would be a better word. He was certainly not a man of the world.'

'That may have been his downfall, Miss Linnane.'

'As a silversmith, however, he obviously had a promising future ahead of him. When he talked about that coffee pot, he came alive for the first time. I felt that he was a kindred spirit – bewitched by the magic of silver. He spoke with such intense pride about his work.'

'He also mentioned a sister, I hear.'

'Yes, Inspector. The poor creature only has one week's holiday a year. Mr Kellow was saving up to take her to Margate. He was a very caring brother.'

'So it seems,' said Colbeck. 'What else can you tell me about him? Did you see, for instance, if anyone was at the station to meet him when the train pulled in?'

'I saw nobody waiting for him.'

'But there might have been someone.'

'The platform was very crowded and I had to make sure that my luggage was unloaded properly. By the time we left the railway station,' she said, 'Mr Kellow had long disappeared. Yet instead of delivering that coffee pot, he was in this very hotel – being killed only yards from my door!' She put the back of her hand to her forehead as if about to swoon, an attitude, Colbeck recalled, that she had struck as Desdemona. 'Nigel actually identified the body. He told me that it was a frightening spectacle. *I* could never have gone into that room.'

'That's why the superintendent didn't call upon you.'

'I prefer to remember Mr Kellow as he was on the train.'

'That's a sensible policy, Miss Linnane.'

'It's the only way I can get over the shock of it all,' she said, then she seemed to dismiss Kellow entirely from her mind. Her manner was conversational. 'Will you be staying long in Cardiff, Inspector?'

'I'll be here until the case is solved.'

'Then you'll have the time to visit the Theatre Royal.'

'I'll make a point of doing so,' said Colbeck. 'On my way there yesterday, I was given a playbill by one of the company – a charming young lady named Miss Tremaine.'

Kate frowned. 'She has some decorative appeal on stage, I grant you,' she conceded, 'but she's far too wooden to be an actress. Handing our playbills is more suitable employment for her.'

Colbeck heard the note of contempt in her voice. For the second time, he had a surge of sympathy for Laura Tremaine. While the actor-manager and leading lady enjoyed the luxury of the Railway Hotel, Laura would be staying in some squalid boarding house in the suburbs, dreaming, probably in vain, of the time when she would take leading parts in the classical repertoire. One thing was clear. The young actress would get neither help nor encouragement from Kate Linnane. The only person in whom she was interested was herself.

'Thank you, Miss Linnane,' he said, getting up. 'You've been very helpful. I'll intrude on you no longer.'

'Having you here has reassured me greatly.'

'I'm glad to hear that.'

'If this case is left in the hands of bumbling local policemen, it would never be solved.'

Colbeck sprang to his friend's defence. 'You do Superintendent Stockdale a disservice,' he said with polite firmness. 'He's extremely competent and polices this town well.'

'I found him a trifle vulgar,' said Kate.

'We must agree to differ on that score.'

She produced her most bewitching smile. 'I suspect that we'd agree on most other things, Inspector.'

She offered her hand and he placed a token kiss on it before letting himself out. Colbeck felt as if he had been watching a performance rather than having a normal conversation. To a woman like Kate Linnane, even one person constituted an audience. As he walked along the passageway, he had the uncomfortable sensation of being watched and he threw a glance over his shoulder. Nobody was there yet he still sensed a presence. It was unsettling. When he turned the corner, therefore, he came to a sudden halt after a few steps then flattened his back against the wall. He inched his way towards the corner so that he could peer around the angle. He was just in time to see the shadowy figure of a man going into Kate Linnane's room before closing the door behind him.

* * *

'Where the devil have you been, man?' roared Edward Tallis from behind his desk. 'I expected you ages ago.'

'I had some calls to make, Superintendent,' said Leeming.

'Your first call should have been here so that you could tell me what happened yesterday evening. Instead of that, you stay away for hours. You'd better have a very good reason for doing so.'

'I visited the house where Mr Kellow lodged.'

'Did you learn anything pertinent to the investigation?'

'I believe so, sir.'

'Well, spit it out,' ordered Tallis. 'And don't stand there dithering like that – sit down.'

Victor Leeming obeyed, sinking on to the chair in front of the desk. It did not get any easier. No matter how many times he went into his superior's office, he still felt like an errant schoolboy hauled up before a tyrannical headmaster. Tallis had the authority of a man who had spent most of his career in the army, commanding soldiers in war-torn parts of the Empire. Now in his fifties, he was beak-nosed, broad-shouldered and portly, a shock of grey hair contrasting sharply with the rubicund hue of his cheeks. A well-trimmed moustache decorated his upper lip like a third eyebrow. His rasping voice made his question sound like an accusation.

'What have you done since you left here yesterday?'

'I did as you instructed, sir,' replied Leeming, 'and called on Mr Voke. Some interesting facts emerged.'

Tallis issued a challenge. 'Then interest me.'

The sergeant gave his report. Colbeck had taught him to keep a written account of every interview that he conducted so that it could be referred back to at a future date. Leeming had memorised what he had put down on paper yet – unsettled by the basilisk stare of the superintendent – he still stumbled over some of the words. When the report reached the point where Leeming had departed from Wood Street the night before, Tallis wanted to clarify one point.

'And you're sure that you warned Mr Voke that the duplicate set of keys had been stolen?'

'Inspector Colbeck sent me there for that express purpose.'

'Did you examine the premises before you left?'

'No, sir,' said Leeming.

'It never occurred to you to advise him about the security of his premises?'

'I didn't think it was my place to do so. Mr Voke has had that shop for many years. He knows how to guard his stock. A silversmith would not remain in business if he didn't lock all his doors at night.'

'Locks can be opened,' said Tallis.

'Only by the right keys, sir,' Leeming pointed out.

'Someone appears to have had them.'

'What do you mean?'

'According to this,' said Tallis, picking up a sheet of paper, 'a Mr Leonard Voke reported a burglary at his premises during the night. It appears that his safe was completely emptied.'

'I did tell him to be on his guard.'

'You obviously didn't tell him loudly enough. Nor did you have the sense to check every door to the premises to see if they could in any way be made more secure. Our task,' he went on, sententiously, 'is not merely to solve crime. We also exist to prevent it.'

Leeming was abashed. 'Yes, sir.'

'Since you chose to act on your own initiative this morning, the very least you could have done was to return to Mr Voke's shop to check if anything untoward had happened during the night.'

'I thought it was more important to visit Mrs Jennings.'

'Was she Mr Kellow's landlady?'

'Yes, Superintendent,' said Leeming. 'She showed me his room.'

He gave an account of his visit to the house, hoping to receive at least a hint of praise for what he had learnt. Tallis, however, was unimpressed. Stroking his moustache, he pondered.

'Mrs Jennings has told you little of practical use,' he announced at length. 'Your visit there was hardly productive.'

'I learnt much about the murder victim's character, sir.'

'That brings us no closer to identifying his killer.'

'I believe it does,' argued Leeming. 'It seems clear to me that the prime suspect is Mr Stephen Voke. He was fired by revenge. From what I can gather, Mr Kellow not only supplanted him as a silversmith, he also took young Mr Voke's place in his father's affections. That must have rankled with him.'

'Yes,' conceded Tallis, 'I can detect a plausible motive there.'

'Stephen Voke would also have known to whom that coffee pot locomotive was being delivered and had a very good idea as to when work on it would be completed. More to the point,' said Leeming, 'he would know his way around the premises in the dark.'

'Then he needs to be brought in for questioning.'

'That may be difficult, sir.'

'Why – Mr Voke told you where his son worked.'

'I called on the proprietor, Mr Solomon Stern. He didn't speak well of Stephen Voke. Apparently, his work was very satisfactory at first but he became lax. Also, his timekeeping was poor. He began to arrive late and leave early. What annoyed Mr Stern,' he remembered, 'was that a young lady was always loitering outside the shop in the evening. As soon as he saw her, Stephen Voke left.'

'Are you telling me that you never actually met Voke?'

'He no longer works in Hatton Garden.'

'Did his employer give him the sack?'

'Mr Stern never had the chance to do so,' replied Leeming. 'He has not seen hide nor hair of Stephen Voke for a week. The young man has terminated his employment there without warning.'

'Then you should have sought him at his lodgings.'

'I did, sir. I went to the address given to me by Mr Stern.'

'Was Stephen Voke there?'

'No, sir,' said Leeming, 'and he never has been. He gave a false address to his employer. Nobody seems to know where he is. Stephen Voke – and, presumably, the young lady – has vanished into thin air.'

Tegwyn Rees was a tall, angular, emaciated man who looked as if he should be lying on the slab beside the corpses he dissected. When he was introduced to Colbeck by Jeremiah Stockdale, he regarded the inspector through cold, almost colourless eyes.

'Why do we need detectives from London?' he said with undisguised resentment. 'The crime was committed on Welsh soil. I'm sure the superintendent could have solved it without interference.'

'I came to help, Dr Rees,' said Colbeck, 'and not to interfere. In any case, Superintendent Stockdale is very much involved in the investigation. His officers are making enquiries about the source of that sulphuric acid even as we speak.'

'Yet they are under the direction of a complete stranger.'

'Don't be so territorial, Tegwyn,' said Stockdale, jovially. 'The inspector is no stranger to me. And if you think a Welsh murder can only be tackled by Welsh policeman, it rules me out. I'm as English as Cheddar cheese – and just as delicious. Now tell us what the post-mortem revealed.'

They were in Rees's surgery, a room as neat, chilly and sterile as the man himself. He consulted a sheet of paper before speaking.

'The cause of death,' he began, 'was heart failure brought on by a massive dose of sulphuric acid. Its corrosive properties can be seen in the disfigurement around the mouth and in several internal organs. The wound on the scalp and the bruising were caused before death.'

'I realised that when I saw the blood,' said Colbeck. 'As soon as the heart stops, so does the circulation.'

'Let me finish, please,' said Rees, tetchily. 'There were also bruises on the chest and arms of the victim, suggesting that someone may have been kneeling on him.'

'That disposes of your idea that the killer was a female,' said Stockdale to Colbeck. 'No woman would have been strong enough to hold him down.'

'She wouldn't have needed strength if he'd willingly submitted to being tied up,' returned Colbeck before giving Rees an apologetic smile. 'Do go on, sir.'

Rees clicked his tongue. 'Thank you,' he said with sarcasm. 'Need I remind you that I was the one who conducted the autopsy? All that you saw were the more obvious external signs. As it happens, Inspector, your wild guess has some foundation. The victim's wrists were tied tightly enough to leave a mark and there were similar weals on his ankles. In other words, he was spread-eagled on the bed.'

'That's what Inspector Colbeck suggested,' said Stockdale. 'He felt that Mr Kellow may have been seduced by a woman and that being tied up was part of some ritual.'

'There is some supportive evidence for that theory,' said Rees, glancing at his notes. 'There was a discharge of semen in the victim's underwear, consistent with high sexual excitement. It may even be the case that some of the bruising was a deliberate part of any ritual. There are – believe it or not – people who actually derive pleasure from pain and who pay others to administer it.'

Stockdale grinned. 'You don't need to tell me that, Tegwyn,' he said. 'When we raided a house in Charlotte Street last month, we found a man hanging naked from the rafters while a woman in a black mask flayed him with a cat o'nine tails.' He pulled a face. 'I don't mind telling you that it's not my idea of pleasure.'

'We're still working on assumptions,' Colbeck reminded them. 'It would be mistake to build too much on them. Explain one thing to us, Dr Rees, if you can,' he went on. 'Even someone who enjoyed pain to a certain point would surely have cried out when he was struck on the head with a blunt instrument that broke open the scalp.

'You're quite right, Inspector.'

'Then why did nobody hear the noise?'

'You should have been there when I examined the back of the victim's neck,' said Rees, loftily. 'There were unmistakable marks of something having been tied very tightly against it. My considered opinion is that, before he was killed, the victim was bound and gagged. He could neither move nor speak. The gag was only removed when the acid was about to be poured down his throat.'

'That would explain the cry for help,' said Colbeck. 'One of the guests heard it as she walked past and it was quickly stifled.' He gritted his teeth. 'Whoever committed the murder did not simply wish to kill Hugh Kellow. They were determined to make him *suffer*.'

CHAPTER SIX

Since he perceived the definite link between the murder in Cardiff and the burglary in Wood Street, Edward Tallis decided to accompany Leeming to the silversmith's shop. They found Leonard Voke in a state of utter despair. Having closed his shop for the day, the old man was wandering around the premises in a daze. The visitors noticed that he had forgotten to shave that morning. Voke took them into the back room and flopped into a chair, his head in his hands.

'I'm ruined,' he kept saying. 'I'm absolutely ruined.'

'We're very sorry that this has happened, Mr Voke,' said Leeming with genuine pity, 'but I did warn you that the keys had been stolen.'

'I have three locks on some doors.'

'They were not enough, sir.'

'What exactly was taken?' asked Tallis.

'*Everything*,' groaned the old man. 'Everything I hold most dear. The safe contained my most valuable stock as well as commissioned items not yet finished. Clients will demand their deposits back when I tell them that I won't be able to deliver the items they requested.'

'Can't you start work on them again?'

Voke looked forlornly up at him. 'I could never do that on my own. It would take me years to replace everything. If I still had Hugh beside me, then there's a chance I could rebuild. He worked quickly as well as meticulously. Without him, Superintendent,' he said, 'I'm lost. It's like having a right hand cut off. Besides,' he added, wincing as if a nail had just been driven into his body, 'I kept all my tools in that safe. The burglar stole them as well. That really hurt me.'

'This was no random crime, sir,' said Leeming. 'The only person who would steal your tools is either someone who knew how much they meant to you or someone who might have planned on using them himself. That leads us to one particular person.'

'Don't mention his name under my roof!' snarled Voke, wagging a finger. 'I told you, Sergeant, if you want to speak to that detestable young man, you must go to Hatton Garden.'

'That's what I did, sir, but the bird has flown.'

Voke winced again. 'He's run away?'

'Yes,' said Tallis, taking over, 'and we have reason to believe that he was not alone. Was your son – this young man we're talking about, that is – married?'

'No, Superintendent, he was not. He claimed that I never paid him enough to support a wife.'

'Did he have anyone in mind?'

'Not that I know of,' said Voke, sourly. 'He never brought anyone home but I knew that he frequented places where young women could be found in abundance. That disgusted me more than I can say. I thank God that my wife died without knowing about his habits.'

'We need to contact him as soon as possible,' said Tallis. 'Can you give us any advice on how to do that? Did he have male friends with whom we could talk?' Voke shook his head. 'Well, can you give us the name of the places where he went drinking?'

'I wish I could, Superintendent. I want him caught as much as you do. But the truth of it is,' he went on, 'we lived our lives in different ways. What I had to offer here was not enough for him. He sought excitement elsewhere.' The lines in his brow deepened. 'And you say that he left Hatton Garden?'

'I spoke to Mr Stern himself,' said Leeming.

'I'll be too embarrassed to do that myself. Sol was a good friend until this happened. He's a hard task master and I thought he might do a certain person some good. How can I look Sol Stern in the face now this has happened? I told you,' he said, mournfully, 'I'm ruined.'

The two detectives did their best to console him but he was beyond help. After some futile attempts to get useful information out of him, Tallis decided that it was time to leave.

'We're wasting our time here, Sergeant,' he said as they left the building. 'We'll have to find Stephen Voke *without* his father's help.'

'Somebody must know where he is,' observed Leeming.

'We're not just looking for him, I fancy. My instinct tells me that there's a woman involved here as well. Did you get a description of Stephen Voke from his employer?'

'Yes, sir.'

'Then it needs to be given to the newspapers,' said Tallis with rancour. 'It's high time the press actually did us some good for a change instead of just sneering at our efforts.'

The locomotive belonged to the Firefly class. It emerged from the tunnel with clouds of thick, dark, acrid smoke billowing in its wake. Legs braced, the driver stood on the footplate and stared at the line ahead. His fireman was reaching into the tender for more coal to feed into the firebox. A railway policeman in top hat and frock coat stood near the opening of the tunnel, right arm outstretched to signal the 'all clear.' His dog waited obediently beside him. Four figures were resting against a wall nearby, taking no interest in the clanking monster that was powering its way past them on the next stage of its journey on the Great Western Railway.

It was Madeleine Andrews' favourite drawing, lithographed in colour to give it more character and definition. Her only regret was that she was not the artist. It was the work of John Cooke Bourne, a London lithographer, who had taken it upon himself to produce a series of illustrations for his *History and Description of the Great Western Railway*. Some early copies had been available in 1843 but Madeleine had the main edition published three years later. It was a gift from Robert Colbeck, a spur to her own artistic ambitions and proof that she was not the only person in thrall to the railway system. Whenever she needed encouragement in her own work at the easel, she invariably turned to the volume.

Caleb Andrews always reproached his daughter for spending so much time with her head in a book about a railway company that was a fierce rival of his own. He urged her to look at Bourne's *Drawings of the London & Birmingham Railway* because that company had been incorporated into the one for whom Andrews worked as a driver. Madeleine knew that his reprimands were half-hearted because she had often caught him studying the volume about Brunel's railway. Bourne's work was a remarkable record of its early development and she admired the accuracy of its detail every time. When she had finished scrutinising the lithograph, she turned to something that she always read before closing the book. It was the message that Colbeck had inscribed for her on the title page. His firm hand had expressed the hope that the book might serve to inspire her. Madeleine smiled. The very fact that he had bought it for her did that.

Sir David Pryde was a big, bluff, middle-aged man with a mop of sandy hair and a full beard. He reminded Colbeck of a businessman he had once prosecuted for embezzlement during his time at the bar. Pryde had the same booming voice and easy pomposity. He was not pleased with what his two visitors had told him.

'Why bother me?' he demanded. 'You surely can't think that I have anything to do with the theft of Winifred Tomkins' infernal coffee pot? I have no interest in it at all.'

'I understand that you recommended the silversmith,' said Colbeck, 'so we were bound to wonder why.'

'Isn't the answer obvious, Inspector? I felt that Voke had earned the kind word I put in for him. See for yourself,' he urged, pointing to a large silver yacht that stood on the mantelpiece above the huge fireplace. 'That's only one of the things he made for me. Voke is a genuine craftsman and his prices are not as exorbitant as most London silversmiths.'

The three men were in the drawing room of the Pryde residence, a Regency mansion standing in its own estate. It was impossible to miss its owner's connection with the sea. Model ships, boats and yachts stood on almost every surface in the room, turning it into a kind of naval museum. Pryde himself was evidently a sailor in his own right. Silver cups that he had won in yachting races occupied the remaining space on the mantelpiece.

Jeremiah Stockdale stood with his peaked cap under his arm.

'When exactly did you make the recommendation, Sir David?' he asked with elaborate respect. 'Can you remember the date?'

'What relevance has that got?' rejoined the other.

'It must have been some time ago. According to Mrs Tomkins, you and Lady Pryde are no longer regular guests at their home.'

'It's the other way around, Stockdale – not that it's any of your business. Mr and Mrs Tomkins have ceased to be part of our circle.'

'I find that surprising,' said Stockdale, fishing gently.

'I'm not interested in your reaction. It's a private matter and will always remain so. Now, Inspector,' he said, confronting Colbeck. 'Perhaps you'll tell me exactly why you came here?'

'Of course, sir,' replied Colbeck. 'I wish to speak to anyone who was aware that the coffee pot locomotive had been commissioned by Mrs Tomkins.'

Pryde laughed harshly. 'Then you'd better speak to half the people in Cardiff,' he advised, 'because they all heard her bragging about it. Winifred Tomkins is a woman with a compulsion to impress all and sundry.'

'Several people may have heard about it, Sir David,' said Stockdale, 'but very few knew when it would be delivered. Mrs Tomkins said that you and Lady Pryde were among them.'

'The devil she did!' snorted Pryde. 'You should have known better than to listen to her, Stockdale. Winifred is just trying to stir up trouble. That's typical of the woman.'

'*Did* you know that the item was being delivered yesterday, Sir David?' asked Colbeck, levelly.

'No, I did not.'

'What about Lady Pryde?'

'I can't speak for my wife,' said Pryde after some hesitation. 'It is conceivable that she'd been given that information but she most certainly did not commit a murder in order to lay her hands on the silver coffee pot. That's a preposterous notion.'

'I'm sure that it is,' agreed Colbeck. 'I just wondered if you or Lady Pryde happened, in an unguarded moment – and I mean this as no criticism of either of you – to have mentioned details of its arrival to anyone else.'

'My wife and I do not consort with criminals, Inspector.'

'That's not what I'm suggesting. In a public place, you may have been overheard, that's all I'm saying. Such information patently got into the wrong hands.'

'Well, neither I nor my wife put it there.'

'Lady Pryde does have a large circle,' noted Stockdale.

'If you mean that she's involved in many charities and sits on several committees, then you're right. But we are very selective about whom we allow into our home and it is only in the ears of close friends that comments about the silver coffee pot would be made.'

'It is a highly unusual item,' said Colbeck. 'It's probably unique. It was bound to arouse comment. Is there any chance that we might talk to Lady Pryde about it?'

'No, there isn't,' said Pryde, sharply. 'I refuse to let you bother my wife in this way and I resent your taking up my time.' He put his hands on his hips and took a combative stance. 'Was there anything else, Inspector?'

'You have our apologies, Sir David,' said Colbeck, signalling to Stockdale that it was time to withdraw. 'You've told us all that we needed to know, sir. Thank you.'

Stockdale waited until the two of them had left the house.

'What did you make of him?' he said.

'He reminded me of a businessman I once prosecuted. The physical resemblance is very close. They both resort to bluster in an identical way.'

'Sir David always does that when he's hiding something.'

'Yes, I felt that he was not entirely honest with us.'

'He's the kind of man who swallows nails and shits screws,' said Stockdale, heartily. 'I wouldn't trust him an inch. Can you imagine what Carys Evans sees in that ogre?'

Colbeck smiled. 'I'm sure that his bank account is very fetching,' he said, wryly. 'Wealth has a remarkable power to improve someone's appeal.'

'There are few people wealthier than Sir David Pryde – though Clifford Tomkins would run him close and so would the Marquis of Bute when he finally comes of age. By the way,' he said, turning to Colbeck, 'what happened to that businessman you prosecuted?'

'He went to gaol for six years,' said Colbeck.

The Detective Department of the Metropolitan Police Force had an uneasy relationship with the press. When it came into being in 1842, the new branch was greeted with cynicism. Its failures were cruelly mocked and its successes, Superintendent Tallis felt, were not trumpeted as they should have been. His dealings with newspapers usually left him in a state bordering on apoplexy and he had never forgiven one of them for ridiculing him in a cartoon. What added insult to injury was that he had caught some of his detectives sniggering at the pictorial attack on their superior. Notwithstanding his ingrained dislike of the press, he accepted that it had its uses. When he and Victor Leeming returned to Scotland Yard by cab, he was given ample proof of the fact.

A young woman was waiting to see him. She was sitting on the edge of a chair with a folded newspaper in her lap. Informed that the superintendent had come back, she leapt to her feet and intercepted him in the corridor.

'Excuse me, sir,' she said, deferentially, 'but I've come about that reward notice in the newspaper. My name is Effie Kellow.'

'Then you must be Hugh Kellow's sister,' said Leeming.

She gasped in horror. 'It *was* him, then,' she said. 'I was afraid that it might be. No name was given in the report but I feared the worst when I saw that the crime happened in Cardiff. That's where he was going yesterday.' She began to sway. 'My brother was *murdered*.'

Leeming nodded sadly then moved swiftly to catch her as she collapsed. Tallis ordered him to bring her into his office, going ahead to open the door then finding a bottle of brandy in a desk drawer. As Leeming lowered her gently on to a chair, her eyelids fluttered. The superintendent supported her with one hand and, as she slowly recovered, held a glass to her lips. One sip of the brandy made her cough and sit up. Leeming was amazed at the tenderness shown by Tallis. He was a confirmed bachelor who avoided female company as a rule yet here he was, treating their visitor with all the care of a doting father. It was an aspect of his character that had not been caught by the newspaper cartoonist.

'Thank you, sir,' said Effie Kellow, straightening her hat. 'I'm sorry to put you to any trouble.'

'It's no trouble at all,' Tallis assured her, going back to his desk and taking the opportunity to swallow the rest of the brandy as he did so. 'It was a perfectly natural reaction.'

'I'd never have known about if Mr Dalrymple hadn't shown the newspaper to me,' she said, holding back tears. 'I work at his house. He knew that Hugh had been working on a funny coffee pot because I'd told him. Mr Dalrymple said that I should come here to find out the truth. I simply *had* to know.'

'I appreciate that, Miss Kellow.

'Hugh was such a wonderful brother.'

Effie Kellow was a pretty, petite, auburn-haired young woman who had put on her best dress for the visit. She opened her reticule and took out a letter.

'This came only days ago,' she explained, giving it to Leeming. 'Hugh said that he was going to Cardiff to deliver that coffee pot. He was thrilled that he'd be in first class on the train.' Leeming passed the letter to Tallis who read through it. 'We weren't able to see each other very much but we kept in touch. Hugh's letters were always more interesting than mine,' she admitted, meekly. 'Nothing much happens in my life.'

Tallis returned the letter to Leeming so that he could read it as well. It was quite short and couched in a natural affection for a sibling. He noted that Kellow had used the address of his employer in Wood Street rather than that of Mrs Jenning's house. Folding it up, he handed it back to Effie. She read it wistfully.

'What exactly happened to him?' she asked, looking up.

'The sergeant is better placed to tell you that than I am,' said Tallis, shifting the burden of explanation to Leeming. 'He and Inspector Colbeck went to Cardiff to view the scene of the crime.'

'I'd rather not go into details,' said Leeming, trying to spare her more distress. 'Suffice it to say, that your brother was killed in a hotel room in Cardiff and the coffee pot locomotive he was carrying was stolen.'

'Why did he have to be *murdered*?' she cried. 'If someone wanted that coffee pot, why didn't they just steal it?'

'That's a question we've been asking, Miss Kellow.'

'Yes,' added Tallis. 'It's one of many to which we need answers.'

'I want to see him,' declared Effie.

'Oh, I don't think that would be wise,' cautioned Leeming as he remembered his encounter with the corpse. 'Mr Kellow was badly injured in the attack. You would only upset yourself even more.'

She was adamant. 'I want to see him,' she insisted. 'It's my right. I'm his next of kin. I need to identify the body. I won't believe that it's my brother until I actually see him. Mr Dalrymple said that I could go to Cardiff to reclaim the body.'

'Mr Voke has offered to do that,' Leeming told her, 'and he also agreed to bear the expenses of his funeral. You'll see the body when it's brought back to London.'

'I'm going to Cardiff today,' affirmed Effie with determination, 'and if you won't help me, I'll go on my own.'

'That won't be necessary,' said Tallis, coming across to touch her on the shoulder with almost paternal concern. 'The sergeant will take you there directly.'

Leeming was startled. 'Will I, Superintendent?'

'Inspector Colbeck needs to be told about recent events here. In any case, we can't let Miss Kellow travel by herself.'

'I can buy my own ticket,' she said, bravely. 'Hugh sends me money and I've brought some of my own savings as well.'

'Sergeant Leeming will take care of the tickets,' promised Tallis, 'and see that you come to no harm. I'm told that your brother's hat had his name in it and there were items in his pocket to confirm that he was Mr Kellow. But we always

100

prefer a positive identification from the next of kin – if you feel able to make that effort.'

'I *must*, sir,' she told him, 'don't you see that? It's what Hugh would expect of me. I can't let my brother down.'

Archelaus Pugh was anxious to make his own small contribution to the murder investigation. When he saw Colbeck crossing the foyer of the hotel, he scurried over to speak to him.

'May I have a word with you, Inspector?' he said.

'Of course, sir,' replied Colbeck.

'Let me first apologise for being so unhelpful yesterday. I was so completely bewildered by what had occurred in that room that I could not think straight. Indeed,' he went on, 'it was only when I went into the kitchens a while ago that my memory was jogged. We took a delivery around noon yesterday.'

'That's close to the time of the murder.'

'I wondered if the delivery man had seen anything odd when he unloaded provisions at the rear of the hotel. So I sent one of my assistant managers off to question him. The warehouse is in Butetown and, luckily, the man was there.'

'Did he have anything useful to say?'

'That depends, Inspector,' said Pugh. 'I leave you to judge. The fellow didn't even know that a crime had been committed here and that he might have witnessed something relevant to it.'

'What did he remember?' asked Colbeck.

'There was a lot to unload from the cart so he was there some time. What he recalls is someone coming out of the rear entrance in a hurry and walking off in the direction of the railway station.'

'Was he able to give a description, Mr Pugh?'

'It's only a hazy one,' apologised the manager. 'The man was young, well-dressed and carrying a large bag. It seemed strange that he should be leaving by the back door. It's only a servants' entrance, used by staff and by people making deliveries. Most guests would be unaware of its existence.'

'Oh, I think this young man may have taken the trouble to learn the geography of the hotel. Thank you, sir,' said Colbeck. 'It was very enterprising of you to secure this information. It's possible, of course, that this person has no connection whatsoever with the crime but the timing of his hasty exit is significant – so is the detail about his luggage.'

'If he caught the train, he could be hundreds of miles away.'

'He's bound to have left clues here in Cardiff. When we gather enough of them, we'll track him down wherever he is.'

After thanking him again, Colbeck left the hotel and strode briskly down St Mary Street. It took him less than twenty minutes to reach the house in Crockherbtown where Carys Evans lived. It was a large, stone-built cottage with a well-established garden at the front. When first constructed, it had stood in splendid isolation but was now cheek by jowl with other houses. Jeremiah Stockdale rarely missed an opportunity to speak to Carys Evans but he felt that Colbeck might be able to question her more effectively if he was not there to distract him. Admitted to the cottage by a servant, Colbeck was shown into a large, low-ceilinged room with exposed beams and oak furniture. In spite of its size, it had a cosiness that reached out to enfold him.

Carys Evans rose from her chair to greet him and he had a strange feeling that she was expecting him. She showed none of the surprise or hostility of Sir David Pryde.

'Do sit down, Inspector,' she said, indicating a chair. 'Can I offer you any refreshment?'

'No, thank you, Miss Evans,' he said, taking a seat.

Sitting opposite, she appraised him. 'I must say, that you don't look like a policeman. They tend to be rather large, hefty, clumsy men like Superintendent Stockdale.'

'You might have thought the same of me when I was in uniform.'

'I doubt that, Inspector Colbeck.'

Holding his gaze, she gave a half-smile of interest. Carys Evans was a striking woman in her late twenties with pale, elfin features offset by dark hair that hung in ringlets. She wore a shade of green that exactly matched her eyes and had a large silver brooch in the shape of a dragon on her bodice. Hers was a natural, unforced beauty that relied on none of the cosmetics used so artfully by Kate Linnane. Carys was relaxed and self-possessed. What gave even more appeal to Colbeck was the lilt of her voice with its soft, melodic cadences.

'You've come to talk about the murder, I presume?' she said. 'Not that I can help you in any way, I fear. I read the report in this morning's paper and was horrified. I also felt sorry for Winifred Tomkins. I know how eager she was to have her coffee pot.'

'Mrs Tomkins is not the only person with a fondness for silver,' he remarked, noting the ornaments in various parts of the room. 'You have your own collection.'

'It's my only indulgence, Inspector.'

'The one thing I don't see is a coffee pot.'

'It's kept in the kitchen,' she explained, 'and, before you ask me, it is not in the shape of a steam engine. I like to think my taste is more refined. A coffee pot is for pouring coffee and a locomotive is for pulling a train. They are incompatible.'

'Not according to Miss Kate Linnane,' he said. 'She's appearing as Lady Macbeth at the Theatre Royal this week.'

'I know – I'm going to watch the first performance this evening as the guest of the mayor. Miss Linnane is a wonderful actress, by all accounts. How does she come to have an opinion on coffee pot locomotives?'

'She and Mr Buckmaster travelled from London with the young man on his way to deliver the item to Mrs Tomkins. He showed them the silver coffee pot and both have described it to me as a work of art.'

'Works of art are for display,' she argued, 'not for functional use. I could never drink coffee that was poured out of the funnel of a locomotive. The very notion would make me cringe. Lady Pryde had the same reaction as I did.'

'I thought she and Mrs Tomkins were not on speaking terms.'

She was impressed. 'You've picked up the local gossip very quickly, Inspector.'

'How long has this situation been going on?'

'You'll have to ask the ladies concerned. When I was in their company a fortnight ago, they seemed to be on good terms.'

'Is the rift between the two wives or the two husbands?'

'I don't see that it matters either way,' she said, evenly, 'and it certainly has no bearing on the crime you are investigating. One thing I can assure you is that Lady Pryde was not responsible for the theft of that coffee pot. When she first saw the sketch of it, she laughed. That really hurt Winifred. Lady Pryde thought the coffee pot absurd.'

'And so did you, by the sound of it, Miss Evans.'

'I thought it far too large. Imagine how much coffee it would hold – enough to serve a dozen people or more. It belongs in a hotel and not in a private house.'

'Mrs Tomkins wanted it to commemorate her father.'

'I can think of more fitting memorials.'

'She had a keen interest in railways.'

Carys was amused. 'I have a keen interest in racing, Inspector,' she riposted, 'but that doesn't mean I'd commission a silver coffee pot in the shape of a thoroughbred stallion. It might provide a talking point for my guests but that would be its only virtue. Do not mistake me,' she added, seriously, 'I respect the right of Winifred Tomkins – or anyone else for that matter – to follow their own inclination, and I hope you can retrieve the coffee pot for her so that she can enjoy it to the full.'

'Were you aware that it was being delivered yesterday?'

'Yes, Inspector, but I was only one of a number of ladies. Some of them were expecting to be drinking coffee out of it this morning.'

'I don't follow, Miss Evans.'

'Winifred Tomkins wanted to put it on show the day after it arrived,' she told him. 'We were all invited to the celebration. I gave a polite refusal but Lady Pryde, I suspect, was a trifle more blunt.' She offered him a radiant smile. 'To answer the question you came here to ask, Inspector Colbeck,' she continued, smoothly, 'I was one of several people who knew the day and the time when that silver coffee pot would steam into Cardiff General Station. You'll have a lot of calls to make if you wish to speak to every one of us.'

CHAPTER SEVEN

Because of his dislike of travelling by train, all journeys on the iron way were a severe trial for Victor Leeming. None, however, had been as boring, uncomfortable and seemingly interminable as the one between Paddington and Cardiff that day. When he had made the same trip with Colbeck the previous afternoon, the inspector had helped to defeat time with conversation about the case in hand. No such diversion was open to Leeming on this occasion. His companion did not say a single word. Effie Kellow sat hunched in a corner of the compartment, her eyes vacant and her mind preoccupied. Whenever they stopped at a station, she did not even toss a glance out of the window. As a result, Leeming had to remain silent for the whole journey, feeling every jolt and judder of the train, listening to the snores of the elderly gentleman who sat beside him, and fearing that he would not be at home with his family that night.

When they finally reached their destination, he got swiftly

onto the platform, one hand on his stomach to keep at bay the travel sickness that threatened. Effie followed him. To his amazement, she was ready to talk to him now.

'Where are we going, Sergeant?' she asked.

'To the Railway Hotel,' he replied.

'Is that where Hugh…where it happened?'

'Yes, Miss Kellow. It's also where Inspector Colbeck is staying and you'll need to speak to him before you're allowed to see the body.'

She looked anxious. 'He won't try to stop me, will he?'

'I don't think so.'

'Mr Dalrymple said I was entitled as next of kin.'

'That's true.'

'Then why do I have to speak to Inspector Colbeck?'

'He's in charge of the investigation.'

'Has he caught the man who killed my brother yet?'

'I think that highly unlikely, Miss Kellow,' said Leeming, 'but we will certainly do so in the fullness of time. The inspector will leave no stone unturned to find the person we're looking for.'

They joined the passengers thronging around the exit, the fierce hubbub making any further conversation difficult. Though he was barely ten years older, Leeming felt more like a parent to her and had a father's reluctance to expose her to anything as unpleasant as viewing the corpse of a murder victim. Yet Effie had a kind of inner strength which had made her insist on coming to Cardiff and he hoped that it would sustain her through the ordeal.

'Have you been to Wales before?' he asked.

'I haven't been anywhere,' she said, dully.

'Where were you born?'

'Watford – we moved to London when I was a child and I've been there ever since. Hugh was going to take me to Margate this year,' she went on, brightening momentarily. Her face crumpled. 'That won't happen now. I'd always wanted to go to Margate.'

'It sounds as if he really looked after you, Miss Kellow.'

'Oh, he did, sir. Hugh was much more than a brother to me.'

Leeming wondered how she would cope without him. Her future was bleak. Effie Kellow seemed doomed to spend the rest of her life in service. With the death of her brother, her one real escape route had been blocked. For such an attractive woman, there was the possibility of marriage but it would only to be to someone on the same social level. The one consolation was that, according to her, Effie had a very considerate employer. Leeming knew of many cases where rapacious householders had taken advantage of female members of staff who had been forced to comply rather than risk dismissal. He was relieved that she had at least been spared that torment.

To the sergeant's relief, Colbeck was at the hotel when they got there. It meant that Leeming no longer felt *in loco parentis*. Colbeck was interested to meet Effie and he put her at ease immediately by agreeing to let her identify the body of her brother.

'Thank you, Inspector,' she said, grasping his hand.

'Sergeant Leeming will doubtless have warned you what to expect,' he said, looking at his colleague. 'The body was viewed by someone who travelled with your brother on the train but I'm not sure how much credence can be placed on his identification.'

'I'm the only person who ought to have seen Hugh.'

'Granted, Mrs Kellow, but we had no means of getting in touch with you. Fortunately, the reward notice and newspaper report came to your attention.'

'Can I see him now, sir?'

'Are you sure you wouldn't like some refreshment first?' offered Leeming. 'It must be a long time since you've eaten and you must be hungry – I know that I am.'

'I suggest a meal afterwards, Sergeant,' said Colbeck.

Leeming read his meaningful glance. If she viewed the corpse on a full stomach, there was always the possibility that Effie Kellow would be violently sick. It had happened many times with other relatives of murder victims. Leeming mimed an apology to Colbeck.

'Where is my brother?' she asked.

'We'll take you to him at once,' said Colbeck.

'I *have* to see him, Inspector.'

'I understand.'

'It's the only way to put my mind at rest.'

Leeming squirmed inwardly. He feared that the sight of her brother's corpse would have exactly the opposite effect.

Clifford Tomkins had spent many years regretting his decision to marry Winifred Armitage. At the time, of course, she had seemed like a good catch, a handsome young woman from the landed gentry with a vivacity kept just inside the bounds of convention. Unlike any other female of his acquaintance, she had shown a sincere interest in his work and been willing to live in Merthyr, the greatest iron town in the world, a noisy, dirty, over-crowded, rough and ready place that would have deterred many potential wives. She had produced five children, gaining weight and losing more of her dwindling appeal after each birth, and devoted herself to spending increasing amounts of his vast wealth. As he looked at her now, in the wild-eyed and bellicose state to which she reverted so easily, he could not believe that her beauty had ever ensnared him or that he had foolishly endured a lengthy and highly regulated betrothal in order to wed her.

'I must have that coffee pot back, Clifford!' she asserted.

'You will, my dear,' he soothed.

'Otherwise, I'll be the laughing-stock of Cardiff.'

'Nobody will laugh at a brutal murder.'

'They all knew how much store I set by it. How they must be rejoicing now! Lady Pryde will be cackling, Carys Evans will be clapping her hands and the rest of them will be taking immense pleasure out of my misfortune.'

'You do them wrong, Winifred,' he told her. 'Your friends will have genuine sympathy for you. Lady Pryde might wrest some cruel enjoyment out of your predicament, perhaps, but Carys and the others will all feel sorry. They know how much that coffee pot meant to you.'

'There'd be nothing else like it in the whole of Wales.'

'You always did have a sense of originality, my dear.'

He gave a noncommittal smile. They were in the drawing room of their house and Tomkins was forced to listen to yet another outburst of self-pity from his wife. A silver coffee pot in the shape of a locomotive struck him as a rather bizarre and totally unnecessary object to commission, especially at such a high price. But it was an opinion he would never dare to vouchsafe to his wife.

'We must put our trust in this Inspector Colbeck,' he resumed.

'I'm not sure that I can, Clifford.'

'Why not?'

'Well, I don't have much faith in a man who doesn't even bother to call on us. If he is in charge of the investigation, it was his duty to inform us in person of the loss we sustained. Instead of doing so, he sent that oaf, Superintendent Stockdale.'

'Be fair to the man,' said Tomkins, remembering the occasion when Stockdale's discretion had saved him from being exposed as a client of a certain brothel in the town. 'The superintendent is no oaf. He does a difficult job very well even if he is somewhat heavy-handed at times.'

'He let us down,' she accused.

'I don't think so.'

'The crime occurred not long after noon yet it was *hours* before we were told about it. We should have been contacted at once.'

'You can understand the delay, my dear. Stockdale had a murder on his hands. That took precedence over the theft. He was probably waiting for Inspector Colbeck to arrive before he took any major decision.'

She was enraged. 'Whose side are you on?'

'It's not a question of sides, Winifred.'

'Then why are you defending the superintendent?'

'I'm defending nobody, my dear.'

'You're the one person I felt I *could* rely on,' she said, hotly. 'When my property was stolen, I should have been told instantly.'

'I quite agree,' he said, choosing dishonesty as a means of appeasing her. 'I'll make that point to Stockdale when I see him.'

'Inspector Colbeck is the person we ought to be seeing. Out of common courtesy, he should have been in touch with us.' She drew herself up to her full height. 'Does he know who we *are*?'

He swelled with pride. 'Everyone in South Wales knows who we are, Winifred,' he boasted. 'As for the inspector, we must bear in mind what Stockdale said of him. He comes with an excellent reputation for solving crimes.'

'I haven't been impressed with what he's done do far. According to him, someone would be trying to sell that coffee pot back to us. I believed him at first,' she said, 'but I think it's an absurd idea now. My fear is that the coffee pot is no longer even in Cardiff.'

'We'll get it back somehow, my dear.'

'Will we?'

'If all else fails, I'll commission another one.'

'That would take *ages*, Clifford. I want it now.'

'Then you'll simply have to keep your fingers crossed.'

Before she could reply, she was interrupted by a tap on the door. It opened to reveal the butler who came into the room with something on a silver salver.

'This just arrived for you, Mr Tomkins,' he said.

'Thank you, Glover – rather late for any mail, isn't it?'

'It's not franked, sir,' said the butler as Tomkins took the envelope. 'Someone put it through the letterbox and slipped away unseen. I just found it there.'

'I see. That will be all.'

The butler nodded and left the room, closing the door behind him. Tomkins, meanwhile, opened the letter. He blenched when he read it.

'What is it?' demanded his wife.

'It's a ransom demand,' he gulped. 'Inspector Colbeck was right.'

Since there was no mortuary in the town, the dead body was kept in a cold, dank cellar that helped to delay decomposition slightly. Herbs had been scattered to combat the stench of death. An oil lamp hung from a beam, casting a circle of light around the slab. Colbeck was glad to have the body identified by a family member and grateful that Dr Rees had cleaned the scalp wound and wiped away the blood from the corpse. It was no longer as gruesome a sight as it had been. How Effie Kellow would respond, he did not know but he and Leeming stood either side of her as a precautionary measure. They left it to Rees to draw back the shroud. As soon as the dead man's face came into view, Effie needed only a second to confirm that it was her brother. Staring in horror, she reached out to touch the corpse tenderly on the shoulder and seemed to be on the point of leaning forward to plant a farewell kiss on her brother's forehead. Changing her mind, she averted her eyes. Effie clearly needed time to recover. Colbeck waited a full minute before speaking.

'I'm sorry we had to put you through that,' he said.

'It's Hugh,' she said, chewing her lip. 'It's my brother.'

'Let's get you out of here, Miss Kellow.'

'Who could have *done* such a terrible a thing?'

'We'll find his killer, I guarantee it.'

'It's so unfair – Hugh wouldn't have harmed a fly.'

Colbeck wanted to ask her if she could suggest any reason why her brother had been in that particular hotel in the first place but it was obviously the wrong moment to do so. Effie, in any case, had gone off in a private world, her face contorted with grief and her head moving to and fro. A flood of tears then came. Colbeck was ready for them, pulling a handkerchief from his pocket to give her and placing a gentle arm around her shoulder by way of comfort. He was moved by the sheer hopelessness of her situation.

'Miss Kellow can't return to London in this condition,' he told Leeming. 'We'll have to find a room for her at the hotel.'

The first night of *Macbeth* was a glittering occasion. The cream of Cardiff society converged on the Theatre Royal in its finery. Carriages of every description arrived in an endless procession to drop off those attending the opening performance. The mayor and mayoress were among the first to arrive, the one wearing his chain of office and the other in a blue silk taffeta dress that would not have been out of place in the presence of royalty. A small knot of people had gathered to watch their social superiors, marvelling at the elegant men and the bejewelled ladies arriving in waves. There was so much colour, action and affectation on show that it seemed as if a drama was being enacted outside the theatre as well as upon its stage.

Sir David and Lady Pryde descended from their phaeton with aristocratic poise, ignoring the watching hoi polloi before sweeping in through the portals of the theatre. Swathed in a black and cerise silk dress that accentuated, rather than concealed, her bulk, Martha Pryde wore a silver tiara and flicked an ivory fan ostentatiously beneath her double chin. She was a hefty woman in her fifties with an arrogant strut. As she and her husband were shown to their seats, her beady eyes scanned the whole auditorium.

'She's not here,' she said, gleefully.

'What's that?' asked her husband.

'Winifred Tomkins is not here. She can't face us now that her outlandish coffee pot has been stolen. I know that she was invited but I can't see her anywhere. Can you, David?'

'I haven't really looked.'

'Well, look now. I can't believe that I've missed her.'

'Very well, Martha,' he said, reluctantly shifting his gaze from Carys Evans with whom he had been exchanging a secret smile. 'Although why you should be bothered with them, I really don't know. They no longer exist as far as I'm concerned. If I bump into either of that dreadful pair, I shall cut them dead.'

'Winifred hasn't got the courage to appear in public.'

'Forget the egregious woman.'

'After what happened – how can I?'

'She's not here – be grateful for the fact.'

'Oh, I'm more than grateful,' said his wife as she took her seat beside him. 'I'm delighted. The thief who stole that coffee pot of hers deserves congratulations. He's wiped that haughty smile off her ugly face.' She smiled triumphantly.

'I feel wonderful. I don't think I've ever been so ready to enjoy a performance. Wherever she is, I hope that Winifred is in pain.'

'What do we do, Inspector?' asked a querulous Winifred Tomkins.

'I suggest that the ransom is paid,' said Colbeck.

Tomkins was scandalised. 'Pay twice for the same thing?' he said in alarm. 'That goes against the grain.'

'Nevertheless, sir, it's what I advise. And, if I might correct you, the full price for the item has not yet been paid. Mr Kellow was to have collected the balance. All that you have parted with is a deposit.'

'Fifty pounds is not a trifling amount.'

'Much more is now required. I'd urge you to pay it.'

'You mean to let the thief get away with it?'

'He's a murderer as well as a thief, Mr Tomkins, and he will be arraigned for both crimes. Until we arrest him, you must comply with the demands in the ransom note.'

'I refuse to bow to his wishes.'

'Then you can wave farewell to any hope of recovering the item.'

'Don't say that, Inspector!' exclaimed Winifred. 'I can't bear such a thought. Superintendent Stockdale led us to believe that you would retrieve that coffee pot for us.'

'I'm endeavouring to do just that, Mrs Tomkins.'

Neither she nor her husband was persuaded. They remained hurt, fearful and sceptical. Colbeck and Leeming had been summoned to the house to be shown the anonymous ransom note. The inspector was completely

117

at ease in the sprawling mansion but his sergeant was perturbed. Leeming always felt intimidated by the sight of wealth and, since their arrival, had been shifting his feet and holding his tongue.

'Have the money ready for tomorrow, sir,' suggested Colbeck.

'I might as well toss it on a fire,' said Tomkins, sullenly.

'At least I'd get my property back,' his wife put in.

'Winifred, it's not worth twice the asking price.'

She shot him a look. 'It is to me.'

'You won't lose a penny of the money, Mr Tomkins,' said Colbeck, 'and you'll have the satisfaction of seeing the thief put behind bars. The person to thank will be my sergeant.'

Leeming was taken aback, 'Me, sir?' he said.

'Yes, Sergeant, you will be involved in the exchange. All that the note has told us is how much money is required. The details of the exchange will come tomorrow.'

'Then why can't you lie in wait to catch the thief when he delivers the message here?' asked Tomkins.

'This person is far too clever to be caught that way. We're dealing with someone who plans ahead very carefully. When the exchange is made, for instance,' prophesied Colbeck, 'it will be somewhere in the open so that the sergeant can be watched.'

'What then, Inspector?' said Leeming.

'You ask to see the coffee pot before you hand over the money, and when you see no deception is involved – you make the arrest.'

'Where will you be?' wondered Tomkins.

'A respectable distance away, sir,' said Colbeck. 'At the

slightest sign of a police ambush, the exchange will be cancelled and the coffee pot will disappear forever.'

'No!' shrieked Winifred.

'Sergeant Leeming is an experienced detective. It's not the first time he's been in this situation. He'll know what to do.'

'A lot of money is at stake here,' Tomkins reminded him.

'Not to mention my coffee pot,' added his wife.

'Don't worry,' said Leeming, pleased to be given such a pivotal role. 'The money and the coffee pot will be returned when I catch him.'

Colbeck looked at the ransom note. 'Why do you assume that you'll be dealing with a man? I'm no expert on calligraphy,' he went on, passing the note to Leeming, 'but I'd say that was definitely a woman's hand – wouldn't you?'

In defiance of its record of catastrophe, *Macbeth* was a huge success. There were none of the anticipated mishaps – no falling scenery, no actors taken ill onstage, no sudden failure of the gas footlights and no unfortunate accidents in the auditorium. Laughter was confined to the scene featuring the Porter. At all other times, the audience was in the grip of a searing tragedy. Nigel Buckmaster excelled himself, letting the poetry soar to its full height, committing a foul murder yet somehow managing to retain a degree of sympathy. Kate Linnane was the personification of evil, giving a performance of equal range, brilliance and intensity. The rest of the cast was competent but completely eclipsed by the two principals. When the curtain call was taken before rapturous applause, it was Macbeth and Lady Macbeth who occupied the centre of the stage, he bowing low and she dropping a graceful curtsey, both of them lapping up their due reward for minute after ecstatic minute. They had brought the spectators to their feet. In her costume as Lady Macduff, Laura Tremaine tried at one point to come forward but she was thwarted by Kate Linnane who simply stepped sideways, swished her dress and made the younger actress retreat back into anonymity. No other woman would be allowed to steal one moment of the leading lady's glory.

When the curtain finally fell, Buckmaster turned to blow a kiss of thanks to the entire cast. They dispersed happily to the dressing rooms. The actor-manager took the trouble to catch up with Laura.

'Well done, Miss Tremaine!' he congratulated. 'I couldn't fault you this evening.'

'Thank you, sir,' she replied, excitedly.

'Your Lady Macduff was a minor triumph.'

Laura giggled with pleasure and went off with the others. Kate Linnane was less complimentary as she walked past Buckmaster.

'A minor triumph!' she said, acidly. 'Miss Tremaine was a positive embarrassment. I've seen better Lady Macduffs in the ranks of amateurs!'

'One has to offer encouragement,' he said.

'She should be encouraged off the stage altogether.'

Flouncing off into her dressing room, she slammed the door behind her. Buckmaster knew better than to follow her.

Jeremiah Stockdale joined them in their hotel room to report his findings and to review the situation. Colbeck had asked for a bottle of whisky and three glasses to be sent up.

Resigned to spending at least one night in Cardiff, Leeming sipped his drink and confided his worries.

'Do you think that someone should be looking after Miss Kellow?' he said, concernedly. 'Not one of us, of course,' he went on. 'That would be quite improper. But there must be a female member of staff whom the manager could recommend.'

'I think she's best left on her own, Victor,' said Colbeck. 'She's very volatile at the moment. Company might unsettle her. She wants to be alone to mourn in private.'

'When will she go back to London?'

'That's up to her but she won't budge without her brother.'

'The body is now with an undertaker,' said Stockdale. 'Tegwyn Rees has finished with it so it will be ready to leave tomorrow.'

'Then we may have to call on you, Superintendent. Somebody must accompany Miss Kellow back to London and Victor will be involved here. Could you spare a man to go with her?' asked Colbeck. 'It's not right for a grieving sister to travel alone with her brother's coffin. We have a duty of care here.'

'Consider it done,' said Stockdale. 'I know just the man – Idris Roberts. He's spent the whole day tramping around chemists' shops so he'll appreciate a job where he can sit down. Yes, and I'll make sure that Idris is not in uniform,' he decided. 'We don't want this girl to look as if she's under arrest.'

'Did Constable Roberts find anything of interest?'

'I'm afraid not, Inspector. Some of the chemists would supply the most venomous poison to a total stranger but none would ever admit it. They all swore that nobody had bought sulphuric acid.'

'Perhaps it was brought from London,' said Leeming. 'As I explained, I'm fairly certain the man we're after is Stephen Voke.'

'Then he must be here in Cardiff,' said Colbeck.

Stockdale ruffled his beard. 'I thought you told us a delivery man had seen someone leaving by the rear exit around the time of the murder and hurrying off towards the station.'

'I'm beginning to think that he was laying a false trail. The man with the large bag *wanted* to be seen heading that way. Had he left by the front entrance like every other guest, nobody would have thought it unusual enough to remember. Someone behaving suspiciously at the rear of the hotel, however,' argued Colbeck, 'was expecting to be noticed by someone.'

Leeming had made up his mind. 'Stephen Voke is still here and so is that coffee pot.'

'Don't forget the woman in the case, Victor.'

'She must be the one seen waiting for young Mr Voke in Hatton Garden. The two of them are in this together. They plotted to steal that coffee pot then sell it back to the owner.'

'They certainly didn't try to get rid of it here,' said Stockdale. 'My men called on every jeweller and silversmith in Cardiff. None of them had been offered that coffee pot – not even Wlaetislaw Spiridion.'

Leeming grinned. 'He doesn't sound very Welsh to me.'

'This is a cosmopolitan place. Walk around Cardiff and

you'll bump into many nationalities. If you want a real Welsh town, you'll have to go up the valleys.'

'Let's turn our minds to the morrow,' said Colbeck, pensively. 'Miss Kellow must be on the earliest possible train with Constable Roberts. I don't think it's good for her to spend too long in the hotel where her brother was killed. I'll have to rely on you, Superintendent, to organise the release of the coffin.'

'I'll have it conveyed to the station and put into the guard's van,' said Stockdale. 'Where must it be delivered in London?'

'Mr Voke has volunteered to pay for the funeral,' said Leeming. 'If the coffin is taken to his shop in Wood Street – I'll give you the address before you leave – then he can engage an undertaker and arrange the funeral service.'

'What about the sister?'

'I daresay she'll go back to her workplace in Mayfair.'

'Miss Kellow will be out of the way,' said Colbeck. 'As long as she stays here, she poses a problem. I suggest that you see her off at the station, Victor. I could see how much she trusted you.'

'I wish that I could go back with her, sir.'

'You're needed here to hand over the ransom money.'

'That's worth staying for,' said Leeming, lifted by the thought. 'I like to be in the thick of things. And having seen what that villain did to Hugh Kellow, I want the chance to meet him face to face.'

'I still think you should let me surround the Tomkins residence with my men,' said Stockdale, anxious to be involved. 'They can hide in the trees. When the killer delivers the second ransom note, we arrest him and force him to tell us where that coffee pot is kept.'

'Always respect your opponent,' warned Colbeck, 'He or she is far too slippery to be caught so easily. Remember how much planning went into the exercise. Its success would never be sacrificed by a silly mistake like that. No,' he continued, 'my guess is that a total stranger is paid to deliver the second note. Your men would be arresting an innocent person, Superintendent.'

'And they wouldn't be able to tell you anything useful about the man who asked them to carry the message,' said Leeming, 'because they'd have no idea who he is. We had a case like this last year in London. The person who delivered the ransom note on that occasion was a child, picked at random off the street.'

'I can see that I'd better leave it to you, Sergeant,' said Stockdale. 'As long as you promise that you'll give the bastard one good punch from me.'

'I will, Superintendent.'

'Don't be so sure, Victor,' said Colbeck. 'What if, as I fancy, you may be dealing with a young woman? You're far too chivalrous to strike a member of the fair sex.'

'I'll clap handcuffs on her and make her lead us to Stephen Voke. He's behind the whole thing. I'm certain of it.'

'I agree with the inspector,' said Stockdale, downing some whisky. 'Only a very attractive woman could have tricked Mr Kellow into that hotel room. I think he was tempted by her blandishments. And that raises an interesting possibility.'

'What's that?'

'Mr Pugh happened to mention something to me when

I arrived this evening. It may have nothing to do with the crime, of course, and the manager clearly thinks so. But it is an odd coincidence.'

'Tell us more,' said Colbeck.

'Well, what you're looking for is a beautiful woman who has a passion for silver. I know that because I've often seen her wearing it in some form or other. Around the time of the murder,' Stockdale went on, 'there was someone in this hotel fitting that description perfectly. The manager remembers seeing her leave.'

'Who is she, Superintendent?'

'Miss Carys Evans.'

When the performance of *Macbeth* was over, Carys Evans mingled with the other guests at a reception given by the mayor and mayoress. Nigel Buckmaster and Kate Linnane joined them on behalf of the company, wallowing in the unstinting praise from all sides. Carys managed to speak to the actor-manager alone for a couple of minutes and he was clearly drawn to her. Their conversation was interrupted by the arrival of his leading lady, smiling benignly but unable to hide the proprietary glint in her eye. Carys observed that, when Lady Pryde cornered Buckmaster, Kate made no effort to intervene. An obese, waddling, over-dressed, middle-aged woman with a braying voice offered no threat.

As the guests began to disperse, Carys thanked her hosts and withdrew. But she did not return to her cottage even though it was less than a hundred yards away. Instead, she got into a waiting chaise and was driven out of the town in the direction of Llandaff. It was a pleasant night for a drive with the moon conjuring trees out of the darkness. Largely hidden behind a copse, the house was near the cathedral. Gaslight burnt in the ground floor windows. When she let herself in, Carys was pleased to see that the fire in the drawing room had also been lit to ward off the evening chill. Wine and glasses stood on the table. Everything was in readiness. Slipping off her stole, she closed the curtains then settled down on the couch, arranging her crinoline with care. While she waited, she read through the theatre programme, reviving memories of a performance that had stirred her to the marrow. Nigel Buckmaster had been striking at close quarters but had been far more arresting onstage. It was a Macbeth to lodge in the brain for a long time. Kate Linnane, too, as his wife, had had some magnificent moments and Carys had also been moved by Laura Tremaine in the small part of Lady Macduff. The Porter, she felt, had been deliciously vulgar.

It was almost an hour before someone let himself into the house and locked the door behind him. As he entered the drawing room, he was given a welcoming smile.

'What have you brought me this time?' she asked.

CHAPTER EIGHT

It had been a full day for Madeleine Andrews. She was up early to prepare breakfast and to make her father sandwiches to take to work. Once she had seen him off on his walk to Euston Station, she picked up a large basket and went off to do the first of her chores. She spent a couple of pleasant hours, haggling in the market, window-gazing among the shops, buying some artists' materials and talking to friends and neighbours she encountered along the way. The afternoon was largely taken up with a visit to relatives in Chalk Farm, consoling her aunt over the recent death of a much-loved family pet and chatting with her uncle, a retired stationmaster, about her latest lithographs. It was not until early evening that Madeleine was finally able to do some work at her easel.

By the time that her father returned home, she had a meal ready for him. Caleb Andrews followed a regular pattern. At the end of his working day, he liked to have a pint or two of beer in a public house frequented by railwaymen before strolling back to Camden. More often than not, he brought the day's newspaper with him. His daughter therefore never got to read it until late evening. As he came into the house, he gave her his usual cheerful greeting before hanging up his coat and his hat. The newspaper remained folded up in his coat pocket.

'Where have you been today?' asked Madeleine.

'Crewe was the farthest we went,' he told her, 'and we had an hour or more to look around. It's a railway town in the best sense, Maddy. I really feel at home there. I wouldn't mind living somewhere like that one day. Mind you,' he went on with a chuckle, 'the station does have one problem. If you're not careful, you can trip over a severed head on the platform.'

'That only happened once, Father.'

'It pays to keep your eyes open in Crewe.'

Madeleine understood the jocular reference. The previous year, a hatbox had burst open on the platform when a porter accidentally dropped a trunk on it. Out of the hatbox came a human head. The incident provoked a murder investigation led by Robert Colbeck and culminating in some arrests in the wake of the running of the Derby. Madeleine had been directly involved in the case, finding out vital information for Colbeck and being taken to Epsom on Derby Day by way of thanks. Unfortunately, it was different this time. She could not contribute. A new case had taken him across the Welsh border and excluded her in every way.

'What about you, Maddy?' asked Andrews. 'What have you been doing all day?'

'I'd like to say that I've been sitting down with my feet up,' she replied, 'but there was far too much to do.'

'Did you get across to Chalk Farm?'

'Yes, Father – Uncle Tom and Auntie Dolly send their love.'

'Have they got over losing that mangy dog of theirs yet?'

'Uncle Tom has but Auntie Dolly is still very upset. They had Chum for twelve years and he was like one of the family. Auntie Dolly says that she can't sleep properly, knowing that Chum is not curled up at the foot of the bed.'

Andrews wrinkled his nose. 'It was unhealthy,' he said with disgust, 'having that smelly old dog in their bedroom at night. A kennel is the proper place for an animal like that. Chum should have been in the back yard, guarding the property, not snoring away on the bedroom carpet. Apart from anything else, Chum had fleas.'

'His death distressed Auntie Dolly, that's all I know.'

'My sister should have had him put down years ago.'

'Father!'

'People get too sentimental about animals.'

'You worshipped Blackie when we had him,' she recalled.

'Cats are different,' he said. 'They don't wag their tails at you all the time and expect to share your bedroom. They've got self-respect and they know how to look after themselves. Blackie was easy to have around the house but a dog takes over your life.'

Madeleine did not argue. Her father had a deep dislike of dogs, fuelled by the fact that he was often bothered by stray mongrels on his way to and from work. It explained why he so rarely visited his sister and brother-in-law in Chalk Farm. Now that Chum had passed away, Madeleine hoped, he might feel able to enter their house with a measure of enthusiasm.

'Is there anything interesting in the paper today?' she asked, glancing across at his coat.

'Not really, Maddy,' he answered. 'I don't know why I buy it sometimes. There's another report about the Crimean War and that looks as if it might drag on for years. Oh, yes,' he added, casually, 'there was a brief mention of someone called the Railway Detective.'

'Why didn't you tell me?' she scolded, hurrying across the room to pull the newspaper out of his coat pocket. 'What does it say?'

'Very little – it's barely a mention.'

She opened the paper. 'Where is it?'

'Turn over the page. It's at the bottom.'

Madeleine turned to the next page and ran her eye down the left-hand column. The item at the bottom was short but explicit. It informed its readers that Inspector Robert Colbeck had been called to the Railway Hotel in Cardiff to investigate the murder of a young man from London who had been on his way to deliver a silver coffee pot in the shape of a locomotive. It had been stolen. The victim's name was not given but Madeleine nevertheless felt a surge of pity for him. She was also worried that the crimes might keep Colbeck away from London for some time. When her father had read the item, however, he had been less concerned about the fate of the victim. What interested him was the object that had been stolen.

'A silver locomotive!' he said with a whistle.

'It's supposed to be used as a coffee pot, Father.'

'That would only tarnish the inside.'

'It must have cost an absolute fortune,' she observed.

'I'm sure it did, Maddy – what a wonderful thing to own! I couldn't bear to have a dog in the house but a silver locomotive is another matter altogether.' He gave a cackle of delight. 'Now that's something that *would* stay at the foot of my bed at night – if not on the pillow beside me!'

Expecting to find her still distraught, Colbeck was pleased to see that Effie Kellow was a little more composed on the following morning. She was clearly making an effort to be brave in the face of tragedy. Though small and almost frail, she seemed to have an instinct for survival. She and her brother, he reminded himself, had been orphaned at a young age yet had managed to find a life for themselves that had some promise on the horizon. Robbed of her brother and deprived of her dreams of escape from service, Effie somehow gave the impression that she would not surrender to the vicissitudes of Fate. There was a muted determination about her.

She and Colbeck had breakfast together. While she was patently unaccustomed to eating in a hotel, she had regained her appetite and munched her food gratefully. Leeming joined them at their table, relieved to see that Effie was managing to control her anguish.

'Has the inspector explained what's happening today?' he asked after placing his order with the waiter.

'No,' said Effie. 'I want to take Hugh's body back with me.'

'That's what I've arranged,' Colbeck told her. 'Superintendent Stockdale will have the coffin put on the eight o'clock train and there'll be a ticket bought for you.

Constable Roberts will then travel with you to London.'

She was upset. 'But I want to be alone with Hugh.'

'I think you need company, Miss Kellow, and the constable will have the necessary documents. He'll supervise the transfer of the coffin from Paddington to Wood Street where you and Mr Voke can discuss details of the funeral.'

'Very well,' she said, meekly accepting the decision.

'If you wish, Constable Roberts will make sure that you get back safely to your place of work.'

'No, Inspector – he doesn't need to do that. It's not where I want to go, you see. Not at first, that is. I prefer to go to Mrs Jennings' house.'

'Of course,' said Leeming. 'Anything belonging to your brother is your property now. It's a sort of inheritance.'

'All I want are the books that Hugh showed me,' she said. 'They fired him to be a silversmith. I'd like to keep them because they meant so much to him.' She looked up deferentially at Colbeck. 'May I ask you a favour, Inspector?'

'Of course, Miss Kellow?'

'Could you write me a letter, please? If I tell the landlady that I've come for Hugh's books, she might not believe that I'm his sister. Hugh said that she was very wary of strangers.'

'That's true,' Leeming put in. 'I had a job persuading her who I was. Mrs Jennings would be suspicious of her own shadow.'

'I'll happily jot a few lines down on paper for you,' said Colbeck. 'You won't lose anything of your brother's, Miss Kellow. I daresay there'll be property belonging to him at Mr Voke's shop as well. That will be rightfully yours.'

'It's those books that I really want,' she said, turning to

Leeming. 'Can't *you* take me back to London, Sergeant?' she asked, plaintively. 'You so were kind to me on the way here. I don't know this other policeman.'

'I'm afraid that I have to stay here in Cardiff,' said Leeming, 'but I'm sure that Constable Roberts will look after you – and he won't be wearing his uniform. He'll look like just another passenger.'

'Oh, I see.'

That appeared to allay her fears somewhat and she continued to eat her food. When the meal was over, Colbeck probed for information.

'Did you brother have any enemies, Miss Kellow?' he asked.

'None that I know of,' she returned. 'Hugh was a very friendly person. He could get along with anybody.'

'What about Stephen Voke?'

'They worked together quite well for a time then things changed. Hugh thought that Mr Voke's son was jealous of him. He was always bickering with his father,' she remembered. 'Then one day, he was gone without any explanation. Hugh said that old Mr Voke would never talk about him after that.'

'Did your brother ever mention Stephen having a close female friend?'

'No, Inspector. He told me very little about him. We only met now and again and we had more important things to talk about than Mr Voke's son.'

'What about your own brother?' enquired Colbeck. 'He seems to have been a handsome young man. Was there anyone special in his life – apart from his sister, that is?'

'Yes,' she replied, 'I think there was. Hugh mentioned her in one of his letters,' she said, opening her reticule to look inside. 'He didn't write very often and only when he had something important to say. I carry all his letters around with me.' She took one out and passed it to Colbeck. 'This came over a month ago, Inspector.'

Colbeck read it through. It contained some gossip about his work and about his landlady then it ended on a hopeful note. Hugh Kellow confided that he had met someone called Bridget and that they had become good friends. Colbeck handed the letter to Leeming so that he could read it as well.

'I've no idea who Bridget is,' admitted Effie, 'and I'm worried for her. She ought to be told what's happened to Hugh. I'd hate her to find out the way that I did – by reading the newspaper.'

'But she may already have done just that,' Colbeck pointed out. 'If they were good friends, the chances are that your brother told Bridget he was going to Cardiff with that coffee pot.'

'Mr Voke forbade him to tell *anyone* about that, Inspector. Hugh may have told me but he wouldn't have said a word to anyone else. Well,' she added, searching for another letter, 'I can prove it. I showed this to Sergeant Leeming and the superintendent.'

'That's right,' agreed Leeming, returning one letter to her as she was giving the other to Colbeck. 'The funny thing is that there's no mention of any Bridget in his last letter. Perhaps the friendship didn't last. What do you think, Inspector?'

'We can only speculate,' said Colbeck, reading the letter

before handing it back to Effie and noting the care with which she put it into her reticule. 'Mr Kellow was obviously very secretive about his visit to Cardiff and rightly so. Carrying a valuable item made him a target. What continues to puzzle me is how he ended up in this very hotel.' He turned to Effie. 'Can you throw any light on that?'

'I'm afraid not,' she said.

'Did he ever mention this hotel to you before?'

'Hugh had never been to Cardiff, sir – though he once did some work for a customer here. He was called Sir-Somebody-or-Other and he told Hugh what a good job he'd done.'

'Do you know what the item was?'

'Oh, yes,' she said. 'It was a large silver brooch in the shape of a dragon. Hugh made it last year. He showed me a sketch of the design. It was a wonderful piece of jewellery.'

Colbeck had a strong feeling that he could confirm that. He believed that he had seen that particular brooch being worn by the beautiful woman for whom it had been made – Carys Evans.

Carys Evans alighted from the chaise and went up the steps to the front door. When she pulled the bell rope, there was a loud, jangling sound from somewhere inside the house. The door was eventually opened by the butler. He recognised the visitor at once.

'Good morning, Miss Evans,' he said.

'Good morning, Glover,' she answered. 'Is Mrs Tomkins at home?'

'Yes, but I'm afraid that she's not available to callers.'

'I'm not a caller,' said Carys, easing him aside with a hand so that she could walk across the hall. 'I'm a close friend and I want to know how she is.' She knocked on the door of the drawing room and went in. 'Ah, there you are, Winifred!'

'Carys!' exclaimed the other woman in surprise, leaping to her feet. 'What are you doing here?'

'I came to see how you were, of course. When you didn't make an appearance at the play last night, I feared that you might be ill or something. You'd never miss an occasion like that as a rule.'

'We didn't feel like coming,' said Winifred.

'This business with the coffee pot has upset us both,' said Clifford Tomkins, who had been reading the newspaper when they were interrupted. 'We didn't want to spend an evening at the theatre, fending off questions about the theft.'

'I can understand that,' said Carys, 'though you missed an absolutely splendid performance. And, for once in his life, the mayor managed to provide a reception worthy of the name. You were both sorely missed.'

'We can see the play another night.'

'I'd recommend that you do so, Clifford.'

'I'm not really in the mood for watching *Macbeth*,' said Winifred. 'I find it such a depressing play.'

'It was truly inspiring at the Theatre Royal. Everyone was there. But,' she went on, holding out the letter in her hand, 'I'm forgetting my other duty. I'm delivering your post this morning.'

Tomkins took it from her. 'Where did this come from?'

'It was handed to me at the gate,' explained Carys. 'As we slowed down to turn into your drive, a rather rough-looking individual stepped out of the bushes and asked me to bring this up to the house. I didn't see any harm in doing that.' She noticed the exchange of nervous glances between them. 'Have I done something wrong?'

'Not at all, not at all,' said Tomkins.

'I suppose I should have told that man to deliver it himself. All that he had to do was to walk up the drive and put it through the letterbox. But he lurked outside the gate as if he was frightened of doing that.' She looked from one to the other. 'Why was that, do you think?'

'I really don't know,' said Winifred.

'Did you get a good look at this fellow?' asked Tomkins. 'I mean, would you know him if you saw him again?'

Carys was uncertain. 'I'm not sure,' she replied. 'I remember his clothes rather than his face. They were so grubby. He wasn't a young man and he clearly hadn't shaved for days. Also, he was wearing a hat with the brim pulled down.' She gave a shrug. 'That's all I can tell you, really. Why are you so interested in the man?'

'No reason,' said Tomkins, moving to the door. 'And do forgive our manners, Carys. Come in and take a seat. Now that you're here, I'll organise some refreshments.'

He went off into the hall and the two women sat down. Caught off guard by the sudden visit, Winifred was obviously discomfited. Carys's inquiry was deliberately gentle.

'Is there any news about the coffee pot?'

'No,' said Winifred, 'but the police are looking for it. There's a detective from London in charge of the case.'

'Yes, I had a visit from Inspector Colbeck. He's a most engaging gentleman but I still don't know why he felt obliged to call on me. I don't suppose that *you* suggested he did so, did you?'

'No, no,' lied the other.

'I was sure you wouldn't do a thing like that. It's the sort of thing Martha Pryde might do in the circumstances but not you.'

Winifred's tone was vinegary. 'I suppose that *she* was at the play last night, trying to get as much attention as usual. I really don't know what I saw in Lady Pryde. She turned out to be a real monster.'

'Those of us who know her discovered that long ago.'

'Yet you still continue to see her.'

'Only now and again,' said Carys, 'and not with any pleasure. I'd hate to be thought of as a close friend of hers. I'm more of a distant acquaintance. It's her manner I object to – she will hector.'

She was about to pass some more remarks about Lady Pryde when they were interrupted by Tomkins. Opening the door, he thrust an anxious face into the room.

'Excuse me, ladies,' he said, forcing a smile. 'I wonder if I could have a word with you in private, Winifred? Something has arisen.'

Jeremiah Stockdale arranged for the coffin to be loaded into the guard's van of the train before Effie Kellow even arrived at the station. He felt that she would be upset if she saw her brother's body arriving in a wooden casket. Victor Leeming was touched by his friend's consideration and told him so. The two men stood on the platform to wave the train off. Constable Roberts, pleased to have a day that did not entail

138

pounding his beat in Cardiff, waved back at them through the window. Effie did not even glance in their direction. As on the journey to the town, she sat motionless in deep silence.

Stockdale sighed. 'Poor girl!' he said. 'She'll never get over something like this.'

'I fancy that she will,' argued Leeming. 'Miss Kellow is stronger than she looks. I saw a glimpse of her willpower when she came to Scotland Yard. I think she'll recover in time.'

'I hope so, Sergeant. She's shown a lot more dignity than Mrs Tomkins. Effie Kellow loses her only brother yet somehow bears up well. Winifred Tomkins loses a silver coffee pot and carries on as if she's just had her arms and legs amputated with a blunt axe. When all's said and done,' he commented, 'a stolen coffee pot can be replaced. You can never replace a dead brother.'

'That's true, Superintendent.'

'She's in good hands on that train. Idris Roberts has a daughter of his own. He'll look after Miss Kellow.'

As the train vanished from sight, the two men headed towards the exit. While his sympathy was with Effie, his mind was on another young woman altogether.

'I'd like to know more about Bridget,' he said.

'Who's she?'

'A friend of Hugh Kellow – a special friend, judging by what he said about her in a letter to his sister. She showed it to us this morning. Inspector Colbeck and I had the same reaction,' he went on, 'but we didn't say anything to Miss Kellow, of course.'

'Why not?'

'It would only have alarmed her. If you ask me, the less she knows about the details of her brother's murder, the better.'

'I agree – but who is this Bridget?'

'She could – just could, perhaps – be the person we're after,' said Leeming, thoughtfully. 'Someone led Mr Kellow astray and persuaded him to go into that hotel. From everything we've heard about him, he's not the sort of person to fall into the clutches of a woman who accosts him for the first time in the street. No, it would have to be someone he knew and thought he could trust.'

'Do you believe this woman befriended him on purpose?'

'It's a possibility, Superintendent. She could have wormed her way into his affections. It may even be that they arranged to meet here at the hotel.'

'But the room was booked by a young man.'

'That must have been Bridget's accomplice – Stephen Voke.'

'Maybe,' said Stockdale, unconvinced, 'and maybe not. Do you know anything about this young woman?'

'Nothing at all beyond her name,' confessed Leeming.

'So you could be spitting in the wind.'

'We shall see.'

As they left the railway station, their attention was diverted by the roll of drums. Looking resplendent in their red uniforms, a small detachment of soldiers was marching in ranks towards St Mary Street accompanied by four drummers.

'Recruiting officers,' said Stockdale. 'They're after young men to send off to fight in the Crimea. I lost one of my constables to them this week. I told him it was suicide but he was dazzled by the promise of glory. If the enemy don't shoot him out there, he'll die of fever.'

'The war is happening such a long way away.'

'Don't you believe it, Sergeant. We very nearly had some of the action right here on our doorstep.'

'How could that be?'

'When the war first broke out,' explained the other, 'we had a Russian ship moored alongside a Turkish one in the East Dock. Back in the Crimea, of course, Russians and Turks were killing each other for the sheer love of it. I got word that the Turks were sharpening their scimitars and threatening to cut the Russians into thin slices.'

'What did you do, Superintendent?'

'I ordered the vessels to be berthed on opposite sides of the dock so that the crews weren't looking into each others' eyeballs any more. Then I made certain that the Russian ship left as soon as possible. To stop them from fighting each other at sea,' Stockdale said, 'I found an excuse to keep the Turks here for another three days.'

Leeming grinned. 'That was clever of you,' he said, admiringly. 'It sounds as if you averted a nasty international incident.'

'We do that all the time in Butetown. My men spend a lot of time keeping different nationalities apart. Last month a group of Spaniards started a fight in an opium den posing as a Chinese laundry. And there's always trouble in the brothels when some foreign sailor decides he didn't get what he paid his money for. Cardiff would be a much quieter place if only the Welsh lived here,' he concluded, 'but then it wouldn't be half as interesting. I'd hate a population made up entirely of people like Archelaus Pugh and Tegwyn Rees. They're too religious and well-behaved for my liking. I need a bit of real danger to keep me on my toes. I daresay it's the same with you, Sergeant.'

'It is – and there's always plenty of danger in London.'

'I don't want you to think the town is out of control,' warned Stockdale, 'because we rule the roost here. We raided eighty brothels last year – and you'd be surprised what we found in some of them,' he said as the image of a nude Clifford Tomkins came into his mind. 'Most of the people here are law-abiding or I'll want to know the reason why. And we do have our choirs, concerts and plays. There's always something to see. Talking of which,' he added, 'they had a great success at the Theatre Royal last night.'

'Inspector Colbeck was hoping to go there one evening.'

'Make sure that you go with him.'

'Why?'

'It's a marvellous performance, from what I hear. Harry Probert, the Town Clerk, told me that he was thrilled by it – especially by Lady Macbeth. He said that he couldn't keep his eyes off her.' He laughed merrily. 'Harry's a lecherous old devil and he's going to the play again tonight. He's bought a seat in the front row so that he can ogle Miss Kate Linnane.'

Seated on the couch, Kate Linnane read the card then smiled before putting it aside. A number of admirers had sent her flowers and she was surrounded by them. As she picked up another card, there was a tap on the door.

'Yes?' she called.

'Ah,' said Nigel Buckmaster, opening the door. 'It's not locked this morning.' He closed the door behind him. 'It was different last night.'

'I was very tired and needed my sleep.'

'You could have at least let me bid you good night.'

'I didn't wish to see you.'

'Is that so?' he said, peevishly. 'You changed your tune quickly. When I talked to Miss Evans at the reception after the play, you dragged me away from her like a jealous lover. Yet when we returned to the hotel, you barred the door against me.'

'It had been a long day, Nigel. I was exhausted.'

'So was I – we could have collapsed into each other's arms.'

'I was not in the mood.'

He mastered his irritation. 'Very well, let's leave it at that. I just trust that it won't happen again.' He glanced around. 'You have quite a floral display in here.'

'Certain gentlemen seem to have enjoyed my performance,' she said, holding up the card. 'This one is from the Town Clerk.'

'I, too, had my admirers.'

'Welsh women always have such a peculiarly bovine look to them,' she said, tartly.

'That's not true of Carys Evans – she was radiant.'

'I thought her rather dowdy.'

'Is that why you pulled me so rudely away?'

'I felt it was time to get back to the hotel.'

'After a triumphant performance like that,' he reminded her, 'we usually celebrate. You were wont to be in a more receptive mood hitherto. But,' he said, holding up both hands, 'I won't dwell on that lapse. Let's put it behind us, shall we? The important thing is that we conquered our audience. They will tell their friends and we can rely on full houses all week.'

'The Town Clerk is coming to see us again tonight,' she said as she put the card aside. 'When I told him that we'd be performing *Hamlet* in Newport next month, he promised to come and see that as well – even though he was rather surprised.'

'By what, pray?'

'The fact that I'll be playing Gertrude,' she replied. 'Mr Probert assumed that I'd be Ophelia. He said that I was far too young to play Hamlet's mother whereas you were far too old to play the Prince.'

'That's nonsense!' he cried, stung by the comment. 'It's my greatest role and it's brought me acclaim all over the country. I expect to play Hamlet for at least another decade.'

'At that age, you ought to be playing Claudius – if not Polonius.'

'I need no advice about casting from you, Kate!' he snarled. 'I think you should remember what you were when you first came to my attention. You played non-speaking parts in that execrable touring company. I rescued you from that misery. I saw your true promise. I taught you the essence of the actor's art. Within a year, you were playing Ophelia to my Hamlet.'

'Yes,' she said, pointedly, 'a part that I've now yielded to Miss Tremaine. Where did you pluck that useless creature from, Nigel?'

'Laura Tremaine has a talent.'

'For what – it's certainly not acting!'

He grinned wolfishly. 'Do I detect a note of envy?'

'I could never envy that empty-headed little baggage. Her Lady Macduff is ludicrous but it pales beside her appalling Ophelia. Be prepared, Nigel. When the audience in Newport realises that Ophelia has drowned herself, they'll break into spontaneous applause.'

'Let's have more respect for a fellow-actress, please!'

'Then cast one worthy of the name.'

'A company must pull together, Kate.'

'Spare me, please – I've heard that speech too many times.'

'There's no talking to when you're in such a fevered state,' he said, moving to the door. 'I hope you'll have come to your senses by the time we go on stage this evening – and when we get back here.'

'Knock on someone else's door,' she advised, rising to her feet to strike a pose. 'I daresay Miss Tremaine will leave hers unlocked for you. Lady Macduff would fawn at your feet.'

'Stop it, Kate!' he ordered.

'Or perhaps Miss Carys Evans is more to your taste.'

'I'll have no more of it, do you understand? You're acting like a dog in a manger – *you* may not want something yet you're determined that nobody else will have it.'

'Close the door when you go out, please.'

Buckmaster fumed. 'I'll see you later,' he said, angrily, 'when I trust that you will behave like a grateful member of a company that *I* happen to manage. Remember that.'

Storming out of the room, he left the door wide open.

* * *

Robert Colbeck studied the letter with interest. It was written by the same person who had penned the earlier ransom note. He handed it to Victor Leeming to read. Clifford and Winifred Tomkins had sent for the detectives and now watched them carefully. Winifred was excited at the prospect of getting her coffee pot back while her husband was resenting the cost involved. As a businessman, he had been used to driving a hard bargain, paying the lowest price for something he could sell at the largest profit. It appalled him that he would have to buy back something on which he had already spent fifty pounds deposit.

'These instructions seem quite clear,' said Colbeck. 'The money is to be handed over this evening. Do you have it ready, sir?'

'Yes, Inspector,' said Tomkins, 'but I'm loathe to let it out of my hands. Supposing that the thief simply grabs it and runs away?'

'Sergeant Leeming will make sure that doesn't happen.'

'I'm still unhappy about the whole thing.'

'It's the only way to get my coffee pot back, Clifford,' said his wife. 'You promised me that you'd pay anything to retrieve it.'

'Anything within limits,' he corrected.

'With luck, it won't cost you anything at all. The sergeant will arrest the thief so that the money and the coffee pot are both safe.'

'There is one debt to discharge, Mrs Tomkins,' said Colbeck. 'Mr Kellow died before he could collect the balance from your husband. All that's been paid to Mr Voke so far is the deposit. I'll be glad to take the rest of the money to him on your behalf.'

'Let's make sure that we've still got it,' said Tomkins.

'I've no reason to doubt that, sir.'

'According to this,' said Leeming, handing the letter back to the inspector, 'Mr Tomkins is supposed to hand over the money. If, as we suspect, the villain is Stephen Voke then there could be a problem. We know that he was still working for his father when Mr Tomkins went to the shop to commission the coffee pot.'

'That was a long while ago, Sergeant,' said Tomkins.

'And there's something else you should have noticed,' said Colbeck. 'The exchange is to be made when evening shadows are falling. In bad light, you could certainly be taken for Mr Tomkins, I fancy. Stephen Voke – if, indeed, it is him – will see little of your face.'

'Didn't you say you thought a woman might be there to take the money?' asked Winifred. 'I find that hard to countenance, I must say.'

'Look at the handwriting, Mrs Tomkins,' suggested Colbeck. 'It is patently a woman's. I think that significant. Well, you've both seen the instructions. Has she chosen a good place for the exchange?'

'Yes,' said Tomkins, grudgingly. 'Sergeant Leeming will be seen from a long way off. If the thief has the slightest suspicion, he or she can simply vanish.'

'That's why the sergeant will be alone.'

Leeming grinned. 'Carrying all that money,' he said. 'It will be a new experience for me to be so well off, if only for a short while.'

'Take care of every penny,' urged Tomkins.

'And *please* bring my coffee pot back to me,' said Winifred.

Colbeck held up the letter. 'How was this delivered?'

'There was a man loitering at our gate, apparently,' she explained. 'When a friend arrived in her chaise, he thrust it into her hand and asked her to bring it to us. All she can recall of the fellow was that he was badly dressed and was in need of a shave. Oh, and he was not young.'

'He was probably paid to do exactly what he did. It's unlikely that he has any connection with the murder and the theft. By the way,' he went on, giving the letter to her, 'who was the friend who brought this to your door?'

'It was Carys Evans.'

'How interesting!' said Colbeck, thinking of a silver brooch in the shape of a dragon. 'And were you expecting the lady to call?'

'Oh, no,' replied Winifred. 'She came without warning. Carys had some flimsy excuse about being worried because my husband and I failed to attend the play last night. I think that she just came to enjoy my discomfort at losing that silver coffee pot.'

Colbeck could imagine another reason altogether for the visit.

CHAPTER NINE

Sir David Pryde stood in front of the cheval-mirror as he adjusted his bow tie then ran a palm over his thinning hair. His wife, meanwhile, was seated at her dressing table, putting the finishing touches to her appearance. She issued a command.

'Don't drink so much champagne this evening, David.'

'I like it,' he protested.

'Sometimes, I fear, it does not like you. At the reception last night, I don't think you realised how many glasses you had. And what was the result?' she asked, swinging round to face him. 'You had one of your migraines yet again.'

'It wore off after a few hours, Martha.'

'That may be so but it meant that you spent the night in the other room instead of beside me. I prefer to sleep with my husband.'

'Then that's what you'll do tonight,' he promised. 'I'll take care to drink in moderation. I missed being with you last night but my head was splitting when we got home. It was excruciating. I would not have been good company'

His recurring migraines were a useful invention. They gave him an excuse to leave the marital couch occasionally and slip away from the house for an assignation. His wife was a heavy sleeper. Once she had dozed off, she would not hear the horse's hooves as he rode off into the darkness. When she had been awakened by her husband that morning, it never crossed her mind that he had spent the night near Llandaff Cathedral with another woman.

'Who else is dining with the Somervilles?' he asked.

'I've no idea – as long as it's not Winifred Tomkins and her husband. They're such dreary people. Agnes Somerville maintains high standards at her dinner table so I think we're safe from a brush with Winifred.'

'At the play last night, you actually *wanted* to see her.'

'That was only so that I could crow over her.'

'Had she been there, you should have ignored her altogether. Both she and Tomkins should be ostracised,' he said, testily. 'I won't have anyone speaking to my wife that way or casting aspersions on one of our children.'

'Dorothy does *not* have a squint,' declared Martha, getting to her feet like a combative speaker at a public meeting. 'She has a way of screwing up one eye, that's all. I've always thought it an endearing habit. Winifred only said that because I caught her on the raw when I told her that living in Merthyr was bound to blunt a person's finer feelings. It's an iron town, for heaven's sake – there must be ash and stench and pandemonium there all day long. How can anyone of taste live in such a godless inferno?'

'We should never have admitted them to our circle.'

'It was not merely our daughter whom she attacked. That vicious-tongued harpy made some unkind comments about you as well, David.'

'I don't want to hear them,' he said, having already done so many times. 'Neither she nor that husband of hers are fit to consort with us, Martha. They are *personae non gratae* – not that I'd expect either of them to understand Latin. We should be relieved that they didn't turn up to see *Macbeth*. Everyone of consequence was there.'

'That rules out Winifred.' They shared a brittle laugh. 'Did you happen to notice Carys Evans at the reception?'

'I caught a fleeing glimpse of her, I think,' he replied, turning back to the mirror to brush some non-existent dust off his shoulder. 'I was too busy talking to the mayor about the Council's plans for the town. I never miss an opportunity to mix business with pleasure.'

'She's starting to look her age.'

'Who is?'

'Carys Evans,' she said. 'She may be pretty enough now but her looks will soon fade. She should take advantage of them while she still has them. It's almost indecent for a woman to remain single for so long. I was barely twenty when you proposed to me.'

Pryde smiled. 'You were only seventeen when I first saw you,' he recalled. 'It took me three years to pluck up the necessary courage.' He spun round to face her. 'And I've been the happiest of men ever since, Martha.'

'You used to drink even more champagne in those days. I don't remember it ever giving you a migraine then.'

'I'm starting to suffer the defects of old age, my love.'

'Fiddlesticks! You're as hale and hearty as ever.'

'That's certainly true of you,' he said, dredging up the sort of compliment she required on a regular basis. 'You are still the lovely young bride I took to the altar.'

She was spiteful. 'If you want to see the defects of old age, look no further than Winifred Tomkins. A stranger would take her for seventy or more. Think of those bags under her eyes, that air of decay and that dreadful, unsightly, sagging body.'

He was too diplomatic to point out that his wife was much heavier than the other woman and had even more prominent eye-bags. Lady Pryde liked to inhabit a world where she was always praised and never contradicted. Her friends understood that and indulged her accordingly. It had been Winifred Tomkins' mistake to question the acknowledged perfection of Lady Pryde and her family. Honesty, she had learnt, had no place in any dealings with Martha Pryde.

'David,' she said, crossing to stand in front of him.

'Yes, my love?'

'How did you come to know of that silversmith – the one who made that absurd coffee pot?'

'I've told you that, Martha.'

'Tell me again,' she pressed. 'I've forgotten.'

'Jack Somerville gave me that silver snuff box for my birthday,' he told her. 'When I heard that it was made by a Mr Voke of Wood Street in London, I took note of his name. It was exceptionally well-made. That's why I engaged him to make that silver yacht for me.'

'I remember your going to London to meet him.'

'I was impressed by his work.'

152

'So his reputation rested on that little snuff box?'

'Of course not, Martha,' he said. 'I required more evidence than that before I committed myself. Jack showed me some candlesticks he got from the man. They were superb – solid silver and exquisitely fashioned. That's why I commissioned the yacht from Voke. If you want to blame anyone for putting Winifred Tomkins in touch with that silversmith,' he went on, 'then the real culprit is Jack Somerville – but please don't challenge him about it this evening.'

'I have more tact than that, David.'

After a final look in the dressing room mirror, she was ready to leave. They went downstairs to the hall where the butler was waiting to open the front door for them, inclining his head as they passed. Pryde helped his wife into the phaeton then sat beside her. The driver cracked his whip and the vehicle lurched forward. After a prolonged silence, Martha whispered a question to her husband.

'Do *you* think that Dorothy has a squint?'

Victor Leeming was in high spirits. All that he had to do was to go through the motions of handing over a substantial amount of money before apprehending someone responsible both for murder and theft. By checking the copy of *Bradshaw* that Colbeck always took with him when they left the capital, he had seen that there was a late train to Paddington. If the exchange went as planned, he might be able to shake the dust of Cardiff from his feet and travel back to his wife and family, basking in the fulsome praise he would unquestionably have received from Clifford and Winifred Tomkins. The crimes would be solved within the hour.

'Do exactly as that letter told you,' warned Colbeck.

'I will, Inspector.'

'They'll be watching for any false move.'

'Where will you be?'

'The nearest I can get without arousing suspicion is about a quarter of a mile away.'

'What about Superintendent Stockdale?'

'He's standing by at the railway station in case of mishap.'

'There won't *be* a mishap,' said Leeming, hurt that it should even be suggested. 'I've done this before, Inspector. I know what to expect.'

'I trust you implicitly, Victor. My fear is that, when you arrest one person, his or her accomplice will take flight. The obvious way to escape the town is by rail so that's why the superintendent will be guarding the station.'

Leeming was placated. 'Oh, I see. It makes sense when you explain it like that.' He put on his top hat and looked in the mirror. 'Do you think I'll be taken for Mr Tomkins?'

'I'm sure that you will,' said Colbeck. 'You're a far better double than me. I'm too tall and slim to fool anybody. You're much younger than Mr Tomkins but you're closer to his build – and your face won't be seen in the twilight until it's too late.'

'I'll have the handcuffs on him in two seconds,' said Leeming, taking them out and dangling them in the air. 'Stephen Voke will get the surprise of his life.'

'What if the person you arrest is a woman named Bridget?'

'She deserves the same treatment, sir.'

They were in the hotel room where they had spent the

previous night. Leeming hoped that he would not have to stay there for the second time. It was up to him to ensure that he and Colbeck could catch the late train to Paddington. Putting the handcuffs away, he reached into a pocket to take out a thick wad of banknotes.

'I've never held this much money in my hands before.'

'Don't be tempted, Victor,' teased Colbeck. 'Crime doesn't pay.'

'It pays very well if *this* is what you get by way of a ransom. Stealing a silver coffee pot is far better than kidnapping a person. You don't have the problem of guarding and feeding someone who's been abducted. A coffee pot is also much easier to hide.'

'That's assuming that they actually have it in their possession.'

'They must do, sir.'

'Must they?' asked Colbeck. 'Allow for every eventuality, Victor. It's not impossible that those ransom notes are part of an elaborate hoax. You saw the report in the local newspaper. Everyone in Cardiff is aware that Mrs Tomkins had her silver coffee pot stolen. What's to stop an enterprising local villain from claiming to have it in order to squeeze some money out of a wealthy man? Instead of pursuing a killer tonight, we could be on a wild goose chase.'

Leeming was deflated. 'Does that mean we *won't* be able to catch the late train back to London?' he asked, disconsolately.

As the evening wore slowly on, Clifford and Winifred Tomkins grew increasingly nervous. He was worried about the ransom money he had handed over and she was frightened that her silver coffee pot might have been badly damaged in some way. Doubts arose in her mind.

'How much faith can we place in Inspector Colbeck?'

'He seems to know what he's doing, Winifred.'

'I think that *you* should have taken the ransom.'

Tomkins spluttered. 'And run the risk of being hurt?' he said in alarm. 'We're up against a killer. I think it's very brave of Sergeant Leeming to confront him.'

'But the letter said that it should be you, Clifford.'

'Nobody will know the difference in this light.'

They were in the library, a large, oak-panelled room with well-stocked bookshelves around three walls. Most of the volumes would never even be looked at but Tomkins had felt it important to have a library for show. Crossing to the window, he peered out.

'It's starting to get dark already.'

'I just wish I had more confidence in Inspector Colbeck.'

'Stockdale has been singing his praises aloud.'

'He can't be relied on,' complained Winifred. 'There's corruption in the police force and, according to Lady Pryde, the superintendent takes bribes.'

'That's wicked gossip,' said Tomkins, who had not parted with a penny to secure Stockdale's silence about the nocturnal raid on a particular brothel. 'One or two constables have been dismissed for drunkenness, it's true, and others have been slack in their duties but that's to be expected. There will always be a smattering of drunks and idlers in any organisation. Look at the problems we had with the police in Merthyr – it was far worse there. I think the superintendent is to be commended with the way he runs things here.'

'Lady Pryde knows him better than we do.'

'She thinks that *everyone* is either corrupt or untrustworthy. I'm amazed to hear you quoting her, Winifred. Lady Pryde is a ferocious snob and I'm glad we've severed all links with her.'

'She said the most unforgivable things about Merthyr.'

'That was only because she's never been there.'

'She called it a disgusting and uncivilised hole populated by the dregs of humanity.'

'Sir David should take her for a walk around Butetown at night,' he said, grimly, 'then she'd see just how uncivilised Cardiff can be.'

'She laughed when I told first told her about my coffee pot,' said Winifred, still wounded by the memory. 'That's when I realised how much I loathed her. Well, she may laugh on the other side of her hideous face when everyone tells her what a magnificent object it is.'

'Let's get it back here first.'

'What time is it, Clifford?'

He pulled a watch from his waistcoat pocket. 'It's almost time for the exchange,' he told her. 'In a few minutes, Sergeant Leeming will be apprehending the thief. The money and the coffee pot should be safely returned here before very long.'

From the moment he started to walk along the path, Leeming knew that he was being watched. Though he could not see anybody, he was aware of their presence. Light was fading in the park and trees and shrubs were taking on a ghostly shape. Obeying the instructions in the letter, he was carrying a small bag containing the ransom money. As he walked past a fountain, he lifted the bag up in his right hand to indicate that he was following orders. Then he strolled on, looking neither to right nor left. Heading for a stand of trees in the middle distance, he quickened his step. *That* was where the exchange would be made, he decided. Someone with a telescope was probably watching every step that he took.

Halfway there, he had to go past a clump of bushes. Eyes fixed on the trees, he ignored all else. It was a serious error. No sooner had he passed a large bush than someone jumped up from behind him, knocked off his top hat then struck his head with something hard and heavy. Oblivious to what had happened, Leeming collapsed in a heap. It was some time before he began to regain consciousness. His head was pounding like a drum, the wound was smarting unbearably and blood was trailing down the back of his coat. His brain was on fire. Trying to stand, he keeled over at once. He finished on his hands and knees. When it finally dawned on him that he had fallen into a trap, the ransom money was a mile away.

Nothing that Robert Colbeck said could moderate the passion of Clifford and Winifred Tomkins. They were thoroughly outraged. Tomkins had been relieved of his money and Winifred had nothing to show for it in return. No shred of sympathy was shown towards Victor Leeming.

'You let us both down, Inspector,' said Tomkins, seething

with fury. 'I shall be informing your superior of this fiasco.'

'You misled us,' howled Winifred. 'You assured us that we'd have that coffee pot back where it belonged before nightfall. Now I have no hope of ever seeing it here.'

'Your conduct has been appalling, sir.'

'We feel utterly cheated.'

'Well?' demanded Tomkins. 'What have you to say?'

'My thoughts are with Sergeant Leeming,' said Colbeck, coolly, 'and I'm shocked that neither of you has given him a second thought. He was the person who walked into danger on your behalf. At the very least, that might merit an ounce of gratitude.'

Tomkins was unrepentant. 'He lost my money.'

'No, sir – he had it taken away from him by a brutal attacker. The sergeant had no call to be there,' Colbeck told them. 'That letter specified that you would carry the money, Mr Tomkins. Had you not been spared that task by a brave officer, then it would have been *your* head that was battered with a chunk of stone.' Tomkins put a hand protectively against the back of his skull. 'Would you have had the courage to take part in the exchange, sir?'

'I would not,' conceded Tomkins, shamefacedly.

'Then show some pity for the man who did.'

'How is he?' asked Winifred, much more subdued now.

'The doctor is with him at the moment,' said Colbeck. 'With luck, there'll be no permanent damage but the sergeant has a nasty scalp wound. When I spoke to him, he was still unsure what actually occurred. In the circumstances, I can understand that. If you'll excuse me,' he continued, 'I'll get back to him.'

'Wait!' said Tomkins.

'I'll disturb you no longer, sir. You'll want to write your letter of complaint to my superior. His name is Edward Tallis, by the way. He holds the rank of superintendent.'

'Perhaps I was being too hasty, Inspector.'

'Selfish is the word that springs to mind, Mr Tomkins.'

'I'm entitled to worry about losing that money.'

'And I'm entitled to feel thoroughly upset about my coffee pot,' said Winifred, returning to the attack. 'We're sorry about Sergeant Leeming, of course, but we have to face facts. You promised that everything would go as planned and *this* happens. We're bound to question your judgement, Inspector.'

'Yes,' said her husband, revived by her show of spirit, 'we'll not be made to feel guilty. We're the victims here, after all. Thanks to you, we'll never see that money or that coffee pot ever again.'

'Then you have little insight into the criminal mind, sir,' said Colbeck. 'You've not heard the last of them yet.'

'What do you mean?'

'They will want every penny that they can get from you. It's only a question of time before you get another ransom note.'

Tomkins turned puce. 'Pay for that damned coffee pot a *third* time!' he shouted. 'I simply refuse to do that.'

'To be precise, you've only paid in full for it once.'

'Plus the fifty pounds I paid on deposit.'

'That went to Mr Voke,' noted Colbeck. 'All that you sacrificed today was the full price of the item. If you have another demand – as I'm sure you soon will – it will be for a second payment.'

'They won't get a brass farthing from me.'

'Clifford,' said his wife, warningly.

'I wish I'd never bought that confounded thing!'

Winifred bit back what she was going to say. Containing her rage with palpable difficulty, she gritted her teeth and turned to Colbeck.

'My husband and I need to discuss this matter, Inspector.'

'No discussion is needed!' Tomkins blurted out.

'Could you give us some privacy, please?' she asked.

'I was going to leave in any case, Mrs Tomkins,' said Colbeck, heading for the door. 'My place is with Sergeant Leeming. Please excuse me,' he added with a mischievous smile. 'I know that you and your husband have much to talk about.'

'How does it feel now?' asked Stockdale, bending solicitously over him.

'As if someone is trying to bore a hole in my skull,' said Leeming, gingerly touching the back of his bandaged head. 'It's like being very drunk without the pleasure of having touched alcohol.'

'How much can you remember?'

'Not a great deal, Superintendent – I was striding past some bushes then everything suddenly went blank. I must have walked into an ambush.'

'I wish I'd been closer,' said Stockdale, 'instead of being stuck at the railway station. I should have ringed the whole area with my men.'

'That would have scared them off completely.'

'Maybe – but it would have saved you a nasty headache.'

'Estelle hates it when I get injured in the line of duty.'

'Is that your wife?'

'She thinks that being a policeman is too hazardous. Estelle would prefer it if I worked for her father in his ironmonger's shop. I want more out of life than selling tin baths,' asserted Leeming. 'I need the feeling that I'm doing something really useful.'

They were in the superintendent's office at the police station in St Mary Street. Leeming was slumped in a chair, partially revived by the glass of brandy he had been given but still faintly groggy. The wound had been examined, cleaned and stitched by a doctor and thick bandaging tied in place. It might still be possible to catch the late train to Paddington but – not wishing to return home in that condition – he resigned himself to spending another night in Cardiff. By the next day, he hoped, the agony might have eased and the swirling fog in his mind might have cleared.

There was a tap on the door then Colbeck entered.

'How are you now, Victor?' he asked.

Leeming was stoical. 'I'll survive, sir.'

'I'm sorry I couldn't wait until the doctor had finished. I felt that Mr and Mrs Tomkins ought to know as soon as possible what had transpired.'

'I'd much rather *you* told them than me.'

'I can't imagine that they showed much gratitude for what the sergeant did,' said Stockdale. 'They're a mean-minded pair.'

'You're placing too kind a construction on their behaviour,' said Colbeck. 'They were abominable. They ranted at me for betraying them and took no account of

Victor's injury. I don't think he'd have elicited genuine compassion out of them if he'd been killed in the attack. It's difficult to say which of them is worse – the blustering husband or the wrathful wife.'

'They're tarred with the same brush,' said the superintendent with asperity. 'It's a shame they were not feathered at the same time.'

Colbeck was philosophical. 'They're not the most likeable human beings,' he conceded, 'but we have to remember that they *are* the victims of a crime.'

'So is Victor Leeming – thanks to them!'

'The culprit has so far committed murder, robbery and violent assault,' said Leeming, ruefully, 'and that makes me certain it's a man. No woman could knock me cold like that.'

'They could if you walked around the docks at night,' warned Stockdale with a ripe chortle. 'There are some wild creatures down there – Big Ruth, for instance. She once floored one of my constables with a belaying pin. It took four of them to arrest her.'

'The woman we're looking for is less of a virago,' said Colbeck, 'but her charm is as just as effective as a belaying pin. It's clear that she has a male accomplice to do her dirty work. We'll be hearing from them before too long, I daresay.'

'Won't they simply take the money and run?'

'No, Superintendent – they can sniff an even bigger pay day.'

Leeming gaped. 'Will I have to go through that *again*?'

'I'll go in your place, Sergeant,' offered Stockdale.

'Thank you.'

'I look far more like Clifford Tomkins than you do.'

'Neither of you will be called upon,' decided Colbeck. 'They won't repeat the same trick again because they know we'd be ready for it next time. We tried to fox them and they outwitted us. The rules will be changed for the second exchange.'

'I can't wait to catch up with Stephen Voke,' said Leeming with quiet determination. 'He won't find it quite so easy to get the better of me when my back isn't turned.'

'I look forward to meeting him as well,' said Stockdale, harshly. 'We've got an empty cell all ready for the bastard.'

Colbeck brooded. 'The person who really interests me is the woman,' he said at length. 'All that we know about her so far is that she's beautiful, persuasive and highly resourceful. She must also be utterly pitiless to condone such brutality. I'd love to know what the lady is doing right this minute.'

'I'm terribly sorry I'm so late,' said Carys Evans to her hosts. 'I hope that I haven't held you all up.'

She arrived at the Somerville residence when the other guests were still enjoying a pre-prandial glass of champagne in the drawing room. There were almost a dozen people there and she knew them all well. Everyone gave her a cordial welcome but it was Lady Pryde who bore down on her with a possessive glint. Carys was very glad that someone put a glass into her hand. She took a preparatory sip of champagne.

'There you are!' said Martha, taking by the elbow to guide her into a corner of the room. 'We'd given you up, Miss Evans.'

'I was delayed at the last moment. I'm afraid.'

'Well, at least you're here now. Tell me – do you have any news of that deplorable Winifred Tomkins?'

'I do, as a matter of fact,' said Carys. 'I called at the house this morning to see why she and her husband were absent from the play.'

'What did they say?'

'That they didn't relish the idea of spending a couple of hours being asked about the theft of that coffee pot. To listen to Winifred talk, you'd have thought there'd been a death in the family.'

Martha smirked. 'She's been really hurt by this, hasn't she?'

'Yes, Lady Pryde.'

'*That* will teach her to criticise me! I hope that someone has taken that ludicrous coffee pot hundreds of miles away from here.'

'Then I have to disappoint you,' said Carys, 'because I was given the firm impression that it's still here in Cardiff.'

'What makes you think that?'

'It was their behaviour this morning. As I arrived at their house, I was given a letter for them by a shabby-looking fellow who'd been skulking at the bottom of their drive. He asked me to deliver it then scurried off.'

'Who was this mysterious individual?'

'He was clearly no friend of Winifred and her husband or he'd have delivered the letter himself. When I handed the missive over,' Carys continued, 'Clifford Tomkins went out of the room to read it. The next minute, he put his head back into the room to summon his wife. He looked apprehensive.'

'What did you make of it, Miss Evans?'

'I fancy that the letter might have had some connection with the stolen coffee pot. This is mere speculation, of course, and I may be well wide of the mark but supposing the thief wishes to sell it back to Winifred?'

'Sell it back?' repeated Martha in annoyance.

'At a high price, I daresay.'

'So she may have her coffee pot, after all. This is dire news.'

'It's not news, Lady Pryde – it's pure guesswork on my part.'

'Either way, it's still very disturbing.'

'Good evening, Miss Evans,' said Pryde, descending on them with a broad smile. 'I'm so glad that you've joined us at last.'

'Thank you, Sir David,' said Carys.

'My wife always says that being late is a lady's privilege.'

'I stayed at the cathedral this afternoon rather longer than I intended to – Llandaff is so beautiful in the sunshine.'

'I agree, Miss Evans. It's always a pleasure to visit.' He saw the grimace of Martha's face. 'You look as if you've just eaten something very disagreeable, my dear. Has something upset you?'

'Yes,' grunted Martha. 'That silver coffee pot is still in Cardiff.'

Victor Leeming was a robust man but he had still been shaken up by the attack. Spurning the offer of a meal, all that he wanted to do was to return to the hotel room to rest. Colbeck accompanied him there, leaving the sergeant propped up on pillows so that there was no pressure on the back of his head. The inspector then returned to the lounge to talk with Stockdale over a drink. They went methodically through all the facts at their disposal. Colbeck ventured one possible conclusion.

'I keep coming back to the name of Carys Evans,' he said.

'No,' argued Stockdale, 'I've been thinking about that. I reckon that Carys is far too ladylike to get tangled up in serious crimes.'

'She's not too ladylike to become someone else's mistress and we know that she was actually in the hotel at the time of the murder.'

'There may be an explanation for that, Inspector. Sir David Pryde is a major shareholder in this hotel. One of his perquisites is to have a room permanently reserved for any business associate who visits the town.'

'Are you telling me that he and Miss Evans might have made use of that hotel room on the day in question?'

'It's only a suggestion.'

'Would they be quite so blatant? Why risk being seen together in broad daylight when they could arrange a rendezvous after dark in a less public place? No, I fancy she was here for another purpose.'

'It's the question of motive that troubles me, Inspector.'

'Miss Evans has expensive tastes,' said Colbeck. 'She loves silver above all else and, I suspect, would have no scruples about stealing that coffee pot in order to cause a flutter in the Tomkins household. Though she claims to be a friend of Winifred Tomkins, she is more than ready to ridicule her.'

'The one thing that does support the theory,' said Stockdale, reflectively, 'is that Carys is eminently capable of luring a man into a hotel room simply by looking into his eyes. I can tell you that *I* would not need a second invitation from her.'

'She is a very striking lady and that would incline me to absolve her of any real suspicion.'

'Why?'

'Carys Evans is a woman of quality. She moves among the elite here in Cardiff. If – for the sake of argument – we accept that the killer is Stephen Voke, then we encounter a problem. Would someone like Miss Evans concoct a plot with a young silversmith? How did she meet him? What would she see in such a person?'

'You answered that question earlier, Inspector. She dotes on silver. Who better to woo her than a talented silversmith?'

'But she already seems to have all that she needs.'

'Women always want more,' said Stockdale, cynically.

'She seems to live very comfortably.'

'Much of what you saw there was provided by her admirers. Sir David is only the latest to enjoy her favours. There have been others, squeezed for what she can get out of them and then discarded. I bow to none in my esteem for her,' said the superintendent, 'but I never forget that she is, in essence, a heartless predator.'

'Is she capable of being party to a murder?'

The question hung unanswered in the air. Archelaus Pugh came over to them with a letter in his hand. He gave it to Colbeck.

'This has just arrived for you, Inspector,' said Pugh.

'Who brought it?'

'I can't tell you, sir. It was simply tossed into the foyer.'

As the manager withdrew, Colbeck opened the letter and read the message that was written in large capitals. It berated him for sending someone in place of Clifford Tomkins with the ransom money and gave strict instructions for a second exchange. When he had finished it, he passed it over to Stockdale.

'Is it from the killer?' asked the superintendent.

'Yes,' replied Colbeck. 'He's doubled the price of the coffee pot and insists that Mrs Tomkins hands over the money next time. As you can see from the taunts made to me, he – or she – knows exactly who I am and why I'm here. That will make things much more difficult.'

CHAPTER TEN

Clifford and Winifred Tomkins had shared a frosty breakfast during which neither of them spoke. It was only when the plates had been cleared away that she finally broke the silence.

'I must say that I find your attitude very hurtful, Clifford.'

'I did not get where I am by throwing money away,' he said, pompously. 'I'll not be duped a second time.'

'How little you must care for my feelings!' she complained.

'Your well-being has been the major concern of our marriage.'

'Then why do you turn against me now?'

'I'm not turning against you,' he said, trying to appease her with a flabby smile, 'but you must see sense, Winifred. The thief has no intention of parting with the silver coffee pot. He simply wishes to grab as much money as he can from us. We've already had it dangled in front of our eyes once and you saw what happened.'

'Yes,' she rejoined, 'Sergeant Leeming was assaulted because we did not comply with the instructions we were given. Had *you* handed over the money, you would almost certainly have been given that coffee pot in return.'

'I disagree.'

'We must do as they tell us.'

'Then we give up all hope of capturing these villains.'

'I'm far more interested in retrieving my coffee pot than seeing anyone arrested,' she admitted. 'Just pay up and have done with it.'

'Winifred,' he scolded, 'these people have committed a murder.'

'That's a separate matter and we can leave it to Inspector Colbeck to deal with that. We mustn't confuse the issue. All that we need worry about is our stolen property.'

'I think that you should forget all about it.'

She was indignant. 'I could never do that – Lady Pryde would mock me unmercifully.'

'You no longer have anything to do with the woman.'

'We have mutual friends, Clifford, and she would goad me through them somehow. Don't you see? My social standing in the town is at stake. That coffee pot is not simply a memento of dear Father, it's the one secure way of regaining my position here.'

'That was never under threat, Winifred.'

'I feel that it is.'

The sound of the doorbell ended the conversation. Not used to visitors at that time of the morning, they wondered who it could be. It was not long before the butler came into the dining room.

'Inspector Colbeck is here to see you,' he announced.

Her hopes rose. 'Perhaps he has good news for us!'

'Show the inspector into the drawing room, Glover,' said Tomkins. 'We'll be there directly.'

'Very good, sir,' said the butler, going out.

'It may be that he's made an arrest,' said Winifred.

'I beg leave to doubt that.'

'Superintendent Stockdale's men have been searching the whole town. They might have cornered the villains. Who knows? It may even be that the inspector has brought my coffee pot with him.'

'I think you're being far too optimistic.'

'Why else should he come at this hour?'

'Let's go and find out,' said Tomkins, 'but don't bank on hearing good news. That silver coffee pot is cursed.'

'Don't be nonsensical.'

'It is, Winifred. It's caused us nothing but trouble and my guess is that there's a lot more to come.'

'I don't believe that for a second.'

'We shall see.'

They went into the drawing room and found Robert Colbeck studying a portrait on the wall. To Winifred's dismay, he had brought nothing with him. She looked up at the oil painting.

'That's my father,' she said, proudly. 'He was a far-sighted man. As soon as railways began to be built, he realised that they had a wonderful future ahead of them. He once brought Mr Brunel to the house. Father thought that he was a miracle-worker.'

'I'd endorse that, Mrs Tomkins,' said Colbeck. 'When the

173

notion of the Taff Vale Railway was first discussed, critics said that that it could never be constructed over such difficult terrain. Mr Brunel took up the challenge and made light of the problems.'

'We know that, Inspector,' said Tomkins. 'When the line opened in 1841, I was able to transport iron and steel from Merthyr to Cardiff in less than an hour. Until then, we'd had to rely on road and canal hauliers and they moved like snails.'

'I'd be happy to discuss the topic in more detail with you, sir, but this is not the appropriate moment, alas.' He took out the letter. 'This was delivered to me at the hotel yesterday.'

'Why to you and not us?' demanded Winifred.

'Because the person who sent it feared that this house might be under surveillance. Also, of course, he wanted to issue a warning.'

She started. 'He hasn't threatened to destroy my coffee pot?'

'No, Mrs Tomkins. The warning was aimed at me. I – and, by implication, Superintendent Stockdale – was ordered to keep out of the ransom negotiations altogether.' He gave the letter to Tomkins. 'See for yourself, sir. The instructions are for you and your wife alone.'

Winifred was impatient. 'What does it say? Let me see it.'

'Give me chance to read it first,' said her husband.

'Do they still have my coffee pot?'

'Yes,' Colbeck told her, 'but it comes at a price.'

Tomkins was horror struck. '*Double* the cost,' he yelled in disbelief. 'They expect me to pay double the cost? That's quite inconceivable. In all, it would mean paying three times the value of the item, plus the fifty pounds already paid to Mr Voke as a deposit.'

'Give it to me,' said Winifred, snatching the letter from him and reading it quickly. 'At least, they do have it and they promise that they'll hand it over next time.' The conditions made her shiver. 'They want *me* to make the exchange.'

'Then it's out of the question on two grounds,' said Tomkins. 'I would never part with the sum of money demanded and I refuse to let my wife imperil herself by handing it over.'

'In that case,' said Colbeck, flatly, 'the thieves will simply vanish and try to find a buyer elsewhere. More to the point, our chance of catching them will disappear as well.'

'You're surely not advocating that we agree to their demands?'

'I believe that you should consider doing so, sir.'

'My wife could be bludgeoned to death, Inspector.'

'If you read the letter again, Mr Tomkins, I think you'll find there's a firm promise that your wife will come to no harm. All that they want is the money.'

'They can go to the devil!'

'Clifford!' said his wife, reproachfully.

'I'll not deal with blood-suckers.'

'We have to think this through very carefully,' she said, making a supreme effort to keep calm. 'There has to be a way to get what we want out of this situation.'

'Yes – we ignore this to start with,' said Tomkins, grabbing the letter from her and scrunching it up into a ball. 'Nobody is going to give me orders.'

Colbeck extended a hand. 'If you don't want that, sir,' he

said, 'then perhaps you'd give it to me. It's a piece of valuable evidence. I'm sure that you noticed how different this was from the two earlier ransom notes. It's written in block capitals. There has to be a reason for that.'

'Take the damn thing!' said Tomkins, thrusting it at him.

'But we may need it, Clifford,' cried his wife.

'The whole matter is closed.'

'I refuse to accept that.'

'Winifred, the demands are beyond all reason.'

'They are to you,' she said, 'so I suggest that you are no longer involved in the transaction. I have money of my own. Since you are too grudging even to consider paying for my coffee pot, then I may have to do so myself. Inspector,' she added, holding out her palm. 'May I have it back, please?' Colbeck gave it to her and she unscrewed the paper. 'I need to study this in private – do excuse me.'

'Come back!' ordered Tomkins as she waddled out of the room. He turned to Colbeck. 'Do something, man. We can't have my wife exposing herself to the kind of attack that the sergeant suffered.'

'That's a decision only Mrs Tomkins can take,' said Colbeck.

'You must talk her out of it.'

'I would have thought that was *your* privilege, sir.'

'Winifred can be very headstrong at times.'

'She's clearly determined to get her coffee pot back.'

'But she's taking an enormous risk going there alone.'

'Mrs Tomkins won't *be* alone,' Colbeck reminded him. 'She's been told to travel by carriage so she'll have a driver with her. That, I think, is where we can seize the advantage.

If it were not for the fact that I am clearly known to them, I would suggest that I drove your wife. Instead, one of Superintendent Stockdale's men can pose as the coachman. I'll be concealed inside the carriage, ready to leap out when the exchange is made.'

'The exchange is not going to take place,' decreed Tomkins. 'I refuse to allow it, Inspector. It's up to you to catch these villains and reclaim my wife's property. Don't you have any idea who you're up against here?'

'We do, as a matter of fact.'

'Then why can't you make an arrest?'

'We have insufficient evidence, sir.'

'A murder is committed, a man is robbed and Sergeant Leeming is knocked unconscious – how much evidence do you want?'

'Two possible suspects have been identified.'

'Who are they?'

'I can't tell you that,' said Colbeck, 'until we're certain of our facts. As you know, we believe that we're looking for a man and a woman. A detailed description of the man in question has been printed in the London newspapers. Sooner or later, someone is bound to come forward with the information that we need.'

Edward Tallis was disappointed with the lack of response. In a city as large as London, he felt, there had to be somebody who could give him some indication as to the whereabouts of Stephen Voke. Yet a whole day had passed without anyone coming forward. While it had not linked Voke's name with a murder in Cardiff, the newspaper report had stressed the

Detective Department's eagerness to make contact with him. Tallis had hoped that one of his former colleagues at Solomon Stern's shop might be able to help him but none of them appeared at Scotland Yard. Nor could Leonard Voke provide any real guidance. Demanding his son's immediate arrest, he confessed that he did not have the faintest idea where he might be. Stephen Voke had left no discernible trail behind him.

It was not until the second morning that someone eventually answered the call. Claude Meyrick was a quiet, inoffensive, studious man of middle years with spectacles perched on a long nose and dark hair flecked with grey at the temples. Shown into the superintendent's office, he explained that he had, until recently, been Stephen Voke's landlord.

'At last,' said Tallis, rubbing his hands. 'What can you tell me?'

'I can tell you that Mr Voke was an exemplary lodger. We were sorry to see him go. The only time my wife had to speak to him was when the tapping noise got out of hand.'

'What tapping noise?'

'He was a silversmith. He used a little hammer to fashion the silver into all manner of wondrous shapes. It was not a problem during the day but our other lodgers complained when he worked on into the night. Once my wife spoke to him,' he went on, 'Mr Voke apologised. It never happened again.'

'How long was he living under your roof?'

'It must have been five or six months, Superintendent. Then, out of the blue, he announced that he was leaving us.'

'Did he say why?'

'Yes,' replied Meyrick. 'Mr Voke told us that he'd resigned from his employment so that he could strike out on his own.'

'What – here in London?'

'No, no, he said that there were already far too many jewellers and silversmiths here. Besides, his father was in the same profession.'

'I know,' said Tallis, heavily. 'I've met Mr Voke. He and his son were not on the best of terms, it seems.'

'According to young Mr Voke, his father held him back and refused to pay him a proper wage. I don't know the truth of the matter, sir, and I make it a rule never take sides in family disputes like that. It's foolish to do so. Whenever Mr Voke talked about his father,' Meyrick recalled, 'I just nodded in agreement. My wife and I knew that he would not stay with us indefinitely.'

'Why not?'

'He was an ambitious young man. He wanted to make a name for himself and he could never do that working for someone else.'

'Did he ever mention a Hugh Kellow?'

'Oh, yes,' said Meyrick, 'that was a name that often came to his lips. He was quite bitter about him. He claimed that the worst thing his father ever did was to take on Mr Kellow as an apprentice.'

'Would you say that your lodger was a vengeful man?'

'Not vengeful, sir – just very determined to get what he felt were his just deserts in life. He was single-minded. I admired that.'

Tallis sat back in his chair and tried to assimilate what he had just heard about Stephen Voke. The landlord took a much kinder view of him than Voke's own father did but that was not difficult. Tallis could see that Claude Meyrick had a tolerant and uncritical attitude towards his fellow-men. Preferring to think well of people, he would not look too closely into their faults and foibles. The young man he had known had been a welcome tenant. Meyrick did not realise that Stephen Voke had been disinherited by his father and then had deserted his employer in Hatton Garden. Only the more appealing aspects of his lodger's life and character had been revealed to him.

'Did he have any friends?' asked Tallis.

'I assume that he did, Superintendent,' said Meyrick, 'because he often went out in the evenings.'

'So he brought no young men to the house?'

'None at all, sir – the only person who ever came for him was a young lady.'

'Do you know her name?'

'I'm afraid not. She never actually knocked on the door. She would simply appear on the pavement opposite and Mr Voke would go off with her. Female visitors are not allowed in our lodgers' rooms,' said Meyrick, sternly. 'My wife is very particular on that score. Her father is a clergyman and inculcated the highest moral standards in her. My instincts accord with hers. It's something that all our lodgers must accept if they wish to stay under our roof.'

'I commend that wholeheartedly,' said Tallis, warming to the man. 'There are far too many landlords who allow unmarried couples to cohabit on their premises and who permit all kinds of licence. It is sinful, Mr Meyrick. They are actually encouraging indecency. I'm pleased to hear

180

that you and Mrs Meyrick are more discriminating.'

'It's a matter of conscience to us, Superintendent.'

'Then I applaud you. Coming back to this young lady,' he went on, 'how would you describe her?'

'I only saw her on a few occasions and always through the window, of course. She was well-dressed and looked respectable to me. I thought her attractive and agreeably wholesome.'

'Did she and Mr Voke seem like close friends?'

'Oh, yes – she always took his arm as they walked away.'

'Is there anything else you can remember about her?'

'Only my wife's observation,' said Meyrick, 'and she has sharper eyes for such things.'

'What sort of things?'

'Age and class, sir. She felt that the young lady was a little older than Mr Voke and came from a higher station in life. For all that, they seemed well-suited.'

'When did he actually leave your house?'

'Last Saturday – a cab came to pick him up at the door. I helped him to carry down his luggage. Mr Voke was very grateful. He thanked us for looking after him so well.'

'Do you know where the cab was taking him?'

'Yes, Superintendent,' said Meyrick, 'I heard him tell the driver to take him to Paddington Station. He was leaving London altogether.'

On his way back to the hotel, Colbeck called in at the police station to keep Stockdale informed of the latest developments. When he heard of the reaction to the latest ransom demand, the superintendent was very impressed.

'Winifred Tomkins is a braver woman than I took her for,' he said with mild astonishment. 'I'm not surprised that her husband refused to provide the money even though he could afford to pay fifty times that amount and not miss it. It's the wife that I admire. There are not many women who would take such a risk.'

'I agree,' said Colbeck, 'and that was *before* Mrs Tomkins knew that I intended to hide in the carriage with her. She will not be entirely unprotected.'

'How was the situation left?'

'According to that letter, the exchange will not take place until twilight. That gives them the best part of a day to decide what they're going to do. Mr Tomkins will try to talk his wife out of what he sees as an act of madness while she, I suspect, will hold firm.'

'Even if it means that she has to pay the ransom money herself?'

'*Appear* to pay it,' corrected Colbeck. 'Mrs Tomkins must look as if she's obeying the instructions. As well as keeping her from any harm, I hope to retrieve both her money and her coffee pot.'

'We'll catch them this time,' said Stockdale, confidently. 'I feel it in my bones. It's a pity that the sergeant won't be here to enjoy the moment.'

'What Victor needs to enjoy is the comfort of his wife and family. That's why I put him on the train back to London this morning. He'll have to give a full report to Superintendent Tallis, of course, but he'll be able to sleep in his own bed tonight. That's important to Victor.'

'The love of a good woman is important to any man.'

'Too true,' said Colbeck, thinking of Madeleine Andrews.

'Yet you've remained single, Inspector.'

'Yes, I have.'

'It can't be for want of opportunities,' said Stockdale with grin. 'Even someone as ugly as me has caused the odd female heart to beat faster. A handsome fellow like you could pick and choose.'

'At the moment, I choose to devote all my energies to my work,' said Colbeck, crisply, 'and I know that you're as keen as I am to solve this particular case.'

'I am, Inspector, but these villains are proving devilishly hard to find. They must be in Cardiff *somewhere*,' he said, 'yet we've drawn a blank in all the hotels and boarding houses. There's no sign of them. My men have looked into every nook and cranny.'

'They've been searching for a man and woman but the chances are that the pair of them split up to avoid detection. They'll only get back together again when they're ready to seize the ransom money. And as we've discussed before,' said Colbeck, 'it could be that the woman in question actually lives in the town.'

'Miss Carys Evans.'

'We must keep watch on her, Superintendent.'

'I've been doing just that,' Stockdale told him. 'I paid her a call this very morning. I told her that we'd become aware of the fact that she was in the hotel at roughly the time of the murder and asked her if she saw anything unusual while she was there. Miss Evans said that she did not.'

'Did she explain what she was doing at the hotel?'

'She was visiting a friend though she refused to give me a

name. It could, as we speculated, simply have been Sir David Pryde. From the way that she rebuffed my question, however, I felt that it was not him. It may not even have been a man, of course.'

'Then why was she so evasive?'

'That's in her nature, I'm afraid.'

'Yes,' said Colbeck, 'I noticed that about her.'

'Miss Evans did admit one thing of interest.'

'What was that?'

'She actually visited Mr Voke's shop in London. She went there on the recommendation of a friend – the same one, no doubt, who recommended the silversmith to Mrs Tomkins.'

'Sir David Pryde.'

'Surely, *he* can't be involved in these crimes.'

Colbeck had no time to reply. Someone rapped on the door then it opened to disclose the figure of a burly uniformed sergeant. He told the superintendent that someone was demanding to see him.

'Who is it?' asked Stockdale.

'That actor from the Theatre Royal, sir,' said the man. 'He seems very upset.'

Colbeck's curiosity was aroused. He followed the superintendent through into the outer office where a distracted Nigel Buckmaster was pacing restlessly up and down. When he saw Colbeck, the actor rushed impulsively forward to grab him by the shoulders.

'You must help me, Inspector!' he cried, shaking him. 'We are facing calamity – Miss Linnane has been abducted.'

* * *

It was a new weapon and it was used to great effect. During their long marriage, Winifred Tomkins had always got her way either by nagging her husband incessantly or resorting to a fit of temper. He had usually bowed to her will. She deployed none of her customary tactics now. Retreating into silence, she simply ignored him. Clifford Tomkins did not know how to cope with such treatment. He reasoned, he shouted, he threatened and he even pleaded but all in vain. Her mind was made up and nothing could dissuade her. As she was putting on her coat to leave the house, he made one last intervention.

'This is insane, Winifred!' he cried.

'Out of my way, please,' she said, coolly.

'The bank manager will tell you the same thing.'

'It's my money and I can do what I wish with it.'

'Before he'll sanction it, he'll want to know why you're withdrawing such a large amount of capital at short notice.'

'Then I'll tell him the truth,' she replied. 'The money is to meet an emergency and my husband has declined to help me.'

Tomkins flushed. 'Think how that will make me look!'

'It makes you look like the miserly and unloving husband that you are, Clifford.'

'Now that's unfair!'

'When I really need you, I'm badly let down.'

'Everything I own is at your disposal,' he said, recklessly, 'as long as it's for a worthy purpose, that is. In this case, you're proposing to throw away a large sum on a whim and it's my duty to stop you.'

185

'It's your duty to support me,' she snapped. 'Were Lady Pryde in this position, I'm sure that Sir David would come to her aid without any delay or prevarication.'

'That's a false comparison and you know it. Lady Pryde would never dare to risk her life for a silver coffee pot.'

'You heard what Inspector Colbeck told you – the exchange must go ahead.'

'That's only because he expects to catch the villain when it takes place. His priority is to safeguard you. I'm not sure that he can.'

'You saw what that letter said. On no account must the police be involved at all. Remember what happened to Sergeant Leeming. It will be far easier if I just hand over the money and get what I want.'

'At *three* times its original price!' he exclaimed.

'It would be worth it, Clifford.'

'That coffee pot was supposed to be a gift from *me*.'

'You seem to have forgotten that,' she said, icily. 'When I visit the bank, I will be withdrawing enough money to reimburse you for your loss. That way I'll have paid the full price for it so it will be truly mine. You'll have no cause to harass me then.'

'I'm not harassing you.'

'Then please step out of my way.'

'At least, talk this over sensibly.'

'You're incapable of understanding my point of view.'

'I'm trying to stop you doing something you'll afterwards regret.'

'Oh, no,' she said, nostrils flaring. 'What I regret is that I believed you'd stand by me in a situation like this. We are not really talking about a silver coffee pot, Clifford. Much more is at issue here. The whole basis of our marriage has been rocked. When I look for your uncritical support in a crisis, I find you wanting. Goodbye.'

Sweeping past him, she went into the hall and headed for the front door. The butler was at hand to open it for her and give an obsequious bow. The phaeton stood ready outside. Winifred was about to walk across to it when she noticed a letter on the doormat in the porch. Written across it in bold capitals was her name.

It took Colbeck several minutes to calm the actor down so that he could relate the facts of the case. Taken into Stockdale's office, Nigel Buckmaster went through his full range of dramatic gestures. He explained that he had gone to Kate Linnane's room to take her down to a late breakfast, only to find the door wide open and the room in disarray. Buckmaster reported his findings to the manager and Pugh had immediately questioned his staff. A waiter remembered seeing a woman being hustled down the back stairs by a man in a cloak. One of the cooks had seen the couple leaving by the rear entrance. Both of the witnesses agreed that the woman had looked in distress.

'Kate has been kidnapped!' howled Buckmaster.

'It certainly looks that way,' said Colbeck, 'though I wonder that she didn't cry for help as she was taken past those witnesses.'

'Some kind of weapon must have been held on her under the man's cloak – a knife, perhaps, even a pistol.'

'Who could want to do such a thing?' asked Stockdale.

'I'm sure that she has many admirers but they'd hardly go to those lengths.'

'I don't think we're looking for someone who reveres Kate,' said Buckmaster, 'but a rival who detests and envies me. He's determined to wreck my company because it's had such resounding success. What lies behind this crime is artistic jealousy of the worst kind.'

'That's one possible explanation,' said Colbeck.

'What other one is there, Inspector?'

'The answer to that must lie in Miss Linnane's private life, sir. She's a very beautiful woman. Has there been an entanglement in her past that left someone feeling vengeful towards her?'

Buckmaster was peremptory. 'There's been no such thing.'

'How can you be so certain?'

'Kate has no secrets from me.'

'Then she's unlike any woman I've known,' said Stockdale with a dry laugh. 'Women are secretive creatures – it adds to their allure.'

'I'm not interested in your opinions, Superintendent,' said the actor, treating him to a glare. 'Kate Linnane has been my leading lady for some years now and the trust between us is complete. If there had been any dark shadows in her past, she would surely have told me about them.'

Colbeck remembered the figure he had seen flitting into Kate's room earlier that week. It had obviously not been Buckmaster or there would have been no need for stealth. Colbeck sensed that she had not felt obliged to tell the actor-manager about her furtive caller. What else had she decided not to confide?

188

'Kate's safety is paramount, of course,' said Buckmaster, 'but the fate of the whole company now hangs in the balance. We have a full house for this evening's performance. It will be a catastrophe if we have to cancel it. The damage to my reputation will be irreparable.'

'We'll do our best to find the lady,' promised Stockdale. 'Any woman as striking as Miss Linnane will surely have been seen after she left the hotel. I'll organise a search for her at once, sir.'

'Thank you.' As Stockdale went out, the actor turned to Colbeck. 'I was hoping that you'd take charge of the case, Inspector.'

'I already have my hands full, Mr Buckmaster.'

'This could prove disastrous for us.'

'I sympathise with you,' said Colbeck with unfeigned sincerity. 'Accounts of Miss Linnane's performance have been uniformly glowing. It's been a source of great annoyance to me that I've been unable to see the two of you in *Macbeth*. Unfortunately,' he went on, 'I have no jurisdiction beyond the case that brought me to Cardiff. The superintendent is responsible for law-enforcement in the town and he is known for his tenacity. There is one crumb of comfort, however.'

'I fail to see it.'

'When she was taken from the hotel, Miss Linnane was apparently unharmed. If someone had meant to injure her in order to prevent her from appearing onstage, they could have done that in her room. I would expect her to be found in good health.'

'And when will that be?'

'I trust that it will be in the very near future.'

'I need Kate *now*,' insisted Buckmaster. 'She is more than just our leading lady, Inspector, she is our good luck charm. Without her, we face potential ruin.'

'I think you exaggerate a little, sir.'

'She's a vital part of the company.'

'That goes without saying,' conceded Colbeck, 'but you would not have had such continuous success in your profession if you had cancelled a performance because someone was indisposed. For a role like Lady Macbeth, you must surely have an understudy.'

'I do and I do not,' said Buckmaster, uneasily. 'There *is* someone who could step into Kate's shoes but she's young and untried. What if she lets us down? How can I scale the heights if I am held back by a Lady Macbeth who is floundering in the part?'

'Would the understudy happen to be Miss Tremaine?'

Buckmaster blinked. 'How did you know that?'

'I had the good fortune to meet the young lady when she gave me a playbill in the street,' said Colbeck, smiling at the memory. 'I was taken with her patent dedication. To lose Miss Linnane in this manner is very troubling but your predicament may not be as serious as you fear. I have a feeling that Miss Tremaine will rise to the occasion.'

Laura Tremaine was torn between delight and quiet terror. The message had simply told her to come at once to the actor-manager's hotel for a rehearsal of her role as an understudy. The thought that she might actually play Lady Macbeth opposite Nigel Buckmaster gave her a dizzying thrill. It was beyond anything she had ever dreamt about, expecting to occupy lesser parts for many years before even being considered for a leading role. Yet it now seemed possible. There had been no explanation as to why Kate Linnane was unable to repeat her triumph that evening but Laura knew that she would never yield up a part lightly, especially to someone she openly despised. She tried to put the other actress from her mind. Kate's loss was Laura's gain. She needed to seize the unexpected chance of greatness.

With opportunity, however, came fear and uncertainty. Was she ready? Did she have enough talent to be an adequate substitute for such an experienced actress? Would she let everyone down? Could she remember the lines and repeat the correct moves? She had watched Kate Linnane play the part often enough but that was not the same as taking it on herself. Would Laura Tremaine – whatever her fantasies about theatrical glory– be able to hold her own against a titan of the stage like Nigel Buckmaster? The challenge was both exhilarating and daunting. She would not simply be fulfilling her ambition of taking a leading role, she would be doing so as one of the most famous wives in world drama. In the course of that evening, pretty, young, shapely, well-spoken, respectable Laura Tremaine had to undergo a veritable transformation. Shedding the sweetness of Lady Macduff, she had to turn herself into a murderous fiend.

As she sat patiently in the hotel foyer, she felt the sheer weight of expectation. The whole company would depend on her. Her friends would will her to succeed while her enemies – and she had one or two in the company – would pray for her to fail. Every move she made and every gesture she gave would be subjected to intense scrutiny. And what would happen when Kate Linnane came back to reclaim her rightful role? However well she had played it, Laura would get neither thanks nor praise. Once the imperious leading lady had returned, her understudy would have to slink back into obscurity. It was a thought that made Laura resolve to make the most of her opportunity. She would play Lady Macbeth as if the part had been expressly written for her.

Nigel Buckmaster strode into the hotel and she jumped to her feet obediently. He did not even look at her as he went past.

'Come to my room,' he said. 'We have much work to do.'

Laura followed him up the stairs as if floating on air.

Jeremiah Stockdale did not have a large force at his disposal but he managed to deploy over a dozen men in the search for the missing actress. They questioned anybody who lived or worked in the vicinity of the hotel. It was when one of the constables went to the railway station that firm evidence was at last obtained. Stockdale passed on the information to Colbeck at the police station.

'They caught a train to London.'

'Are you sure about that?' said Colbeck.

'The stationmaster remembered them clearly – a startling young woman and a man in a cloak who had her by the arm. They got into a first class carriage.'

'That sounds like Miss Linnane.'

'One of the porters saw them as well. He thought they were a husband and wife who'd just had a quarrel because the woman was very tense and the man brusque.'

'I'm still surprised that she made no resistance, Superintendent. Miss Linnane is very self-possessed. I can't imagine her letting anyone make her do something against her will.'

'Maybe the porter was right,' suggested Stockdale. 'The man could have been a jealous husband who suddenly leapt out of her past. Or it might have been someone who was blackmailing her. He didn't need to have a weapon because he was holding some guilty secret over her. That's why she went with him. Forget what Mr Buckmaster told us,' he said, airily. 'In my experience, an actress is a lady with a very colourful history.'

'It's not a profession renowned for its saints.'

Stockdale chuckled. 'Sinners are far more interesting.'

'What steps have you taken?'

'I sent two of my men after them on the next train. They can make enquiries at Paddington. It's the second time Idris Roberts has been there this week.'

'Of course,' said Colbeck. 'He was the constable who took Effie Kellow back to London. Was the body delivered to Mr Voke?'

'Yes, Inspector – Idris saw to that. After they'd talked about funeral arrangements, he escorted Miss Kellow to her brother's lodgings and made sure that she got the books she was after.'

'What then?'

'He gave her money for a cab to Mayfair and caught the train back to Cardiff. He was sad to leave her. She was so downcast.'

'The only thing that will lift her spirits is if we catch those responsible for her brother's murder. With luck and with the active cooperation of Mrs Tomkins,' added Colbeck, hopefully, 'I expect to do that this very evening.'

Winifred Tomkins did not even tell her husband that there had been a change of plan. The letter she had found outside her house had given her fresh instructions and she was determined to obey them. Her husband would only have tried to stop her or insisted that she showed the latest missive to Inspector Colbeck. She refused to do that. She had an inner conviction that the only way to get her hands on the silver coffee pot was to pay the excessive amount of money demanded. Her father had bequeathed her over eighty thousand pounds. It seemed appropriate that some of that inheritance should be spent on an item that would keep his memory fresh in her mind.

Clifford Tomkins was surprised when she ordered the carriage that afternoon. He followed her out of the house.

'Where are you going, Winifred?'

'I thought I'd call on Carys Evans,' she said.

'Is she expecting you?'

'I promised to take tea with her one day this week.'

'Would you like me to come with you?'

'Don't be silly, Clifford. You'd only be in the way.'

'We haven't really spoken since you came back from the bank,' he said, worriedly. 'What did the manager say?'

She shot him a withering look. 'You'll have to ask him.'

'I hope you said nothing to my detriment. I'm held in high regard at the bank.' She climbed into the carriage and closed the door after her. 'Do you still mean to go through with the exchange this evening?'

'I'll see you later, Clifford.'

'When shall I expect you back?'

Ignoring his question, she gave the coachman a signal and they pulled away. Once clear of the house, she felt strangely elated. There was an element of danger but it was offset by a sense of adventure. Everything she had done in her adult life had been guided by her relationship with her husband. For once she was doing something entirely of her own volition, something that he would have strongly opposed. It was a small victory and the coffee pot would forever be an emblem of that victory. She was content.

They went for a mile before they reached the designated spot, a stand of trees on the road to Fairwater. Winifred ordered the coachman to stop and the carriage rolled to a halt. Though she could see nobody, she was certain that she was being watched. She suddenly began to tremble with fear, realising how vulnerable she was. The coachman was with her but he was a slight man and unarmed. He would be no match for a desperate criminal ready to commit murder.

'Mrs Tomkins?' called a man's voice.

'Yes, yes,' she answered aloud. 'It's me.'

'Please get out of the carriage.' She did as she was told. 'Do you have the money with you?'

'I do – every penny of it.'

A young man stepped out from behind a tree, his face largely obscured by the brim of his hat. Winifred gasped when she saw that he was holding a pistol in his hand.

'Let me have the money,' he said.

'I want to see my coffee pot first,' she insisted, amazed that she had the courage to say the words. 'I'm ready to pay for it.'

'Then here it is.'

He reached behind the tree and pulled out a large leather bag. Opening it up, he tilted it towards her so that she could see the silver locomotive nestling inside. It glinted in the late afternoon sunshine. Winifred was overwhelmed with joy.

'Here, here,' she said, holding out the money. 'Count it if you must but please let me have my coffee pot.'

'All in good time, Mrs Tomkins,' he said, closing the bag. 'I'll want rather more than the money from you.' He turned the pistol on the coachman and barked a command. 'Get down before I shoot you!'

The coachman jumped down instantly to the ground. The man used the weapon to motion them off behind the trees then he ordered Winifred to give him the money. When she did so, her hands were shaking so much that she dropped some of the banknotes. She scrambled to pick them up. Without bothering to count them, he thrust the money into his pocket then told her and the driver to turn their backs. The next thing they heard was the departing carriage.

'We'll have to walk back,' protested the coachman.

'No matter,' she said, hurrying over to the leather bag. 'We have what we came for – I'd have walked a hundred miles to get this.'

Opening the bag, she took out the silver locomotive to gloat over it but the moment she felt the object, she knew that it could not be silver. It was far too light. Now that she could see it properly, she observed that the workmanship was poor and the detail wanting.

'We've been tricked!' she bellowed. 'This is made of *tin*!'

CHAPTER ELEVEN

Nigel Buckmaster was impaled on the horns of a dilemma. He had always planned to entice Laura Tremaine into bed at some time in the future yet, now that they were alone in a hotel room, he held back from taking advantage of her. Recognising her obvious talent, he felt that he could develop her potential to the point where she was capable of taking on major roles. Eventually, he had hoped, she would replace Kate Linnane as his leading lady and as his mistress. Laura had the same freshness, the same burning ambition and the same eagerness to work hard at her craft that Kate had once possessed. She also had two things that the older woman now lacked – a readiness to obey his every wish and the incomparable beauty of youth.

As he looked at her now, beaming up at him with undisguised infatuation, he had a fierce urge to take her. What held him back was the thought that a large audience would be gathering that evening to watch him repeat his magical performance as Macbeth. An hour's pleasure with

Laura Tremaine was an hour's less rehearsal time. It might also stir up her emotions in a way that would adversely affect her performance onstage. Buckmaster was in a quandary. Should he surrender to lust or put the needs of the company first? Should he drown his anxieties in sensual abandon or prepare a young actress for the biggest test of her career?

While not understanding its implications, Laura could see the indecision dancing in his eyes. She was troubled.

'Is something wrong, Mr Buckmaster?' she asked.

'Yes,' he replied with a deep sigh. 'I'm afraid that there is, alas.' He lowered his voice. 'I must tell you this in the strictest confidence. I know that I can rely on your discretion.'

'I won't breathe a word, sir.'

'I will give out that Miss Linnane is indisposed but the truth of the matter is that she has been abducted.'

'Abducted!' she echoed in alarm.

'Have no fear,' he said, allowing himself to take her reassuringly by the shoulders. 'You are not in any danger. I'll see to that. A search is being conducted for Miss Linnane and I have every confidence that she will return to us. Until then,' he said, letting his hands slide gently down her arms, 'you must step into the breach. We owe it to our audience to carry on and we owe it to ourselves to rise above this temporary setback.'

Laura was resolute. 'I am ready, Mr Buckmaster,' she said. 'I'll do anything you ask of me.'

Desire coursed through him again and he had to fight an impulse to enfold her in his arms and enjoy that first, long, tender, exploratory kiss. She was ready to play Lady Macbeth but was she ready to be his? Buckmaster controlled himself. The time to make that decision was after that evening's performance and not before. If they could wrest success out of misfortune, they could celebrate together. He became businesslike, moving the furniture to the margins of the room to create a space.

'Are you nervous?' he asked.

'A little,' she confessed.

'There's no need to be. If we can harness your talent properly, you will play the part to perfection. I have no qualms.'

'Thank you, Mr Buckmaster.'

'You know the lines – I've been through them with you often enough – but what we do need to address are the deeper aspects of the character. Lady Macbeth is no mere monster. She's a complex woman whose emotions need to be understood and communicated to the audience.'

'Miss Linnane does that superbly.'

'I mean this as no disrespect to a fine actress,' he said, 'but we must dismiss Kate Linnane from our minds. It is Laura Tremaine who will play Lady Macbeth now. That and that alone is all that concerns us. This afternoon, we'll rehearse at the theatre with the rest of the company. What I wish to do now in the privacy of this room is to go through your scenes line by line. Think of me as Macbeth, your loving husband. I want you to grow towards me in every way.'

'Yes, Mr Buckmaster.'

'You must convince *everyone* that you are truly my wife.'

Laura quivered with pleasure. Under his direction, she was ready to throw herself body and soul into a role she had always coveted. Aspiration momentarily got the better of her.

She was glad that Kate Linnane had been abducted and had no sympathy for her. If anything, she felt a suppressed glee. Laura believed that it was her destiny to replace the other actress and she intended to do it on a permanent basis.

'Here I am, sir,' she said, spreading her arms in a gesture of submission. 'Instruct me.'

Winifred Tomkins was inconsolable. The humiliation of having paid out a substantial amount of money for a worthless object was like a stake through the heart. After trudging all the way back home, she took to her bed. Her husband was infuriated by what he heard. He sent immediate word to the police station. Colbeck and Stockdale arrived to find him still aflame with righteous indignation.

'It's not my fault!' he asserted, arms flailing. 'I take no blame at all for this, gentlemen. I did warn my wife. I did caution her against rash behaviour.'

'Then why didn't you stop Mrs Tomkins going?' asked Colbeck.

'I was deceived, Inspector. I was never shown that second letter. How was I to know that the instructions had been changed?'

'You would surely have been told of the new arrangements had you provided the money required, sir. That seems to be the crux of the matter here. Mrs Tomkins only acted on her own because you refused to supply the sum demanded.'

Tomkins reddened. 'I won't be criticised in my own house!'

'Inspector Colbeck is only pointing out the true facts of the situation, sir,' said Stockdale. 'There was a loss of trust between you and Mrs Tomkins. She was driven to act unilaterally and has paid the penalty. The financial loss incurred is hers.'

'And mine,' insisted Tomkins. 'Who do you think paid for the carriage and horses? I'm the victim of a robbery as well.'

'But you did not have to face a loaded pistol.'

'That's beside the point, man.'

'I don't agree, sir,' said Colbeck. 'Mrs Tomkins has lost more than her money. She underwent a frightening ordeal. That was why it was imperative for trained police officers to be with her at the time of the exchange. Had I been hidden in the carriage, I could have waited for the moment to catch the man off guard and overpower him. Nothing would have been stolen then and Mrs Tomkins would not have been tricked by this.'

He indicated the coffee pot locomotive that stood on the table. It had a clear resemblance to the item commissioned but could never withstand close inspection. Made of tin, it looked cheap and hastily finished. There were sharp edges on it everywhere.

'Look at it,' said Tomkins, trying to grab the locomotive and pricking his finger in the process. 'It's utterly useless.'

'Not to me,' said Colbeck. 'It's further proof that the man we're looking for is a silversmith. This was deliberately fashioned so that it could be used as a decoy. Mrs Tomkins, I daresay, was only given a glimpse of it from a distance.'

'The villains have made quite a haul,' noted Stockdale. 'They not only pocketed three times the value of the coffee pot, they still have the object themselves.'

'Don't forget the contents of Mr Voke's safe in London,' Colbeck reminded him. 'The thief now has enough stock and capital to set himself up in business as a silversmith. That makes me even more convinced of his identity.'

'Who is he, Inspector?' demanded Tomkins.

'We believe that he may be Mr Voke's son and that he has a female accomplice with some knowledge of the town. He's a clever man, Mr Tomkins. He exploited your wife's determination to have that coffee pot at all costs and it may even be that she was not the only victim of a decoy. The superintendent and I discussed this on the way here,' said Colbeck. 'At the time when Mrs Tomkins was handing over that money, the police force was distracted.'

'Yes,' explained Stockdale. 'The leading lady from the theatre company has been kidnapped. It's a possibility that the crime was committed in order to divert our attention away from events here. Only time will tell.'

'My feeling is that the two things are unrelated,' said Colbeck, 'but the coincidence is strange. The abduction needed immediate attention from the superintendent and his men.'

'Why *me*?' cried Tomkins. 'What have I done to deserve it? Why has all this disaster been visited upon me?'

'I'd say that you've come off rather lightly, sir,' remarked Stockdale. 'It's Mrs Tomkins who's really suffered here.'

'Then there's Sergeant Leeming,' added Colbeck, 'who was assaulted in your place. As for Miss Linnane, victim of a kidnap, we can only guess at the horrors she has been put through. Compared to others, sir, your problems have been relatively small.'

'That's all *you* know!' said Tomkins under his breath.

He was thinking of the difficulties that lay ahead, of the reproaches that were to come when his wife recovered and of the permanent damage done to their marriage. Winifred thought his behaviour had been unforgivable and she was a woman who harboured grudges forever. In failing to support her at a time of need, he had guaranteed himself years of bitter recrimination. Only the restitution of his wife's money and of the silver coffee pot could save him from sustained misery.

'We must catch these devils!' he shouted.

'We'll endeavour to do so, sir,' said Colbeck, 'but, in losing your wife's confidence, you made our task much more difficult. Had I been present at the exchange, there was a good chance of catching the man we're after.'

'You can't be certain of that outcome.'

'I accept that, Mr Tomkins. That's why I had another line of defence. If the killer had escaped from me, he and his accomplice might well have tried to leave the town by train with their booty.'

'I'd have been waiting for them at the railway station,' said Stockdale, 'and I was expecting to do just that this evening. I was unaware that the exchange would take place so soon.'

'It all comes back to your failure to stand by your wife, sir. You forced her to take independent action and two dangerous criminals have slipped through our fingers as a result.'

'I refuse to acknowledge any responsibility,' insisted Tomkins.

'I can only tell you how we view it,' said Colbeck, looking

him in the eye, 'and I venture to suggest that your wife will see it in exactly the same way.' Tomkins swallowed hard. 'Now could I please trouble you to give me the second letter that arrived here today? It might just confirm a worrying little thought I have at the back of my mind.'

It was much more testing than Laura Tremaine had thought. When she had rehearsed the role of Lady Macbeth before, she had simply copied the way that Kate Linnane had played the part. Now that it was hers, Nigel Buckmaster insisted that she put her individual stamp on it and he worked hard to bring that about. She did the letter-reading scene over twenty times before he was satisfied with the interpretation and he went over every syllable of her famous speeches to tease out their meaning and emotional impact. Laura was humbled and exhausted by the exercise but she was also uplifted. Somewhere inside her was the performance of her lifetime and Buckmaster was slowly bringing it out of her. Hours glided by as they exchanged iambic pentameters.

'That's enough!' he decreed at last. 'I think we have earned some refreshment. It is time for the royal couple to feast.'

'Thank you!' she said, overjoyed at his approval.

'We have made great strides and we'll make even more when we rehearse with the full company. I am beginning to have a real sense of you as my wife, my lady, my lover.'

'My performance owes everything to you.'

'We must complement each other in every possible way.'

'Yes, Mr Buckmaster.'

'Oh, I think we can dispense with formalities in private,'

he said, slipping an arm around her shoulders. 'Feel free to use my Christian name, Laura.'

'I will, sir – I mean…Nigel.'

After a late luncheon, they adjourned to the theatre to meet the rest of the company. Actors thrived on rumour and superstition and the place was buzzing. Opinions varied as to whether Kate Linnane had been killed, wounded, dismissed, abducted or struck down by a crippling disease. What everyone knew for certain was that she would not be taking part in the play that evening. Conducting Laura to the stage, Buckmaster clapped his hands to silence the hubbub.

'Ladies and gentlemen,' he said, scanning the faces below him, 'I want no more idle speculation about Miss Linnane. All that you need to know is that she is unable to be here this evening. In her place,' he went on, 'I am delighted to tell you that we will have Miss Tremaine.'

There was a burst of spontaneous applause from most of the actors though one or two were less enthusiastic. Laura did not mind. Later that evening, she would be enjoying an ovation from a full audience, signalling the arrival of a new star in the firmament of British theatre. The moment for which she had secretly yearned had finally come. She would shine in one of the greatest tragic roles ever devised for an actress and she would do so in the company of the legendary Nigel Buckmaster. It was true bliss.

The euphoria lasted until she reached her dressing room. Cold reality then set in. As she looked at her costume, she knew that she could never hope to fill it with the same distinction as Kitty Linnane, especially at such short notice. Many of the things that Buckmaster taught her in his hotel room had already vanished from her brain. There was simply too much to learn. Declaiming lines in private had been thrilling. Adapting her performance to those of the other characters in the play would be far more difficult. She suddenly felt her immaturity. Buoyed up by ambition, she had thought herself ready for anything. Now that she was there, now that she was in a dressing room that had so many vestiges of Kate Linnane, now that she took full measure of the challenge she faced, Laura was forced to admit that she was too young, inexperienced and ill-equipped for the role. Her mouth went dry, her stomach heaved and her heart was like a galloping horse. She was in the iron grip of stage fright.

They were true. All those stories about bad luck attending any production of *Macbeth* had some foundation. Laura had never believed the tales before but the facts were inescapable. They were doomed. The company had been struck by a triple disaster. Murder had greeted their arrival in the town, their leading lady had been kidnapped and Laura Tremaine had been cast as Lady Macbeth. She could turn out to be the biggest disaster of them all.

Robert Colbeck wanted to eliminate one possible suspect before he left Cardiff. Though he doubted if she would condone a murder, he still wondered if Carys Evans was in some way linked to the series of crimes. Accordingly, he paid another call on her cottage. The servant who answered the door was reluctant to admit him.

'Miss Evans is not expecting you, sir,' she said.

'I won't trouble her for long,' promised Colbeck.

'Perhaps you could come back at another time.'

'I need to speak with her now.'

'It's not really convenient.'

'Then I'll stand out here until it is.'

'Miss Evans is rather busy at the moment.'

'I'm never too busy to spare the Inspector a few minutes,' said Carys, appearing in the hall with a welcoming smile. 'Let him in, Maisie.'

'Yes, Miss Evans,' said the servant, dutifully.

She opened the door fully then stood back so that Colbeck could step into the hall. Carys led her visitor into the drawing room. He thought he detected the faintest hint of cigar smoke. It was from the same brand of cigar favoured by Edward Tallis so it was familiar to his nostrils. Offered a chair, he sat down beside the fireplace. Carys, he noted, was still wearing her silver brooch in the shape of a dragon.

'I hope I'm not interrupting you, Miss Evans,' he said.

'Not at all,' she replied, sitting opposite him.

'I had the feeling that you had a guest.'

'I did, Inspector.' She picked up a book from a side table. 'A very special guest, as it happens – Lady Charlotte Guest. I've been reading her translation of the *Mabinogion*.'

'Have you read it in the original Welsh?'

'Of course,' she said, putting it aside again. 'But let's not pretend that you came to discuss my literary tastes. You have infinitely more charm than Superintendent Stockdale but you are here for precisely the same reason that brought him to my door. It appears – for some unknown reason – that I am under suspicion. Please don't talk in circles like the superintendent. Ask me bluntly what you wish to know.'

'Very well,' he said, 'how have you spent the day?'

'I awoke early, went for my usual walk after breakfast then called on Lady Pryde to take coffee from a silver coffee pot that did not pretend to be anything else. Then I returned home and have been here ever since. Maisie will vouch for that.'

'I'm sure that she will.'

'Now you can ask me about the day of the murder.'

'I've no intention of doing so,' he said with a disarming smile. 'If a lady does not wish to disclose whom she was visiting in the privacy of a hotel room, I respect her right to do so. No, Miss Evans, what I'd like to touch on is a visit you made to a silversmith in London.'

She became more guarded. 'Go on, Inspector.'

'You called at Mr Voke's shop in Wood Street, I hear.'

'Is there any law against that?'

'None at all, Miss Evans,' he said. 'I just wondered if this was before or after you acquired that beautiful brooch you're wearing.'

'It was afterwards, Inspector. I was so impressed with it that I wanted to meet the silversmith who made it. Mr Voke introduced me to his assistant, Mr Kellow, a very pleasant young man.'

Colbeck thought of the corpse at the hotel. 'I met Mr Kellow under more distressing circumstances.'

'I was not in London specifically to visit to the shop,' she explained. 'I have friends with whom I stay occasionally. While I was with them, I took the opportunity to seek out Mr Voke.'

'Did you commission anything else from him?'

'I did, as a matter of fact – it was a silver bracelet.'

'And who was instructed to make it?'

'I asked for Mr Kellow to work on it.'

'Were you pleased with the result?'

'I was very pleased,' she said, 'but I had no further dealings with the firm. After my first visit, I was approached by Mr Voke's son who was working at his father's shop at the time. He told me that he could make me jewellery of the same high quality but at a lower price. When he showed me examples of his work, I could see that he was a good craftsman. So I commissioned a silver necklace from him.'

'Are you telling me that you *knew* Stephen Voke?'

'Yes, Inspector, we had a business arrangement.'

'Was the necklace satisfactory?'

'It was a fine piece of work at a bargain price.'

'Then you must have gone to his new place of employment in Hatton Garden to collect it from him.'

'No,' she replied. 'Young Mr Voke delivered it by hand.'

Colbeck was alerted. 'Stephen Voke actually came to Cardiff?'

'This is not the end of the world, Inspector,' she said with a teasing laugh. 'As you discovered, we are only a train ride away from London. And I was very grateful to have the necklace brought to my door. I know that your visit to the town has been very disagreeable but young Mr Voke liked what he saw of Cardiff. He appreciated that it was a place with a future.'

'I share that view. It's patently set to grow and grow.'

'He even talked about moving here one day because he was anxious to get away from London. He likes Wales.'

'Have you commissioned anything else from him?'

'Not in person, Inspector,' she said, extending a hand, 'but a friend of mine was kind enough to purchase this ring for me. None of our local silversmiths could have made anything like this.'

The ruby ring set in silver had the same delicate workmanship as her brooch even though the two items had been made by different craftsman. Both of them had been apprenticed to Leonard Voke and he had schooled them well in the trade. The ring was created by a son who was disowned and the brooch by the young man who had taken his place. In looking at the two pieces together, Colbeck felt that he was studying a motive for murder.

Jeremiah Stockdale was writing a report in his office when she called in to see him. Winifred Tomkins was an unexpected visitor and it had obviously taken an effort of will for her to be there. She looked weary, hurt and repentant. He held a chair for her to sit down then resumed his own seat. Since she had difficulty finding the right words, he tried to prompt her.

'Is there anything that I can do, Mrs Tomkins?'

'Yes, Superintendent, there is.'

'Well?'

There was another long pause. Her tongue moistened her lips.

'I'd like you to accept my apology,' she said.

'To be honest, I'm not sure that one is in order.'

'I believe that it is.'

'In that case,' he said, 'perhaps it's I who should be

apologising to you. We did our best to reclaim your stolen property and we failed.'

'The failure was on my side,' she confessed. 'I was so eager to have my coffee pot back that I was blind to everything else. What could I – a weak and defenceless woman – hope to do against a ruthless criminal? It was madness. I can see that now. You must think me very silly.'

'I think you acted with more bravery than sense, maybe, but I would never describe your actions as silly.'

'I feel so foolish, Superintendent.'

'The villains took advantage of your innocence, that's all. You were an easy prey. It's nothing to be ashamed of, Mrs Tomkins. A criminal will always look to exploit the unwary,' he told her. 'That was why you were ordered to have no more dealings with the police.'

'I was too reckless.'

'Luckily, you survived the ordeal.'

'I thought I knew better,' she said, morosely. 'And all I was doing was exposing myself to danger and letting myself be robbed of a great deal of money. I can't tell you how embarrassed I feel.' She produced a handkerchief to wipe away a stray tear. 'My enemies will never let me forget this. I'll be the butt of their derision for years.'

'That's not true at all, Mrs Tomkins.'

'I've made myself look totally ridiculous.'

'That may be your opinion,' he said, 'but it's certainly not mine. Besides, who outside a tiny circle is going to *know* what happened? I will not be voicing it abroad and nor will Inspector Colbeck. Apart from you, your husband and the coachman, of course, nobody else has any knowledge of what

213

took place and there's no earthly reason why they should.'

Winifred brightened. 'Do you *mean* that, Superintendent?'

'You are unlikely to tell anyone and your husband will hardly want to draw attention to the fact that he refused to provide the money for the exchange. As for your coachman, I daresay you've made sure of his silence.'

'On pain of dismissal,' she said, firmly. 'He'll say nothing.'

'Then you have nothing to worry about.' Stockdale gave a sly smile. 'There is, however, one other person who knows the full details of what occurred on the road to Fairwater and that's the young man who relieved you of that money.'

Her fear returned. 'Do you think that *he'll* spread the word?'

'No, Mrs Tomkins, I don't. No criminal with any sense will boast about a crafty scheme he devised or the public will be forewarned. That would make it difficult for him to use the same stratagem quite so easily again. You are safe from your enemies,' he assured her. 'They will never hear of this unfortunate episode.'

Stockdale had never believed that he would ever feel sorry for Winifred Tomkins. She was a bossy, selfish, odious, pampered woman with a sharp tongue and he could well understand why her husband sought pleasure elsewhere, even to the extent of paying for it. Seeing her now in such distress, however, the superintendent softened towards her. Her real fault had been her gullibility. Driven to possess the silver coffee pot, she had been coaxed into a situation where she was robbed, tricked and mortified beyond endurance. It was a private wound that would never heal. Notwithstanding that, she had somehow found the courage to come to the police station to offer an apology to someone she feared would join in the general mockery of her. Stockdale was glad that he could give her some peace of mind.

'Will I ever get my coffee pot back?' she asked, meekly.

'Oh, yes,' he affirmed.

'How can you be so certain?'

'Inspector Colbeck will pursue them until he finally runs them to ground. He never gives up, Mrs Tomkins. The chase will continue for as long as necessary and your property will be retrieved.'

'All that my husband can talk about is our carriage.'

'That, too, will be recovered and so will your money.'

She bit her lip. 'I should have trusted Inspector Colbeck,' she said with regret. 'You and he deal with criminals all the time. I was stupid to ignore your help.'

'Thank you, Mrs Tomkins.'

'The person who really deserves an apology is the inspector.'

'I'd agree with that.'

'Where can I find him, Superintendent?'

'I wouldn't advise you to go in search of him just now.'

'Oh – why not?'

'Because he's on a train somewhere between here and London,' said Stockdale, wryly. 'Inspector Colbeck thought that the man we want might have a female accomplice here but he's now satisfied that that is not the case. Having no reason to stay on in Cardiff, he's gone back to Scotland Yard. He'll continue the investigation from there.'

* * *

In spite of his reputation for being a hard taskmaster, Edward Tallis was not entirely without compassion. When Victor Leeming had returned that morning, the superintendent had listened to his report with interest then sent him home to reassure his wife that his head injury was not as serious as the heavy bandaging suggested. Though he had been given the rest of the day off, the sergeant insisted on going back to Scotland Yard to take part in the investigation. He was pleased to hear from his superior that progress had been made.

'The most helpful person was Claude Meyrick,' said Tallis. 'He was Stephen Voke's landlord here in London. Mr Meyrick was able to tell me the day and time of his lodger's departure from the house. Given that information, I was able to work out an approximate time of arrival at Paddington Station.'

'That was clever of you, sir,' said Leeming.

'Thank you.'

'It's worthy of Inspector Colbeck.'

Tallis frowned. 'I can act on my own initiative, you know,' he said, tartly. 'Because I knew when he'd be at the station, I was able to make a list of the trains he was most likely to catch.'

'How many of them were there?'

'They were four in number – two of them went to Cardiff.'

'That puts Stephen Voke exactly where we thought he would be.'

'There's more, sergeant,' said Tallis, fingering his moustache. 'I wanted confirmation so I despatched men to the station to talk to the porters. Mr Voke was not alone. He was travelling with an attractive young lady. Since they were quitting London, they would have had a lot of luggage with them and needed the assistance of a porter.'

'Did anyone remember them?'

'They did, fortunately. Thousands of people go to and fro every day and very few of them stand out. But one sharp-eyed porter did recall two people who fitted the description he was given and who caught a train on the day stipulated. The man – I'm certain that it must have been Mr Voke – gave the porter a generous tip.'

'I can see why it stuck in his memory, sir.'

'He stacked their luggage on the roof of the carriage.'

'I think I can guess where the train was going.'

'To Cardiff,' said Tallis, 'and on the day before the murder.'

'It all fits, Superintendent,' decided Leeming. 'However, while we know a lot about Stephen Voke, we know precious little about his companion and Inspector Colbeck feels that she was crucial to the whole scheme. It was the young woman who led Hugh Kellow astray in the first place. I'd love to know who she is.'

'Mr Meyrick could not help us there. Neither could anyone at Solomon Stern's shop. I visited the place myself. Mr Stern and his staff told me that they all knew the young lady by sight but not by name. What they did recall was Stephen Voke's eagerness to leave the shop whenever she appeared.'

'Could it be that *she* is the real culprit here?' said Leeming.

'The two of them are clearly in this together.'

'Yes, I know, but I'm wondering if she is like Lady Macbeth, urging him on to a deed he might not otherwise have committed. As far as I know, Stephen Voke had no record of breaking the law before this happened. This young woman may have been the catalyst.'

Tallis was astounded to hear mention of a Shakespeare play on the lips of his sergeant and his use of the word 'catalyst' had also been arresting. Leeming was not known for his cultural interests. Tallis doubted if he had ever seen a Shakespearean tragedy performed. Yet here he was, making an interesting point with a valid cross-reference from the world of drama. Having impressed the superintendent, Leeming immediately gave the game away.

'At least,' he said, 'that's what Inspector Colbeck mentioned at one point but only because *Macbeth* was being staged at the theatre in Cardiff. Two members of the company actually travelled to the town in the same carriage as the murder victim.'

'Evil is not solely a characteristic of the male sex,' said Tallis, solemnly. 'Women can be equally corrupt, if not more so. Stephen Voke would not be the first man driven to commit a murder at the behest of a scheming female. That's not to excuse anything he's done, mark you,' he added, 'but this accomplice of his may bear the greater part of the blame.'

Edward Tallis had a distrust of the opposite sex that sometimes threatened to spill over into misogyny. Leeming had heard his views on the subject a number of times. He feared that he was about to do so again but he was spared another lecture. There was a firm tap on the door. In response to Tallis's command, Robert Colbeck entered. After an exchange of greetings, the newcomer put a friendly hand on Leeming's shoulder.

'What are you doing here?' he asked. 'You should be at home, resting and being spoilt by your wife.'

'That's exactly what I told him,' said Tallis.

'He's *earned* it, sir. Being so modest, he'll not have told you about the bravery that he showed in Cardiff. In pursuit of a killer, the sergeant risked his life.'

'Then he deserves congratulation.'

'I want to be here,' said Leeming, 'taking part in the search for the man who gave me such a headache. When we catch up with him, I have a score to settle.'

'That time will soon come,' Colbeck told him.

He took a seat and delivered a succinct report on events in Cardiff. The other men were shocked to hear that Winifred Tomkins had spurned the assistance of the police and tried to deal directly with the thief. They both felt that she had been lucky to escape without physical injury and were angry that she had prevented Colbeck from being present at the exchange and therefore in a position to make an arrest. The report provoked Tallis into a familiar tirade.

'That's another aspect of the female character that appals me,' he said, reaching for a cigar from the box on his desk. 'Women do have a propensity to meddle, to get involved in things over which they can never have any control. Mrs Tomkins is a perfect example. With help on offer in the shape of Inspector Colbeck, she blithely decided to take matters into her own hands. She thought, in effect, that she could do what a policeman is trained to do and she learnt that she had severe shortcomings.' He bit off the end of the cigar. 'When will women learn that they have no place whatsoever in the fight against crime? They'd only get in the way and invite injury.' He lit the cigar and puffed hard on it. 'Thank heaven we don't have them here in the Detective Department to hinder us.'

'I've never found that women hinder us,' said Leeming, loyally. 'If anything, my wife does the opposite. Estelle is a great help.'

'Yes,' added Colbeck, 'and I disagree that they have no place in the fight against crime. The time will surely come when we are glad to welcome women into the police service.'

'It had better not come in *my* time,' grumbled Tallis.

Colbeck could have told him that, in a sense, it already had because he had enlisted the aid of Madeleine Andrews on a number of cases and her contribution had always been valuable. Knowing that the information would only bring certain condemnation from Tallis, he held his peace and inhaled the aroma of the cigar. It reminded him of the faint whiff he had sniffed at Carys Evans's cottage, evidence that Sir David Pryde was also a cigar smoker.

'What has been happening while we've been away?' he asked.

'We've not been sitting on our hands,' replied Tallis.

'Do you have any news of Stephen Voke?'

The superintendent repeated what he had earlier told Leeming. Colbeck absorbed the intelligence before reaching a decision.

'I'll leave from Paddington first thing in the morning,' he said.

Leeming was puzzled. 'Are you going back to Cardiff, sir?'

'No, that's the one place he wouldn't dare to show his face after all that's happened. Stephen Voke left London with the intention of starting up in business elsewhere. One of the towns he considered,' Colbeck went on, 'was Cardiff. My guess is that he chose somewhere within relatively easy reach of Wales by rail. On the day that he and his accomplice left London, they would have needed to unload their luggage at the new abode before going on to Cardiff unencumbered.'

Tallis braced himself. 'I fear that you're about to spring another of your infamous theories on me, Inspector.'

'It's less of a theory than a piece of intuition, sir,' said Colbeck. 'I think that Stephen Voke would choose a town with a railway station so that he could be easily reached by potential customers. I know for a fact that he travelled to Cardiff to deliver an item he made for a client. If he's in a small town, he'll need custom from a wider circle. The search for him must therefore begin on the Great Western and on the South Wales Railways. Somewhere between here and Cardiff, I think we'll find Stephen Voke settling into a new life.'

'He could be in a different part of the country altogether,' argued Tallis. 'Railways go everywhere.'

'I happen to know that he's especially fond of Wales.'

'I'm not surprised,' said Leeming. 'Wales has been very good to him. It's given him a silver coffee pot, a large amount of money, a carriage and two horses. Those are rich pickings

221

for a few days' work. I've learnt to rely on your intuition, Inspector,' he declared, 'so I'll come with you tomorrow.'

'You're looking for a needle in a haystack,' complained Tallis.

'Perhaps, sir,' returned Colbeck, 'but it will be a very large needle in a very small haystack. When two people move into a new community for the first time, they are bound to get noticed, especially if one of them opens a shop as a silversmith. Mr Voke's occupation narrows the search immediately. We'll find them.'

'It's a pity we can't call on the assistance of Superintendent Stockdale,' said Leeming, wistfully. 'He was a tremendous help to us in Cardiff and would like to see this case through to the end.'

'No doubting that, Sergeant. Unfortunately, he's preoccupied with another crime at the moment – a kidnapping.'

'Oh – who was kidnapped?'

'Miss Kate Linnane,' said Colbeck, 'the celebrated actress. She was due to play Lady Macbeth this evening. I sincerely hope that they manage to cope without her.'

They all knew. Laura Tremaine had given a competent performance at the rehearsal but it never took wing. Unable to conquer her nerves, she managed nothing more than a brave stab at the part. Nigel Buckmaster was the first to congratulate her afterwards but he knew that she was no Kate Linnane. He assured her that she would grow fully into the role in front of the audience but that prospect only served to increase her dread. Laura was going to take the stage as the unworthy substitute of an actress who had brought real venom to the part. All that the new Lady Macbeth had achieved was petulance. While everyone in the company knew her deficiencies, they tried to ignore them. Laura received nothing but praise and encouragement.

As the time of performance drew near, her feelings of sheer inadequacy were intensified. Her dresser burbled away happily about the triumph awaiting her but Laura was not persuaded. Even during the rehearsal, when Buckmaster had given a deliberately muted version of Macbeth, she had been totally eclipsed by him. When he released his full power that evening, she would trail helplessly in his wake. Panic set in once again. Buckmaster tried to rally her, coming into her dressing room in his costume and false beard.

'You can do it, Laura,' he told her. 'I know that you struggled this afternoon but that was your first attempt. Put those troubles behind you now. Destiny beckons. This is your moment.'

'I feel sick,' she admitted.

'So do I and so do all of us. It's one of the perennial hazards of this profession. The moment you step on to that stage, the discomfort will vanish in a flash. You'll be Lady Macbeth in every particular.'

His words gave her enough confidence to believe that she might get through the performance without any real mishap but there was no question of matching him. Instead of being a steely wife exhorting him to commit murder, she would be making a polite request for him to assassinate a king. Her Lady Macbeth would have surface value but no depth. Nigel Buckmaster, the man she looked upon as a theatrical paragon, would never forgive her. Instead of being the start of a brilliant career for her, *Macbeth* would bring her dreams to an end.

In the event, she never even got to utter a single word of her new role. With barely twenty minutes before the curtain was raised, Kate Linnane flung open the door of the dressing room and stormed in like an avenging angel. She eyed Laura with contempt.

'How dare you!' she exclaimed, eyes blazing. 'What on earth are you doing in my costume?'

Afflicted by a blend of horror and relief, Laura was speechless.

'Get this person out of my dressing room,' ordered Kate, 'and bring me my costume back.'

Laura was hustled out by the dresser and Kate slammed the door after them. Arms akimbo, she confronted the staring Macbeth.

'Stop looking at me as if I'm Banquo at the feast,' she said. 'It's me, Nigel. Do you really think I'd let some ambitious minx replace me as Lady Macbeth – never in a hundred years!'

'We thought you'd been abducted,' he gasped.

'What ever gave you that absurd idea?'

'I expected you for breakfast.'

'I had an invitation to eat elsewhere,' she explained, 'and I could hardly refuse to see my brother.'

'You went off with your *brother*?'

'Michael was in Cardiff for a few days on business and wanted to spend time with me. He's in the audience right now. Oh, by the way,' she added, 'don't worry about the time. I told them to hold the curtain for half an hour so that I have some leeway to change.'

'You did this on purpose, Kate,' he said, glowering at her. 'You staged the whole thing to give us a fright. According to the police, you were seen getting on to a train to London with a man in a cloak.'

'It was my brother and we only went as far as Gloucester. That's where he lives now. I always intended to return for the performance. Unless, that is,' she went on, throwing down the challenge, 'you'd prefer that little baggage, Miss Tremaine, to play Lady Macbeth. If that's what you wish, Nigel, you can have her.'

It was a defining moment and he was quick to recognise it as such. Kate Linnane was too shrewd not to notice the designs he had on Laura Tremaine but she was not ready to be supplanted yet. To show her resentment and to let Buckmaster see how indispensable she was to the company, Kate had conspired with her brother to prove her point. In pretending to be abducted, she had produced all manner of alarums and excursions in the company. Buckmaster had been forced to promote Laura Tremaine into a role for which she was plainly not yet ready. The new Lady Macbeth would have marred the evening's performance. At least, they had been rescued from that. Wanting to throttle Kate for the trouble and anxiety she had inflicted on him, Buckmaster instead embraced her warmly.

'Welcome back, my love!' he said, effusively. 'I knew in my heart that you'd never let us down. I was rightly chastised. Let's put all that behind us and give the audience a performance to remember.'

'Are we friends again?'

'We are and always will be, Kate, you wondrous creature!'

'Good,' she said, kissing him passionately. 'If you kill Duncan for me, you may find the door of my hotel room unlocked again tonight. That's the best place for us to settle our differences.'

CHAPTER TWELVE

Her friendship with Robert Colbeck had not only brought her intense pleasure, it had also broadened the mind of Madeleine Andrews in every way. Even before she met him, she had been interested in books but had never been able to find enough suitable reading matter. Colbeck solved that problem. From his own extensive library, he loaned her a whole series of volumes. While many were related to the history of railways, he took care to provide her with a variety of novels as well. As she sat at home that evening, reading by the light of the lamp, she realised why Colbeck had urged her to read *Dombey and Son*. Two of the scenes in Dickens' novel had been set in Camden and depicted the upheaval caused when the London to Birmingham line cut right through it. Madeleine had been a child when the railway had been built nearby but her father, who now travelled on it daily as an engine driver, had vivid recollections of the clamour and disruption. Charles Dickens was recreating it for her.

Because she expected to hear Caleb Andrews' footsteps

at any minute, she read on with her ears pricked. When a cab rattled down the street and stopped outside, her first thought, therefore, was that he had been injured at work and sent home. Putting the novel aside, she rushed to open the door only to see Colbeck paying the cab driver. Madeleine let out a cry of joy. Doffing his top hat, he gave her a kiss then followed her into the house. He noticed the book immediately.

'Ah, you've started it, have you?'

'Yes, Robert. It's wonderful to see Camden portrayed in a novel. Thank you so much for recommending it.'

'There are four railway scenes in all,' he said, 'and they're very well-written. However, I'm not going to let Dickens come between us. I came here to see you and not to talk about him.'

'I've missed you so much,' she said, squeezing his hands. 'What have you been doing and where have you been?'

'I've been hunting a killer in Cardiff and he's proving to be extremely elusive – so is the young lady, for that matter.'

'What young lady?'

'The one involved in the murder.'

They sat close to each other and he gave her a carefully edited version of the crimes he was investigating. Though she was intrigued to hear details of the case, Madeleine was also interested in the mention of Nigel Buckmaster's theatre company.

'You took me to see him playing Othello,' she recalled. 'I didn't understand everything that was going on but I was deeply moved by Desdemona's plight. She was such a helpless victim.'

'Miss Kate Linnane excelled herself in the role,' he said, 'and, by all accounts, has been magnificent as Lady Macbeth. I only wish that I could have taken you to see it at Saturday's matinee performance.'

'Is there no hope of that, Robert?'

'Probably not – this investigation may occupy me for some time. Besides, we might not, in any case, be able to see Miss Linnane in person. Before I left the town, we had a report that she'd been kidnapped and the police are still looking for her.'

Colbeck was unaware that the leading lady had now rejoined the company and he had been wondering how the young understudy had fared in her place. Madeleine was distressed to hear about the abduction and hoped that the actress would soon be found. She was also worried for Colbeck's safety.

'Murder, robbery and kidnap,' she said in dismay. 'Cardiff sounds like a very dangerous place.'

'It pales into insignificance beside the rookeries of St Giles or Seven Dials,' he told her, 'and, though it could do with more men, it has an efficient police force. You'd feel quite secure walking alone down the main thoroughfares of Cardiff. With regard to the murder, of course, we're not dealing with local criminals. The two people we have in mind came into the town from England to commit their crimes.'

'What about the kidnap?'

'I'm not in charge of that case, Madeleine.'

'You must know something of the details.'

'I've been too preoccupied with my own investigation to

pay much attention to the fate of Miss Linnane,' he admitted, 'but I have the feeling that she'll soon be found. Jeremiah Stockdale, the police superintendent, is very capable. It will not be long before he tracks the lady down.'

Stockdale simmered with anger. Having paid a rare visit to the Theatre Royal to watch *Macbeth*, he had expected Nigel Buckmaster to be playing opposite an understudy. Instead, he was startled to see Kate Linnane appearing as Lady Macbeth at a time when Stockdale's men were still out searching for her. It spoilt the performance completely for him. While the rest of the audience was captivated by the swirling drama, he remained wholly uninvolved. When rapturous applause echoed around the theatre at the end of the play, Stockdale did not join in. Instead of clapping together, his hands were bunched tight like those of a prize fighter. He was livid.

There was no point in accosting them there. Nigel Buckmaster and Kate Linnane would be surrounded by admirers the moment they stepped out of the building. Among those rushing to the stage door would be the Town Clerk, who had come to worship at the feet of the leading lady yet again. There would be dozens like him, lonely and impressionable men enthralled by the beauty, passion and nobility of Lady Macbeth. Stockdale had to bide his time. Pushing his way through the milling crowd outside, he strode purposefully back in the direction of St Mary Street. He had a lengthy wait. It was almost two hours before the actor-manager and his leading lady finally returned to the Railway Hotel. Stockdale ambushed them in the foyer.

'I wonder if I could have a word with you?' he asked in a voice that made it clear they had no alternative.

'Why, it's *you*, superintendent,' said Buckmaster with a flamboyant gesture. 'I didn't recognise you out of your uniform. You cut a fine figure in evening wear, I must say. Was this transformation brought about for any particular occasion?'

'Yes, sir – I attended a performance of *Macbeth*.' The others traded an uneasy glance and began to mouth excuses. 'Perhaps we should discuss this in private,' Stockdale said, interrupting them. 'I promised the manager that I wouldn't arrest you in public.'

Buckmaster goggled. '*Arrest!*'

'We've done nothing wrong,' protested Kate.

'That's exactly the point, Miss Linnane,' said Stockdale. 'Nothing wrong was done. I have been investigating a crime that never actually took place.' His smile was glacial. 'Shall we go upstairs?'

Followed by the superintendent, Macbeth and Lady Macbeth went up to Buckmaster's room. They were not acknowledging an ecstatic audience now nor were they garnering praise from their enthusiastic well-wishers at the stage door. They were compelled to produce a very different performance and it was one they had never rehearsed. When they reached the room, Buckmaster unlocked the door with his key. After helping Kate remove her cape, he took off his top hat and cloak before turning up the gaslight to brighten the room. Taking a stance in the middle of the carpet, he launched into his defence.

'We are deeply sorry, Superintendent,' he said, one hand

to his breast. 'Common courtesy dictated that we should have told you of Miss Linnane's miraculous escape from her kidnapper. The truth of the matter is that we simply didn't have the time. Twenty minutes before the curtain was due to rise, Miss Linnane burst into the theatre and announced that – in spite of the appalling trial she'd had to undergo – she would honour her commitment to the company and take on her role. I'm sure you'll agree that she did so with the brilliance we've come to associate with her.'

'Thank you, Mr Buckmaster,' said Stockdale, curtly, 'but I've heard enough speeches from you this evening and I don't propose to listen to any more – even though you no longer wear that kilt.' He turned to Kate. 'What have you to say, Miss Linnane?'

'I'm still haunted by the memory of it,' she claimed, looking anguished. 'I was snatched from my room, forced to travel to London and kept in a dark cellar for hours on end. When I managed to escape, I hastened back to Cardiff to play the part for which I'd been engaged. All else went from my mind.'

'Who abducted you?'

'It was a crazed fellow who has been stalking me for months, Superintendent. When he saw his opportunity, he pounced.'

'Then I must ask you the question that Inspector Colbeck first put,' said Stockdale. 'Why did you not resist and call out? You almost screeched down the walls of the castle on stage tonight so I know that your lungs are in good order. What happened to your voice during the kidnap? Did he threaten to kill you if you raised the alarm?'

'Yes, yes,' she said, clutching at the suggestion. 'That was it.'

'Now you know the full story,' concluded Buckmaster, 'so you must excuse us. We are very tired and Miss Linnane has been through a very harrowing day.'

'So have my men,' said Stockdale. 'Constable Roberts and Constable Parker made a totally unnecessary trip to London in pursuit of this mythical kidnapper and several other policemen went searching for witnesses in Cardiff itself. I put it to you, Miss Linnane, that this whole episode was devised by you for some personal reason, as a result of which the Cardiff Borough Police were needlessly distracted from pursuing real criminals.'

'I was abducted!' she cried, falling back on defiance.

'Do you subscribe to this lie, Mr Buckmaster?'

'I stand by what Miss Linnane has told you,' said the actor.

'Then perhaps you'd explain something to me, sir. When Miss Linnane returned to Cardiff after her dramatic escape from a dark cellar, why didn't you inform us immediately of her return?'

'I told you – we didn't have time.'

'The performance was delayed by half an hour. That gave you plenty of time to send someone to the police station. One of your underlings could run the distance in less than five minutes.'

'We are actors, Superintendent,' said Buckmaster, grandly. 'The play must always come first. Our public awaited us.'

'I've been awaiting you as well,' said Stockdale, grimly, 'and I got into conversation with the manager while I did so.

Mr Pugh is a shrewd gentleman. He suggested that it was unlikely that anyone would simply charge in off the street and drag Miss Linnane out. To begin with, how would this fellow know where to find her room? Mr Pugh had the answer to that. He wondered if the kidnapper was already staying here as a guest.' Kate clenched her teeth. 'He allowed me to look through the register and do you know what I found? There's someone who booked in two days ago by the name of Michael Linnane.' The two of them wilted under his glare. 'Do I need to say anything more?'

After a night at home in the bosom of his family, Victor Leeming looked much happier and healthier. The bandaging around his head obliged him to wear his top hat at a rakish angle and he collected some curious stares as he and Colbeck walked along the platform at Paddington Station, but he was unperturbed by the attention. When they found an empty carriage, they removed their hats then sat down opposite each other. Leeming's good humour was not only occasioned by the fact that he was hoping to arrest the man who assaulted him. He was relieved that they would not be staying away overnight and that he could return to the comforts of the marital couch in due course.

'I've been looking at a map of where we're going,' he began.

Colbeck patted his pocket. 'I've brought one with me, Victor.'

'The one I saw had part of South Wales on it and what puzzled me was this. Why didn't they build a railway bridge across the River Severn? That would have been the most direct route.'

'The most direct and the most sensible,' agreed Colbeck, 'which is exactly why it was suggested when the line was first mooted. There was a proposal for a long bridge across the river west of Gloucester. Local objection, alas, was so powerful that the scheme had to be abandoned. The line was diverted through the Forest of Dean so Mr Brunel had no need to bridge the Severn. His engineering skills were, however, put to the test.'

'Yes, Inspector – I saw the viaducts at Chepstow and Newport.'

Colbeck was amused. 'You're improving, Victor. There was a time when you hardly looked out of the window of a train.'

'I'm usually too busy praying that we'll arrive safely.'

'Accidents on the railway are not that common.'

'Tell that to the passengers on the Brighton express,' said Leeming. 'The ones who survived the crash last year, that is.'

It was a case that still troubled Leeming. The express had been involved in a head-on collision with a ballast train. He remembered the devastation caused. Though the accident had been deliberately engineered, Leeming's fears were not stilled. Whenever he was tugged along at high speed by an iron monster breathing fire and pulsing with energy, he thought about the Brighton express and longed for the more leisurely days when the stagecoach was the principal mode of transport.

'Where do we start, Inspector?' he asked.

'In Gloucester,' replied Colbeck. 'It's a cathedral city with a pleasant aspect. It could well attract two refugees from London.'

'You can see why they told nobody where they were going.'

'They wanted to cut their ties with the past and start afresh. At least, that's the way it looks. There was nothing to keep Stephen Voke in London and we must assume that the same is true of the young lady who went with him.'

'All that we have is her Christian name – Bridget.'

'I'm not convinced of that,' said Colbeck. 'If she did set out to entrap Hugh Kellow, she might well have given a false name. I've also been thinking about those ransom letters sent to Mrs Tomkins. Two of them were written by a woman but the others – in block capitals – could just as easily have been penned by a man.'

'What do you deduce from that, sir?'

'I'm not sure. It worries me.'

'Perhaps the young woman was not even in Cardiff at the time the last two letters were sent,' observed Leeming. 'The only person involved in the exchange was a man. He was operating alone.'

'I doubt that,' said Colbeck. 'He'd have used his accomplice as a lookout. They've always been extremely careful in the past. We are up against people who take no chances.'

'Then how do we catch them?'

'We exploit their weakness.'

'I didn't know that they had one, sir.'

'They do now, Victor,' said Colbeck. 'Their venture into crime is over. They committed murder and, with the keys stolen from their victim, they emptied Leonard Voke's safe. They used the silver coffee pot cleverly to fleece Mrs

Tomkins. Now that they've got what they want, they'll have left Cardiff to begin a respectable new life. In short, they'll think they got away with it. That's their weak spot – they believe they're completely safe.'

'What about that carriage?'

'You mean the one stolen from Mrs Tomkins?'

'Yes, Inspector – it would bring in a tidy sum if they sold it along with the two horses.'

'It would also arouse suspicion,' said Colbeck, 'and that will deter them. Stephen Voke, I fancy, does not look like someone who is a legitimate owner of a splendid carriage. There's another thing to consider, Victor. Have you ever driven a vehicle with two horses between the shafts?'

'I'm not stupid enough to try, sir. They'd be a handful.'

'Mr Voke will be no coachman either. I think he only stole the carriage in order to buy time for his escape. At the rate she walks, it would have taken Mrs Tomkins some while to get home and report what happened. The villains might have left Cardiff by then.'

'What will they have done with the carriage?'

'Abandoned it, more than likely,' said Colbeck. 'It's no use to them now. It would only get them noticed when they seek anonymity. No, it will turn up in due course.'

'Where was it found?' asked Clifford Tomkins, looking at the carriage.

'A few miles from here,' replied Stockdale. 'It was standing beside a stream well away from the main road. The horses were cropping the grass. If it hadn't been for a man who went fishing in that stream, the carriage might still be there.'

'He deserves a reward.'

'He's already had it, sir. He was a poacher trespassing on private property. I overlooked that offence in return for the information he gave me.'

They were standing on the forecourt of the Tomkins' residence. A policeman had driven the carriage there with the superintendent as his passenger. Stockdale seized on the offer of money.

'You're very fortunate to get it back in this condition, sir,' he pointed out. 'The horses could have been harmed and the carriage damaged. You'd have incurred a sizeable debt. Since you are minded to give a reward, might I suggest that a donation to the Borough Police Force is in order?'

'You shall have it, Superintendent.'

'Thank you, sir. We need money to fight crime.'

'I think you've earned it.'

Tomkins was not speaking from a philanthropic impulse. The ironmaster was recalling Stockdale's discretion with regard to his nocturnal antics in a brothel. That deserved recognition. They were still talking when Winifred Tomkins came out of the house.

'We've got it back!' she cried, coming over to them.

'I'll explain all the details later,' said Tomkins.

'That's one load off my mind, Superintendent. We've had that carriage for years. One grows attached to things like that.' She peered at it more closely. 'Is it damaged in any way?'

'No, Mrs Tomkins,' said Stockdale. 'We inspected it carefully. I suggest that you get your coachman to take it round to the stables. After all this time, the horses need to be 'unharnessed – they're very restive, as you can see.'

'I'll organise that at once,' said Tomkins, walking away.

'Thank you *so* much, Superintendent,' said Winifred. 'I've been having nightmares about that carriage.'

'I did promise that you'd get it back – *and* your money.'

'Strictly speaking, it's not mine any more.'

'Oh?'

'Clifford – my husband – came round to my point of view in the end. Since he commissioned the coffee pot as a gift, he accepted that he should bear any costs pertaining to it. He's agreed to pay me every penny that I lost.'

Stockdale suppressed a grin. 'That's very handsome of him.'

'Now that we have our carriage back, he can't keep blaming me for losing it in the first place.'

'You didn't exactly *lose* it, Mrs Tomkins. It was taken from you by a man with a pistol. In those circumstances, your husband would have yielded up the carriage as well.'

'That's exactly what I told him.'

'You'll be able to sleep more soundly from now on.'

'Oh, I will,' she said with gratitude. 'You saved us from so much embarrassment, Superintendent. What happened with respect to the coffee pot can be kept secret but we could not have hidden the fact that our carriage had been stolen. Tongues would have wagged. You know the kind of rumours that can spread.'

'They've been nipped in the bud, Mrs Tomkins.'

He looked up to see her husband returning with the coachman and pointing to the carriage. Strutting along with his chest out and his stomach pulled in, Tomkins gave the impression that he had retrieved the vehicle in person. He snapped his fingers and the coachman took over, first patting the horses to calm them down then climbing up on to the seat to drive the carriage away.

'I can see why you wanted it back,' said Stockdale. 'It's a very comfortable ride.'

'Far more comfortable than Lady Pryde's phaeton,' Winifred interjected. 'I can assure you of that.'

'I'll have to take your word for it, Mrs Tomkins. I can't envisage myself ever being invited to sit beside Lady Pryde.'

'Then you should be grateful.'

'What happens next, Superintendent?' asked Tomkins. 'When will you recover my money?'

'More to the point,' said his wife, 'when will I finally have my silver coffee pot?'

'I'm in no position to answer either of those questions,' said Stockdale, 'because I am no longer involved in the investigation. It's moved outside Cardiff and thus out of my hands. Inspector Colbeck is pursuing the matter elsewhere. I have to confine myself to finding kidnapped actresses and recovering stolen carriages.'

Winifred's brow creased. 'Kidnapped actresses, you say?'

'There was a slight problem with the theatre company, Mrs Tomkins, but it's been resolved now. Mr Buckmaster was so grateful that he gave me several free tickets for Saturday's performance. He was also kind enough to donate some money to us.'

'But who was kidnapped?'

'Nobody – it was all a misunderstanding.'

'Well, the theft of that coffee pot was not a

misunderstanding,' said Tomkins, sulkily. 'It's cost me almost as much as the locomotive on which it was modelled. I hope that Inspector Colbeck realises that.'

The fugitives were not in Gloucester. That was established without any difficulty. After alighting at the railway station, Colbeck and Leeming walked to a silversmith near the centre of the city and asked him if he was expecting to have more competition in the area.

'Not if I can help it,' said Jack Grindle, gruffly. 'There's barely enough work to keep the rest of us going.'

'This looks like a fairly prosperous town,' said Colbeck.

'People don't always want to spend their money on jewellery, Inspector. When farmers make a profit, they buy more stock and their wives have little desire for my handiwork. New dresses and pretty bonnets are what they prefer. There's over 17,000 people living in Gloucester and most of them work in the docks, the foundries, the timber mills, the flow mills and such like. You won't find much interest in silverware there. It's a luxury they can't afford.'

It was a small shop but the silverware on display was of a high quality. Grindle had an apprentice and an assistant in the back room so he clearly had enough work to justify their wages. He was a big, raw-boned, hirsute man in his forties with the build of a blacksmith yet his hands were small and delicate. He blinked constantly.

'Where would *you* go, Mr Grindle?' asked Leeming.

'I'm staying right here,' rejoined the silversmith, truculently. 'This is my shop and nobody will turn me out of it.'

'That's not what I meant, sir.'

241

'Then why not say so?'

'What the sergeant is asking,' explained Colbeck, 'is only a hypothetical question.'

Grindle was baffled. 'And what's *that* when it's at home?'

'Supposing that you *did* want to move elsewhere and start afresh, which part of the country would you choose?'

'It would have to be London. That's where the money is.'

'The person we're interested in has just left the city. We think that he might have headed in this direction.'

'Then he'd better not show his nose in Gloucester.'

'Is there anywhere in the area that might attract him?'

Grindle scratched his head. 'I can't name a place, Inspector,' he said with a sniff, 'but I can tell you this. If I was starting up again, I'd choose somewhere that was close to rich folk in large country houses. It's the aristocracy and the gentry that like silver tableware. Find someone who wants plate and cutlery and you find a good living.'

'Where would you suggest that we look?' said Colbeck.

'Anywhere but here,' was the blunt reply.

'And you're sure that nobody has made enquiries in the city?'

'If they had, I'd have got to hear about it. We stick together for our own protection in this trade. We won't let any Tom, Dick or Harry stroll in and open up a shop just because he likes to hear cathedral bells on a Sunday. No,' said Grindle, 'the people you're after never came near Gloucester. You'll have to look somewhere else.'

'Thank you, sir,' said Colbeck. 'You've been very helpful.'

He and Leeming left the shop and closed the door behind him.

'I don't think he was any help at all,' said Leeming. 'If he's as rude as that to customers, he won't keep many of them.'

'Mr Grindle is exactly what we need, Victor.'

'Is he?'

'Yes – he guards his own territory and bristles at the slightest hint of a fresh rival. In five minutes, he saved us the trouble of looking anywhere else in the city.'

'So what do we do now, sir?'

'We go on to Chepstow,' said Colbeck, happily, 'and we find someone exactly like Jack Grindle, Silversmith.'

Leonard Voke had been a principal victim of the crimes and despair had eaten into his soul. Since his safe was ransacked, he had had neither the confidence nor the need to open his shop. Without his tools he could make nothing. He spent most of the day sitting in his back room amid the ruins of his livelihood. Edward Tallis called on him and discovered Voke more demoralised than ever.

'There is no God,' said the silversmith, despondently. 'If there had been, I would never have had to suffer like this. My assistant has been murdered, my safe has been emptied and my ungrateful son is responsible for both crimes. Where is God's mercy in all that?'

'This is not the time for a theological discussion,' said Tallis, 'but I can assure you that there is a heaven. God looks down on us all with true pity.'

'I'm not aware of it, Superintendent.'

'You are still dazed by the shock of what happened to you.'

'Dazed?' echoed Voke. 'I've been smashed into pieces.'

Feeling that the old man deserved to be informed of the latest developments, Tallis had made the journey to Wood Street. There was no hope of cheering the silversmith up but he felt able to tell him that his detectives were closing in on the culprits. Voke listened to it all without comment. His mind was elsewhere.

'It's in two days' time,' he murmured.

'What is, Mr Voke?'

'The funeral – the arrangements have been made though there'll be precious few of us to see dear Hugh lowered into the ground.'

'There'll be his sister,' said Tallis, 'and I'm quite certain that his landlady, Mrs Jennings, will be there. Mr Kellow must have friends who need to be informed of the details.'

'I've put a notice in the newspapers.'

'That should bring some people in. Did his sister make any special requests for the service?'

'No,' said Voke, 'she was grateful to leave it all to me. After all that's happened, the poor creature can't think straight.'

'The sudden death of a loved one can have that affect. When that death is of such a violent and unnatural kind, of course, the agony is more searing.'

'Oh, I know all about agony,' groaned the old man.

Tallis did not let him wallow in his misery. He still felt that Voke, unbeknown to him, might have information tucked away at the back of his mind that could be of use in the investigation. The silversmith had so far refused to talk about his son unless it was to unleash a stream of vituperation. Hoping to provoke him into a more considered discussion, Tallis decided to tell him something about Stephen Voke that his father did not know.

'When your son left your employment, he changed somewhat.'

'Yes – he began to plot my destruction!'

'I was talking about his work,' said Tallis. 'I know that you thought him lazy but he seems to have applied himself to his craft. Not, I should add, when he was at Mr Stern's shop. This was when he was on his own. According to his landlord, Mr Meyrick, your son would spend almost all his spare time working on commissioned items for private customers.'

Voke was roused. 'Is this true?'

'He was so dedicated that he worked on into the night until there were complaints about the noise he was making with his hammer. Evidently, the walls in the house are rather thin.'

'I knew it!' yelled Voke. 'He stole my clients from me. I often wondered why people who had been very pleased with our work suddenly went elsewhere. Stephen must have poached them.'

'He could only do that by offering lower charges. The point is that he was not the complete wastrel you described to me. Your son obviously had a new incentive in life and it must be linked to the young woman who came into his life.'

'*Which* young woman, Superintendent – there were many.'

'This one concentrated his mind.'

'Yes,' said Voke, 'on how to abuse his father.'

'If he was prepared to run away with the lady, he was clearly committed to the liaison.' Tallis pulled a face. 'I'm bound to tell you that it's something I frown upon. Young men and women should not be allowed such free access to each other. It leads to depravity. There are social rules to obey. Unmarried couples should never be allowed to set up house wherever they choose. In some ways,' he conceded, 'this young woman seems to have been a good influence on your son. In other ways, I fear, she has led him off the straight and narrow path. Who *is* she, Mr Voke?'

'How should I know?'

'This is your *son* we're discussing.'

'He never brought friends home because he knew I'd disapprove of them. He shut me out of his life, Superintendent.' Something stirred in his memory. 'What about the advertisement you put in the press? Did anybody come forward apart from his landlord?'

'Not at first,' replied Tallis. 'Indeed, it took Mr Meyrick a while before he showed his face. Two other people did call on me but they were acquaintances of your son's rather than friends. They used to drink with him at some hostelry or other.'

'That's all Stephen ever did at one time.'

'Both of them told me the same thing – that your son wanted to move out of London altogether. Apparently, he kept talking about a holiday he'd had when he was much younger. It had made a big impression on him. The problem was,' Tallis went on, 'neither of them could recall the name of the place where you took him.'

Voke's eyes glazed over. 'I can tell you,' he said, wistfully. 'It was when Stephen was still a boy. My wife had a cousin who offered us the use of her cottage for a week. That was the only reason we went there. We had very few holidays after that. And yes,' he added, touched by the thought of happier times. 'Stephen did enjoy it. We were a real family then. We did things together.'

'And where exactly was this cottage, Mr Voke?'

'It was in Caerleon.'

Chepstow was a charming town that overlooked the River Wye near its junction with the Severn. Its forbidding castle was a reminder of the days when the Normans conquered England and extended their overlordship into Wales. Colbeck and Leeming were not detained there long. They spoke to three silversmiths and to the landlord of the town's largest public house. All four confirmed that nobody else intended to open a jewellery shop. Of these witnesses, the landlord was the most unequivocal, assuring them that very little happened in Chepstow that escaped his notice. After thanking this local oracle, the detectives adjourned to the railway station to await the next train.

Leeming was beginning to lose heart. 'Will we have any more luck in Newport, sir?'

'Wait and see,' said Colbeck.

'The next stop after that will be Cardiff.'

'They won't stay there for obvious reasons, Victor. They'll want to put a little distance between themselves and the scene of their crimes. They could, however, have moved further west to Swansea.'

'Do we have to go *that* far?' asked Leeming, worried that his hopes of returning home that night would disappear. 'And why should anyone in their right mind want to live here when they don't speak that peculiar language?'

'You'll find a lot of English people in South Wales,' said Colbeck, 'especially among the ironmasters and coalmine owners. They knew how to exploit the rich mineral resources there. Then, of course, there's Jeremiah Stockdale, another Englishman who settled down on this side of the border. We could do with his help now. He knows Newport very well.'

'I'm not surprised. He told me he was sent here a few years ago to quell riots during an election.'

'I was thinking of a much earlier visit than that. In 1839 there was a Chartist demonstration in Newport. Violence broke out.'

'That's right,' said Leeming. 'The superintendent made his most famous arrest in Newport. I remember him telling us about it.'

'The arrest was actually made in Cardiff. Zephaniah Williams, one of the Chartist ringleaders, escaped there and hid in the Sea Lock Hotel waiting for a ship to carry him to France. The superintendent disguised himself as a sailor,' recalled Colbeck with an admiring smile, 'and was rowed out to the vessel that would have taken Williams to safety. He made the arrest before the fugitive was fully awake.'

'I wish that *we* could make an arrest,' said Leeming, glumly.

'The time will come, Victor.'

'When?'

'Very soon, I trust.'

'Do we have to visit many more shops like the ones we've already been in? I find it so depressing, sir.'

'Why is that?'

248

'They're full of things I could never afford to buy. That last place had a silver tankard worth more than my house.'

'It *was* made in the reign of Charles II,' said Colbeck, 'and you have to admit that it was beautifully decorated. But I can see that that wouldn't carry any weight with you.'

'Tankards are to drink out of and not just to look at.'

'I'll spare you any more silverware in Newport. There may be another way to find what we're after.'

'And what's that, sir?'

'Well, I've been thinking about something that Miss Evans said to me. Stephen Voke made a ring for her but not while he was working at Solomon Stern's shop. It was made at his lodging. In other words,' Colbeck went on, 'he was working on private commissions in his own time. Perhaps he has no intention of opening a shop at all. He may be able to earn a living by getting commissions and working from home. We must search for his house.'

'How will we ever find it, Inspector?' wondered Leeming as a train steamed towards them. 'Newport is much bigger than Cardiff. They must have thousands of houses there.'

'Granted, Victor, but they won't all have changed hands recently.' He raised his voice above the approaching roar. 'We need to speak to someone who sells property in the town.'

There were times when Jeremiah Stockdale disliked his job because it gave him a disturbing insights into the depths to which human beings could sink. A week earlier, he had led a raid on a house in notorious Stanley Street where no fewer than fifty-four people were found crammed into four rooms. The pervading stink of poverty and degradation had stayed in his nostrils for days. Now, however, he was relishing his reign as the town's police chief. He was brimming with optimism. He had forced Nigel Buckmaster to pay full compensation for the time wasted by his men on a pointless search for a supposedly missing actress. He had been able to return a stolen carriage and horses to Clifford Tomkins and earn a generous reward. He had endeared himself even more to Winifred Tomkins. And such was his unwavering confidence in Robert Colbeck that he knew the murder at the Railway Hotel would be solved in time, bringing with it lavish praise for Stockdale's part in the investigation.

When he returned to the police station, therefore, he was in a cheerful mood. As he entered the outer office, he found a letter awaiting him on the desk. After exchanging a few jovial words with the custody sergeant, he opened the letter and read it with interest. An anxious look came into his eye and he read the missive again with more care. An expression of horror spread slowly across his face.

'Inspector Colbeck needs to see this,' he said. 'Urgently.'

It took much longer than Colbeck had expected. A large number of properties in Newport had acquired new owners in recent months. None of the auctioneers and house agents they approached had ever heard of Stephen Voke, leading the detectives to wonder if he had changed his name. It was only after hours of trudging from door to door that they were eventually given the information they sought. Colbeck immediately hired a trap and they set off for Caerleon.

'This is the way to travel,' said Leeming, contentedly.

'Only over short distances,' argued Colbeck. 'Had we set

out from London in this trap, it would have taken two days to get here.'

'What sort of a place is Caerleon, sir?'

'We'll find out before too long, Victor. It's not all that far.'

'That man said that we had to go on beyond the ruins.'

'Yes, Caerleon was a Roman town. It was the headquarters of a legion so it must have been a place of importance. Now, it seems, it's a trading centre through which iron and tin are shipped.'

'What about silver?'

'I daresay that Stephen Voke will answer that question.'

When they left the outer edges of Newport, they had a pleasant drive through open country. The cottage they were after was in an isolated position on the far side of Caerleon. It was a relatively small, squat building but it was in good condition and slate had replaced the original thatch. There was a well-tended garden at the front and a larger one at the rear given over mainly to vegetables. The whole property was surrounded by a low stone wall. As they came over the brow of the hill, they saw that outhouses ran at a right angle to the cottage itself, justifying the value put on it by the vendor. Leeming had expected something more impressive.

'It's not the home of a rich man, Inspector, is it?'

'Perhaps he doesn't wish to flaunt his wealth,' said Colbeck. 'And it's certainly an improvement on a single room in someone else's house. I think it looks very quaint.'

'It was bought with blood money,' said Leeming. 'Hugh Kellow helped to pay for that cottage.'

'I haven't forgotten that, Victor. These are merciless people. We need to take the utmost care.'

251

Tugging the reins, he turned the trap off the road then pulled it to a halt under the cover of some trees. After tethering the horse, Colbeck removed his hat and put it on the seat. Leeming followed suit, his wound starting to throb at the prospect of a meeting with the man who had inflicted it. They trod stealthily through the undergrowth until they had a good view of the cottage. Colbeck thought he saw a hint of movement through a side window.

'I suggest that you work your way around to the back,' he said. 'Be very careful – remember that they know us by sight. When I see you in position, I'll creep up to the front.'

'Let *me* arrest Voke,' said Leeming. 'He's mine.'

'As long as you're not too precipitate – he does have a pistol.'

'I doubt if he'll have it to hand, sir. Why should he? As you pointed out, he thinks that he's safe. The last thing he'll expect is that we tracked him here.'

'That's what I'm banking on.'

'I'll be off, Inspector.'

'Keep a wary eye on those outbuildings,' warned Colbeck. 'That's the most likely place for him to set up a workshop. There's not enough room in the cottage itself. He may well be at work there right now.'

Leeming nodded then set off. Keeping low and skirting the cottage, he made use of some bushes as temporary hiding places. When the sergeant finally reached the back of the property, he crouched down behind the wall. It was the signal for Colbeck to move. He, too, kept low, moving swiftly between any trees or shrubs that could offer concealment for a few seconds. Reaching the cottage without being seen, he straightened up, opened the wicker gate and strode quickly to the front door. Roses grew around the little porch, framing it attractively. A new doormat covered the flagstone. Fresh paint had been put on the door itself. There was the sense that someone cared for their property.

Colbeck pulled the bell rope and it produced a pleasing jingle. He heard footsteps then the door was opened by a handsome young woman with an enquiring smile.

'Can I help you?' she asked.

'I'm looking for Mr Stephen Voke,' he said, politely. 'Is he at home, by any chance?'

'Yes, he's out in his workshop. Did you wish to talk business with him, sir?'

'I do, indeed.'

'That's very encouraging. We've been here barely a week and already we are starting to have customers.' She stepped aside. 'You'd better come in, sir. May I have your name, please?'

'It's Colbeck – Robert Colbeck.'

'You'll have to duck your head. The beams are rather low.'

Something was wrong. The woman had recognised neither him nor his name. She certainly did not look like someone capable of taking part in a murder. He noted her wedding ring. Colbeck surmised that Voke must have had a different accomplice, one who was kept well away from the peaceful domesticity of his new life in Caerleon. Ducking into the cottage, he saw that it was larger than it looked outside. It was also well-furnished and silver ornaments glistened on the mantelpiece. Most of the furniture was very old but it had been recently polished.

'If you'll excuse me, Mr Colbeck,' she said, 'I'll fetch Stephen.'

Leeming had saved her the trouble. The back door burst open and Stephen Voke was pushed into the kitchen, handcuffs pinning his wrists together behind his back. Leeming shoved him through into the living room with a grin of triumph.

'Here he is,' he announced, 'He didn't put up any fight.'

'What's going on?' exclaimed the woman.

'I don't know,' said Voke, pitifully. 'This man jumped on me and told me that I was under arrest.'

'Who are you?' she demanded, looking fearfully at the bandage around Leeming's head, 'and what do you mean by coming here?'

'Let me explain,' said Colbeck. 'This is my colleague, Sergeant Leeming, and I am Inspector Colbeck. We are detectives from London, investigating the murder of Hugh Kellow and the theft of a valuable silver coffee pot.'

'It must be in that workshop, sir,' said Leeming. 'There's a large safe out there. That's where they keep their spoils.'

'What spoils?' asked Voke. 'As for a murder, this is the first I've heard of it. Are you telling me that Hugh was *killed*?'

'Yes,' replied Colbeck. 'His body was found in the hotel room in Cardiff where you had left it.'

'But I haven't been to Cardiff for several weeks.'

'Then how did you manage to give me this?' demanded Leeming, indicating his scalp wound. 'You must have a very long arm if you could hit me from Caerleon.'

'What my husband is telling you is correct,' said the woman with evident honesty. 'We only took possession of

254

the cottage this week. Until then, we were both in London. Stephen had no reason to go to Cardiff. He's been too busy planning the move here.'

'It's the truth, Inspector,' said Voke. 'I swear it.'

Colbeck pondered. 'Take the handcuffs off him,' he ordered at length. 'Go on.'

'But he could turn violent, sir,' said Leeming.

'Take them off, sergeant.'

'Why?'

'I think we have the wrong man.'

While the sergeant unlocked the handcuffs, Colbeck's mind was spinning like a wheel. Having arrested a large number of people in the course of his career, he was accustomed to the routine denial of guilt. That was not happening here. Stephen Voke was bemused rather than defiant. He showed none of the righteous indignation that criminals often dredged up when confronted with their misdeeds. Nor did he look like a killer. He was lean, trim and of middle height. Around the nose and mouth, there was a clear resemblance to his father. He had an open face and met Colbeck's gaze without dissimulation. When the handcuffs were removed, he did not immediately make a dash for the door. He simply rubbed his wrists before putting a protective arm around his wife.

'We must offer you our apologies, sir,' said Colbeck.

'I'm not apologising,' insisted Leeming. 'If it was left to me, he'd be clapped in irons.'

'Mr Voke is completely innocent, Sergeant.'

'But he *can't* be, sir.'

'We've been pursuing the wrong man.'

Leeming was bewildered. 'Well, if *he* didn't murder Mr Kellow,' he wanted to know, 'then who did?'

'Nobody.'

'That's impossible, sir.'

'I'm afraid that it isn't.'

'*Somebody* must have killed him.'

'Think of those ransom letters,' said Colbeck. 'Two were written by a woman but the two written, as I suspect, by a man were in block capitals. Do you know why that was done?'

'I don't have a clue, Inspector.'

'It was because he didn't want us to recognise his handwriting. He knew that we'd already seen examples of that in those letters to his sister, Effie. We'd have realised how cunningly we'd been tricked.'

'I'm still none the wiser,' said Leeming.

'Nor are we,' added Voke. 'What exactly has happened?'

'We were deceived,' said Colbeck, still working it out in his head. 'Hugh Kellow was not murdered in that hotel and the silver coffee pot was not taken from him. Nor were his keys to his employer's shop, for that matter. He knew exactly what to steal from Mr Voke's safe and made sure that he took his own tools as well as the valuables and the money.' He gestured an apology to Voke. 'You were wrongly accused, sir, and I deeply regret that. We owe your dear wife our sincerest apologies as well. The evidence that brought us here was misleading. The man we really need to arrest is Hugh Kellow.' Colbeck gritted his teeth. 'He's still alive.'

CHAPTER THIRTEEN

Discontented members of the Cardiff Borough Police sometimes complained – though never within his hearing – that their chief constable was a martinet but none of them denied that he worked tirelessly to keep the town under control. Stockdale always pushed himself much harder than any of his men. He was indefatigable. At the end of another long day, he adjourned to his favourite pub where a pint of beer was poured for him the second he appeared through the door. He took a first, long, noisy, satisfying sip. It not only served to quench his thirst, it helped to steady him after the shock he had received earlier. He still wondered if his fears were justified or if it would simply turn out to be an unfortunate coincidence. The place was quite full and he chatted happily to several people on the well-tried principle that he might pick up a nugget of useful intelligence from even the most casual conversation.

As he heard the door swing open, he glanced towards it then reacted as if an apparition had just entered. He could not believe that he was looking at Robert Colbeck.

'I was thinking about you only a moment ago, Inspector.'

'Then you can tell me what you thought,' said Colbeck, 'but only after you let me buy you another pint of beer.'

'That's an offer I can't refuse.' Quaffing the last of his drink, he handed his tankard to the newcomer. 'Thank you, Inspector.'

While Colbeck went to get the beer, Stockdale found a table in a quiet corner. As always, he sat with his back to the wall so that he could keep an eye on everybody. Colbeck eventually joined him, handing over one of the tankards then raising his own in a toast.

'To policemen everywhere!' he said.

'Amen.'

They clinked tankards then Colbeck sat down opposite him.

'I was told that I might find you here, Superintendent.'

'In earlier days,' Stockdale confided, 'you'd have found me on the other side of the bar. I was so poorly paid when I first started in this job that I used to serve in the Boat House round the corner in Womanby Street. I had to find *some* way to supplement my meagre wage. The Watch Committee seemed to think I could live on fresh air and, as your nose must have detected, there's not a lot of that in the town.' He supped his beer. 'But I'm so glad you came, Inspector. I had what could turn out to be alarming news.'

'I think I know what it is,' said Colbeck.

'How could you?'

'We may already be one step ahead of you.'

'I had a report on a missing person, a young man

who came to Cardiff on the day of the murder and whose description fits that of the victim. His father made contact with the police in London. Martin Henley – that was the young man's name – had said that he'd be spending the night at the Railway Hotel here before returning home.'

'But he was unable to do so because he was murdered.'

'It *can't* have been Mr Henley, can it?'

'I'm fairly certain that it was.'

'Then why was he killed by Stephen Voke?'

'He wasn't, Superintendent,' explained Colbeck. 'The sergeant and I tracked Mr Voke to Caerleon where he's now living with his new wife. Neither of them had anything to do with the crimes.'

'But they must have done.'

'We were badly mistaken.'

Stockdale frowned. 'None of this makes the slightest sense.'

'It does if you think it through. If Mr Voke is not the culprit…'

'Then it must have been someone else.'

'One name immediately comes to mind.'

'And who might that be?'

'Hugh Kellow.'

Stockdale was flabbergasted. 'Never!'

'That was my response at first.'

'You mean that he faked his own death?'

'What better way to disappear from sight?'

Colbeck told him about their confrontation with Stephen Voke and how the young silversmith had been completely exonerated. He and his wife, Catherine, had gone to a part

259

of Wales that held fond memories for Voke, who felt that he had enough private work to be able to operate from home.

'Miss Evans has recommended him to a number of friends in South Wales so his future seems assured. I saw a ring he made for her. It was exquisite.'

Stockdale rolled his eyes. 'Everything about Carys is exquisite,' he attested, 'except for her choice in men, of course.'

'They fulfilled their purpose by pressing gifts upon her. My guess is that Sir David Pryde commissioned her ring as well as a brooch in the shape of a dragon. For obvious reasons, he couldn't use a silversmith here.'

'No, it was too risky. A local man would know him and wonder why the items were not made for Lady Pryde. It was safer to use someone in London.' Stockdale was honest. 'How stupid we've been! We were fooled. We were well and truly fooled by Mr Kellow.'

'When I saw the disfigurement on the corpse,' said Colbeck. 'it did cross my mind that the acid had been used to make identification more difficult. But Mr Buckmaster swore that it was Hugh Kellow and recognised his clothing. The sister was even more certain.'

'Her visit settled it as far as I was concerned. Effie was so convinced that it was her brother who'd been murdered.'

'That's what she wanted us to believe. Incidentally, I don't think that Effie was his sister at all. She and Kellow were accomplices who worked in harness. We should introduce her to Nigel Buckmaster. She's such a consummate actress that he could make use of her talents on stage. Talking of which,' Colbeck said, 'did you manage to rescue Miss Linnane?'

260

'That's a long story, Inspector.'

Stockdale gave a concise version of it, proud of the fact that he had shamed Buckmaster into paying hefty compensation and received grovelling apologies from him and his leading lady. He assured Colbeck that Michael Linnane would not escape punishment for his part in the charade. Stockdale had written to the Gloucester police with details of the deception practised on their counterparts in Cardiff.

'They'll send him back to face me,' said Stockdale, 'and I'll make him *squirm*. Nobody distracts my men like that without paying for it. I expect another sizeable donation to our funds – that's *after* a night in the cells to repent of his folly.' About to take another drink, he put the tankard abruptly down on the table. 'I've just thought, Inspector. Suppose that that dead man *was* Martin Henley.'

'He was definitely not Hugh Kellow.'

'Yet he'll be buried instead of him.'

'The funeral hasn't taken place yet,' said Colbeck, 'and I sent Victor Leeming back to London with news of what we discovered. He'll make sure that the undertaker doesn't go ahead with the service until we know the true identity of the corpse. Do you still have the report about Martin Henley's disappearance?'

'No,' said Stockdale. 'Because it seemed so important, I sent it to you at Scotland Yard. Idris Roberts volunteered to take it. I think he's developed a liking for train journeys to London. It was his third in three days. Mind you, he's going to be upset when I tell him that Effie Kellow wasn't the poor little waif we thought she was. Constable Roberts treated her like his own daughter.'

'I'll see the report when I return this evening and I'll get in touch with the police station that sent it to you. The gentleman who raised the alarm will need to identify his son's body.'

'How much will you tell him?'

'Very little,' said Colbeck after drinking some beer. 'He simply needs to know that his son died an unnatural death – if, indeed, it is Martin Henley, of course. Too much detail will only cause him unnecessary distress.'

'Please let me know what happens.'

'Of course – you're involved in this investigation. That's why I took the trouble to come here from Newport. I was so close that I felt I had to bring you up to date with a sensational development.'

'It hit me like a blow.'

'Victor Leeming is the one who was most shocked.'

'Why?'

'When he arrested and handcuffed Stephen Voke, he thought that he'd captured a vicious killer. Instead of that, he'd merely caught a harmless silversmith.'

'Not all silversmiths are harmless – look at Hugh Kellow.'

'I hope to do so very soon.'

'He should be hanged, drawn and quartered.'

'That sentence is no longer in the statute book.'

'Well, it should be. He's caused the most terrible mayhem in the town. I don't think I dare tell Winifred Tomkins that the man who offered her that silver coffee pot was someone who helped to make it in the first place. She'd be even more upset.'

'Is she still grieving over the loss of her carriage?'

'That's been recovered.'

'Good – I assured the sergeant that it would be. What is suitable for a wealthy ironmaster and his wife would look quite out of place in the possession of a young man like Hugh Kellow.'

'What do you think he'll do with that coffee pot?'

'Keep it, I should imagine. It's a trophy. He obviously has a deep personal affection for it and not because he intends to drink a vast amount of coffee out of it. Mr Buckmaster and Miss Linnane both remembered him claiming that he'd done a fair amount of work on it,' said Colbeck. 'I have a suspicion that it was largely his creation and that he was never given full credit by his employer.'

'*He's* the next person in line for a shock,' said Stockdale.

'Yes, it will inflict an even deeper wound on Mr Voke.'

'He's been mourning his clever assistant when, all this time, Kellow has been robbing him blind.'

'To some extent, he was to blame,' opined Colbeck. 'His son told us what a skinflint his father was. He could never understand why Kellow worked for him when he could have earned a lot more elsewhere. Now we know the answer. Kellow intended to steal everything of value from his employer to start in business on his own account. He wreaked his revenge by staging his death and breaking the old man's heart.'

Stockdale gave a mirthless chuckle. 'I wouldn't want to be the one who tells Mr Voke what really happened.'

'Neither would I,' agreed Colbeck. 'On reflection, I think that's a task I'd rather leave to Superintendent Tallis.'

* * *

Edward Tallis never postponed things that required an immediate response nor did he delegate tasks to his men because they might involve some discomfort. When he heard Leeming's report that evening, he summoned a cab instantly and went straight to Wood Street. Leonard Voke had retired to bed early and the superintendent had some difficulty in rousing him. The old man eventually padded down the stairs in a dressing gown and slippers. Once Tallis had convinced him that he had important news, he was admitted to the back room of the shop. The two men sat either side of the table with the oil lamp between them. Tallis plunged in.

'The first thing I must tell you,' he began, 'is that the funeral has been postponed. I despatched Sergeant Leeming to the undertaker before I came on here.'

Voke was disturbed. 'Why should it be delayed?'

'I'll come to that in a moment, sir.'

'But the arrangements have been made. Hugh must be given a proper burial. It's not right for him to have to wait any longer.'

'Mr Kellow will have to wait for some time yet before his funeral,' said Tallis. 'The hangman will have to deal with him first.'

'What are you talking about?'

'The man in that coffin is not your assistant, sir.'

'But he must be,' said Voke, utterly confused. 'The body was identified by his sister, Effie. I spoke to her myself. We cried together over poor Hugh.'

'Poor Hugh is extremely well-off. He's been paid three times as much as that silver coffee pot is worth and still has the contents of your safe. It's no wonder he knew what to take,' said Tallis. 'He must have seen inside it every day. He retrieved his own tools from there and, as a final insult, he also took yours.'

'No, no, this can't be true.'

'The facts are indisputable.'

'What facts?' croaked the old man. 'I'm lost, Superintendent. I was told that Hugh had been murdered and that my son killed him.'

'That proved to be a mistaken assumption.'

'It was no assumption – I knew that my son hated me enough to do what he did. Stephen was jealous of my assistant and that drove him to murder Hugh.' His hands flitted about uncontrollably. 'If my son is not the killer, why did he flee from London?'

'He went to live in Wales with his wife, Mr Voke.'

'His *wife*? I didn't even know that he was married.'

'There are lots of things you don't know about him,' said Tallis with a note of disapproval. 'You turned him against you, Mr Voke. He only stayed here for the sake of his mother. When she died, your son had to get away. According to Sergeant Leeming, who met him and his wife today, he's a reformed character. Stephen Voke has taken on the responsibilities of marriage and is working to develop his own career.'

Voke was stunned. Tallis thought for a moment that he was about to keel over. Eyes wide and mouth agape, the silversmith tried to take in the enormity of what he had been told. The son he had disowned had evidently matured and turned over a new leaf. Yet the assistant he had loved and relied on so heavily had committed the most horrendous crimes. It was a sobering moment. Voke realised that he had to take a major share of the blame for what had happened. In favouring Hugh Kellow, he had alienated his son to the point where Stephen wanted to blot out his past altogether.

'Why didn't he *tell* me he was getting married?' muttered Voke.

'He informed Sergeant Leeming that he didn't think you'd be interested.'

'Stephen is my son.'

'Not any more, Mr Voke. He wants nothing to do with you.'

'Have I really been that terrible?' bleated the old man. 'Both Stephen and Hugh have turned against me. Did I treat them badly enough to merit what's happened?'

'Only you can answer that question, sir,' said Tallis.

Voke shook his head in wonderment. 'So my son went back to Caerleon after all this time – fancy that.'

'Make no attempt to get in touch with him. He was very firm on that point. He made Sergeant Leeming promise to pass on that message. Your son's world is elsewhere now, sir. Don't try to see him.'

'Hugh is the person I want to see,' said Voke, rising to his feet in a rage. 'I did *everything* for him. I took him in, I apprenticed him, I taught him all I knew – and this is how he repays me. I'd like to throttle him, so help me God!'

'Leave that duty to the public executioner.'

'Do you know where he is, Superintendent?'

'No, but we soon shall. He and his "sister" will be apprehended in the not too distant future.'

'I want to see him when you catch him.'

266

'Let justice take its course, Mr Voke.'

'I deserve the right to get at him for two minutes.'

'I can understand your feelings,' said Tallis, 'but you are letting your fury blind you to the obvious. Hugh Kellow is a young man with blood already on his hands. You are more advanced in years. It's foolhardy to think that you could overpower him. No,' he went on, 'leave Mr Kellow to my detectives. Inspector Colbeck will find him.'

Robert Colbeck arrived at the house in Camden in time to act as an arbitrator. Having eaten supper with her father, Madeleine Andrews had cleared the table and washed the plates. When she came into the parlour, she found her father puffing on his pipe as he read *Dombey and Son*. There was a mild argument over the book. Madeleine wanted it back but Caleb Andrews refused to yield it up. Colbeck walked in on the domestic disagreement.

'Tell him, Robert,' said Madeleine, quick to enlist his aid. 'You gave that book to me, didn't you?'

'Yes,' he replied, 'but your father is welcome to read it as well.'

'There you are!' said Andrews with a cackle.

'Though I'd assumed he'd have enough patience to wait until you'd read it first, Madeleine.'

'Father just grabbed it when my back was turned.'

'It's your own fault, Maddy,' Andrews pointed out. 'You told me how wonderful the book was. I wanted to see what it says about Camden. I was *here* when the railway line was built. I remember the deafening noise and the terrible upset it caused.'

'You're the one causing the terrible upset now, Father.'

'Why not take it in turns to read the novel?' suggested Colbeck. 'Mr Andrews is at work all day so you can pick it up whenever you have a moment, Madeleine. The only time he has a chance to read it is in the evenings.'

'I suppose so,' she conceded.

'That's settled then,' said her father, getting up from his chair. 'Anyway, you can't read it while you have company, Maddy. I'll finish this chapter in the kitchen.'

'Before you go, Mr Andrews,' said Colbeck, raising a hand, 'I wanted a word. This is very unlikely to happen now but, if it did, could I have your permission to take Madeleine to the theatre?'

'The answer is yes.'

'I should warn you that the theatre is in Cardiff.'

'Then the answer is no.'

'Father!' protested Madeleine.

'I'm not having a daughter of mine travelling on the Great Western Railway,' said Andrews, good-naturedly. 'I know it links up with the South Wales Railway but that's just as bad. Take Maddy somewhere on the LNWR instead.'

'He was only joking,' she said as her father went into the kitchen. 'Now I have a chance to give you a proper welcome.'

Colbeck embraced her. 'Isn't this better than reading Charles Dickens?' he said before giving her a kiss. 'I've missed you.'

'I've spent the whole day wondering where you were.'

'We went to Gloucester, Chepstow, Newport and Caerleon,' he said. 'Then I sent Victor Leeming back to

London and went on to Cardiff. It's just as well that I like travelling by rail so much.'

'Has the case been resolved?'

'Not exactly, Madeleine – it's taken a new twist.'

'Do tell me about it.'

They sat beside each other and Colbeck recounted the events of the day. She was startled to hear that the real villain was Hugh Kellow and that the woman claiming to be his sister was equally culpable.

'So who *was* the murder victim?'

'A young man named Martin Henley,' he said. 'I've just come from the undertaker's where I took his father to look at the body. He confirmed that it was his son. I'm sorry I've called at such a late hour but I've been rather busy since I got back to London.'

'Call as late as you like, Robert.'

'You might have gone to bed.'

'Then throw stones at my window. You're always welcome here.' He hugged her again. 'But don't take Father's side over that book next time. I want to read it.'

'Would you rather be reading it now?' They laughed.

She became serious. 'Do you have any idea where they've gone?'

'Not yet,' he confessed.

'They could have fled abroad.'

'I think that's very unlikely,' he said. 'They'd have much more difficulty getting established in a foreign country and they'd have to learn the language. That would be enough to deter them. No, I think they've gone to earth somewhere well outside London.'

'They may be difficult to find, Robert.'

'We found Stephen Voke and his wife.'

'That was different – they were not in hiding.'

'They were in a sense, Madeleine. They were in hiding from his father. After listening to some of the things that Mr Voke did to his son, I'm not surprised that he wanted to break off all communication with the old man. But I agree,' he said, 'Hugh Kellow has taken the trouble to muddy the waters. It won't be easy to track him.'

'Where will you start the search?'

'In Mayfair – that's where Effie Kellow worked.'

'But you thought that she might be using a false name.'

'I'm sure that she did.'

'Then why are you bothering to go to Mayfair?'

'Because the name of her employer was genuine,' said Colbeck. 'At least, I believe it is. She showed us a letter from her so-called brother. It was all part of the deception, of course, and was never actually sent through the post. But it was written by him. It was addressed to Miss Effie Kellow, c/o Mr Dalrymple, Chesterfield Street. When she met Victor and Superintendent Tallis, she showed them another letter from Kellow, explaining that he was going to Cardiff. It seemed very convincing. Mr Kellow thought of everything and planned ahead meticulously.'

'Then he must have planned his escape as well.'

'If he's still in this country, we'll track him down.'

'What if he and this young woman *have* gone abroad?'

Colbeck was determined. 'Then we'll go after them, Madeleine. They can run as far as they wish but we'll stay on their tail.'

* * *

Hugh Kellow rubbed the silver to a high sheen then stood back to admire the effect. Effie came into the room and saw him.

'Have you been polishing it again?' she said, clicking her tongue. 'You'll wear it away if you keep doing that, Hugh.'

'It's all mine now,' he told her, admiring the detail. 'And so it should be. I did nine-tenths of the work and Mr Voke passed it off as his. He always did that. Stephen and I slaved over lots of pieces on our own then, when they were sold in the shop, we'd hear Mr Voke taking all the praise for them. It was unfair.'

'You got your own back.'

'He won't ever do that again, Effie.'

Kellow lifted the coffee pot and placed it on the sideboard where it could catch the light from the window. They were in the parlour at the back of a shop that had not yet opened for business. It was a large room with a floral-patterned wallpaper that had appealed to Effie. There were only a few items of furniture at the moment but they had enough money to buy what they wanted now. They intended to go in search of some armchairs that very morning. The one thing they did not need was a bed. It was their first purchase and had been delivered on the day when they moved into their new home. After scattering their spoils on the coverlet, they had made love with celebratory passion in a flurry of banknotes.

'We're going to be *so* happy here,' she said, looking around.

'It will be worth all the effort.'

'Yes, it was an effort, Hugh. It took me weeks to persuade

Martin Henley to meet me in Cardiff and book that hotel room in your name. I had to offer him all sorts of temptations.'

'As long as they were only offered,' he said.

'You know me better than that, Hugh. You're the only man for me. And you told me to pick someone who looked very much like you. That made it a lot easier,' she recalled. 'I could forget that it was Martin and pretend that it was Hugh Kellow.'

'Hugh Kellow is dead.'

She smiled. 'Well, you seemed to be alive enough last night.'

'As far as everyone is concerned,' he boasted, 'I was murdered in a hotel room. They've probably buried me by now with that miser, Mr Voke, weeping tears over my coffin. That's the beauty of it, Effie. We're in no danger because nobody knows that I still exist.'

'What about Martin?'

'He got what he deserved for chasing my girl.'

'That's not what I meant,' she told him. 'He lived at home with his parents. They'll have started to worry about him. They'll go to the police to report him missing.'

'So?' He gave an elaborate shrug. 'People go missing all the time. Nobody will connect him with the corpse at the hotel because they know that was me. His parents will just think Martin ran away – you told me that he hated living at home.'

'He had no real privacy there.'

'Well, he'll have all the privacy he wants in the grave.'

They laughed harshly and hugged each other. Effie was

wearing a new dress that made her look older and more elegant. There was no hint of the servant about her now. She was mistress of her own house. Kellow broke away and appraised the silver coffee pot again.

'I hope you're not expecting me to make coffee in that,' she warned, 'because it's far too big.'

'I prefer tea, Effie.'

'Mrs Tomkins will have to order a new one.'

'Well, it won't be from Mr Voke because he could never make it. His eyesight is really bad now. Without me, he's completely lost.' He smirked. 'I wish I could have seen the look on Mrs Tomkins' face when she took that tin replica out of the bag. That would have been a sight to behold.'

'There's no crime in taking money from rich people.'

'That's what I believe.'

'We earned every penny, Hugh.'

'We did,' he said, 'and when the shop is open and I start to have customers, we'll earn a lot more. Being my own master has always been my ambition and, when I realised that Mr Voke was not going to let me take over his shop, I knew I had to do something drastic. Shall I tell you something, Effie?'

'What?'

His eyes sparkled. 'I *enjoyed* every moment of what we did.'

'So did I – except when I had to let Martin Henley touch me, that is. I hated that bit. He was so desperate. What I did like,' she went on with a giggle, 'was the fun of deceiving people. They believed every word I said – even those detectives.'

'We can forget about them now. Inspector Colbeck will never know the truth of what happened. We're free to live exactly as we want, Effie,' he declared, lifting her up by the waist and swinging her in a circle, 'and that's what we'll do.'

Victor Leeming had never liked venturing into Mayfair. Its abiding whiff of prosperity offended his nostrils. He was much more at ease in the rougher districts of the city, the teeming rookeries and the dark alleys festering with crime. As he and Colbeck sat in a cab that morning, he looked at the fine Georgian houses that went past.

'This area always brings out the Chartist in me,' he said. 'Why should some people have so much money when most of us don't? I can't believe they got it honestly.'

'You can raise the subject with Mr Dalrymple.'

'I still don't believe that he exists, sir.'

'Then you're going to be surprised,' said Colbeck. 'A good liar always uses enough truth to make a lie convincing. I don't think that Effie plucked a name like Dalrymple out of the air.'

'That doesn't mean she actually worked for him.'

'No, Victor, but I'm ready to bet that she did.'

Leeming ignored the offer of a wager. The cab turned into Chesterfield Street with its tall, symmetrical houses of plain brick. Some of the dwellings had been altered by the addition of porticos, stucco facings, window dressings and even extra storeys. The overall impression was that it was a fashionable and civilised place in which to live. They went to the address they remembered seeing on the letters supposedly sent there by Hugh Kellow. When they explained who they were, they were invited into the house and shown into the library. Eliot Dalrymple soon joined them. He was a portly man of medium height with an excessively pale and well-scrubbed face. They also noticed how white his hands were. Although in his sixties, he looked very well-preserved. After introductions had been made, Colbeck took over.

'I believe that you once employed an Effie Kellow,' he said.

'That's not a name I recognise,' replied Dalrymple, 'though I did have a servant who was called Effie below stairs because she hated her given name. Her grandmother had been called Effie, it seems, and she preferred that.'

'What was her real name, sir?'

'Haggs – Bridget Haggs.'

'That's where she got the name from, Inspector,' said Leeming. 'Don't you remember? She said that her brother was friendly with a young lady called Bridget.'

'To that extent,' said Colbeck, 'she was telling the truth. What she omitted to explain was that *she* was that friend.'

'Where is all this tending?' asked Dalrymple. 'I really don't want to press charges against her.'

'Why should you do that, Mr Dalrymple?'

'If you're here about the girl, then I assumed you'd come to ask about the theft. Before she left, she took some things with her. I was annoyed at the time,' he said, 'but the cost involved was not great so I didn't report it to the police. My wife urged me to do so because she was the real victim.'

'What did Effie steal from her?'

'A large sewing box, Inspector,' said the other. 'My wife's

hobby is embroidery. I had to buy her an even larger box to placate her.'

'How long did the girl work for you, sir?' asked Leeming.

'Oh – the best part of a year, I suppose,'

'And was she satisfactory?'

'As far as I know,' said Dalrymple. 'I don't have much to do with the servants as a rule. I'm a great believer in delegation.'

'But if there had been a problem, you'd have been told.'

'Yes, Sergeant – and there never was. Of course, Effie was not always working here in the house. She did some cleaning for me from time to time.'

'Do you have another property in London?' asked Colbeck.

'I'm a chemist, Inspector. I own a number of shops. I also import pharmaceutical drugs.' He gave a self-effacing shrug. 'Since I was not clever enough to be a doctor like my father,' he admitted, 'I went into an allied profession.'

'So Effie would have cleaned some of the shops?'

'Yes,' said Dalrymple, 'either first thing in the morning before opening time or last thing in the evening. I think she liked the work. I caught her in here once, flicking through one of my books. Though what interest she could have in the wonders of chemistry, I really can't imagine. It did prove that she could read.'

'The young lady can do a lot more than that, sir,' said Colbeck.

'That's why we're anxious to find her,' added Leeming. 'Have you any idea where she went when she left you?'

Dalrymple pursed his lips. 'None at all,' he said. 'I don't

keep track of the comings and goings of my domestics. One day she was here and the next, she was gone.'

'Along with your wife's sewing box, it seems.'

'I'm afraid so, Sergeant.'

'Did you write a reference for her?'

'I was never asked to do so.'

'Then she was not expecting to go into service elsewhere.'

'No,' said Colbeck. 'I suspect that Miss Haggs already had another occupation in view. Thank you, Mr Dalrymple,' he went on, 'we're sorry to have troubled you. What you've told us is extremely useful. There is one final question.'

'And what's that, Inspector?'

'Do any of your shops sell sulphuric acid?'

'It's also known as hydrogen sulphate,' said Dalrymple, 'or oil of vitriol. And, yes, we do keep a stock of it because it has a range of uses if correctly mixed. Were you looking to purchase some, by any chance?'

'Not at the moment, sir.'

They took their leave and waited in the street for a cab. Leeming was glad to have escaped from a house whose rich furnishings had made him feel uneasy. He was relieved that he had not accepted Colbeck's earlier bet. Dalrymple did exist, after all. Effie had peppered her lies with truth.

'What did you make of him, Victor?' asked Colbeck.

'I think he spent his entire life washing his hands. Did you see how clean they were? And I've never seen anyone's skin shine like that before. I tell you,' said Leeming, 'that I felt quite dirty standing next to him. What kind of soap does he use?'

'Go back and ask him.'

'No, no – I don't want to go back in there again, sir.'

'That's where Effie lived for a while,' said Colbeck, studying the house. 'She could have done a lot worse for herself, I suppose.'

'Why did she pinch a sewing box before she left?'

'For the same reason that she stole the acid, I expect.'

'And what's that, Inspector?'

'She needed it.'

Effie pored over the book with a look of intense concentration on her face. She did not hear Kellow come into the room and creep up behind her. When he put his hands over her eyes, she screamed in surprise. He smothered the noise with a kiss.

'What are you reading?' he asked.

'It's one of those books I got from Mrs Jennings' house,' she said. 'It's amazing, Hugh. I never realised there was so much to learn.'

'I know that book inside out. I could recite it to you. Next time you want to know something, just ask me.'

'I was trying to understand what these marks meant.'

She pointed to an illustration of a dinner plate. On its reverse side were five separate marks in a line. Kellow used a finger to point to each one in turn.

'These are the maker's initials,' he explained, 'put there as a kind of signature. Then we have the sterling standard mark, that little lion. Next is the crowned leopard's head, the London mark. The letter "P" tells us the date, which is 1810, and the duty mark at the end is the sovereign's head. George III was still on the throne then.'

'I'll never remember all that.'

'You don't have to, Effie. Your job will be to sew tiny jewels on to fabric. I know how quickly you learn. I'll take care of the silver and gold. There's been a flood of cheap gold from California and Australia in the last few years or so,' he told her, 'so we must take advantage of it. We'll be able to work side by side. While you're sewing, I'll be embossing or engraving or doing a spot of forgery.'

She was worried. 'Forgery?'

'Don't be alarmed,' he said, putting his hands on her shoulders. 'Nobody will ever know. I'm too good at it. All the silverware I stole from Mr Voke has the London mark on it and that will be noticed here. The leopard's head will have to be changed to an anchor.'

'What about Mr Voke's initials?'

'I simply change the L to H so that Leonard becomes Hugh. We can leave the V there because I'm not Hugh Kellow any more, I'm Hugh Vernon. And you,' he said, squeezing her gently, 'are my wife, Mrs Vernon.'

She held up a hand. 'I've got the ring to prove it.'

It was a gold ring that Kellow had made for her at the shop in Wood Street. They had decided to live as husband and wife without the normal prerequisite of a wedding. Indeed, they felt that recent events had brought them much closer than any married couples. They had been welded indissolubly together by murder.

'Are you happy?' he said, pulling her up from the chair.

'I am, Hugh,' she affirmed. 'I never dreamt I'd end up in a place like this. I thought I'd spend the rest of my life in service.'

'That was before you met me, Effie. Do you have any regrets?'

'None whatsoever – I won't let you down, Hugh, I promise. I'm not afraid of hard work. When I'm with you, I could do *anything*.'

'Just remember our new name. One slip could ruin us.'

'It will never happen.'

'Good,' he said, kissing her and pulling her close. 'Welcome to your new home, Mrs Vernon.'

As the cab headed east, Leeming became progressively more at ease. They were no longer surrounded by the London residences of the aristocracy or the prosperous middle class. When he saw down-at-heel tenements flash by, he was happy to be in the sort of district where he had once walked on his beat in uniform. Jewellers' shops and splendid houses were not his natural habit. He felt constricted. At the sight of urchins fighting in the street and beggars scrounging from passers-by, Leeming was much more at home.

'I know what the superintendent will ask us,' he said.

'How do we find them?'

'Yes, Inspector, and, to be honest, I don't have the answer.'

'Neither do I, Victor,' said Colbeck, 'but there are a number of avenues we could explore. For instance, Effie Kellow – alias Bridget Haggs – told us that she and her non-existent brother came from Watford. That was almost certainly *her* birthplace though not Mr Kellow's. I don't think she would have invented a detail like that.'

'So?'

'We can visit every church in the town until we find a record of her birth recorded in the parish register. She's still very young. It may even be that the priest who baptised her is still there and can tell us what happened to the family. If he's unable to help us,' he continued, 'then we look for families who baptised children near the very same time and who are still living in Watford.'

'That could take us ages, Inspector.'

'Exactly – we must try a different approach.'

'Do we investigate Hugh Kellow's past instead?'

'I doubt if we could, Victor. He doesn't seem to have one.'

'Someone must know where he came from originally.'

'That's irrelevant now,' said Colbeck. 'Our main objective is to find out where he's likely to be now.'

'Anywhere in the whole country,' said Leeming.

'I think not.'

'Then where is he, sir?'

'He'll have chosen somewhere that can guarantee him a good living as a silversmith.'

'Then he won't be in Gloucester, I know that much. Jack Grindle won't let him set up shop anywhere near the town.'

'We can eliminate Caerleon as well.'

'Can we?'

'Most definitely,' said Colbeck. 'Kellow has higher ambitions than Stephen Voke. He won't settle for rural tranquillity and a life that revolves around private commissions he can deal with in his own home. Kellow desires real success and he has the skills to secure it. He'll have headed for a large town or a city. I'm hoping that Mr Voke will tell us which one.'

'How will he know?'

'He won't, Victor, but he'll make an educated guess. He's

been in the jewellery trade all his life and built up quite a reputation.'

'What use is that to him now?' asked Leeming. 'Hugh Kellow must have reduced him to bankruptcy.'

'Not quite,' suggested Colbeck, 'but he's certainly lost a vast amount of money. According to his son, he had thousands of pounds in that safe along with his most expensive stock. Kellow got away with a fortune.'

'And I'm sure he planned exactly how to use that money.'

'No question about that.'

'So where is he, Inspector?'

'The best person to tell us that is Leonard Voke. If we can coax him out of his self-pity and get him to think hard, I feel certain that he'll point us in the right direction.' He glanced out of the cab. 'It's not long before we get to Wood Street,' he noted. 'It's getting a name as the haunt of drapers, milliners and haberdashers but it has an illustrious silversmith as well.' Colbeck was confident. 'Mr Voke will help us.'

Leonard Voke arranged his surviving stock on the big table in his workshop. Massed ranks of silverware stood to attention like so many soldiers on parade. Sitting in his favourite chair, Voke checked that the weapon was loaded then placed the end of the barrel in his mouth. After a few minutes of recalling happier memories of his time in Wood Street, he looked at his future and was consumed by despair. His beloved wife was dead, his son had deserted him and his assistant had caused his ruin. He had nothing for which to live. All that lay ahead was despair. His finger jerked, the trigger was pulled, and there was a loud bang. The musket ball shot up through the roof of his mouth, into his brain and out of his skull before lodging in the ceiling. The silver army on the table beside him was drenched in his blood.

'He committed *suicide*?' said Tallis in disbelief.

'We arrived there shortly after it happened, sir,' said Leeming. 'Neighbours had heard the noise of a weapon being fired and gathered outside the shop. Inspector Colbeck and I forced our way in. As you can imagine, it was not a pleasant sight but at least we have no doubt about the identity of the corpse this time.'

'What's happened to the body?'

'We had it removed by the undertaker, Superintendent. The inspector sent for a locksmith to repair the door though I can't believe that any thief would want to steal items covered in blood.'

Shaken by the news, Tallis lowered himself into his chair. In his eyes, suicide was both a crime and a sin, an act of wilful self-murder and an offence against God. Yet he did not condemn Leonard Voke. His fear was that he himself was partly at fault. During his visit to the silversmith, Tallis had been characteristically blunt, telling Voke that he had to shoulder some of the blame for what had happened. It now looked as if his words had provoked the old man to take his own life. The sympathy welling up inside the superintendent was therefore tinged with guilt.

'We thought you ought to know as soon as possible, sir,' said Leeming. 'This is one more horror caused by Hugh Kellow. That young man has left a trail of misery behind him.'

'Yes, yes,' said Tallis, coming out of his reverie. 'Thank you, Sergeant. It's very disturbing news and I needed to hear it. But what were you and the inspector doing in Wood Street?'

'We were hoping to speak to Mr Voke. It's clear that his former assistant wanted to set up as a silversmith somewhere else. Inspector Colbeck felt that Mr Voke might suggest a place where Mr Kellow was likely to go.'

'You got there too late for that, obviously.'

'Yes, sir – discovering the body in that state was a real shock.'

'Stephen Voke will need to be informed.'

'I can give you his address, sir.'

'Thank you,' said Tallis, reaching for a piece of paper and dipping his pen in the inkwell. 'But why did *you* bring me this news and not the inspector?'

'He was talking to another silversmith,' said Leeming, evasively. 'Inspector Colbeck wanted some guidance. He sent me back here first then I'm to meet him at Euston Station.'

'Why – where are you going now?'

'We're continuing the hunt for Hugh Kellow.'

Colbeck reached the house just in time. Madeleine Andrews was coming out of the front door with a large basket over her arm. As the cab rolled to a halt, Colbeck jumped down on to the pavement.

'Robert!' she exclaimed. 'What are you doing here?'

'I've come to take you on a journey.'

'But I was on my way to the market.'

'You can do the shopping another time,' he said, 'unless

284

you'd rather not catch a train with me.'

'I can't go anywhere like this,' she protested, indicating her dress. 'You'll have to wait while I change.'

'You look fine as you are, Madeleine,' he assured her, 'though you might want to leave that basket in the house. I'm afraid there's no time for you to change. Victor is waiting for us at Euston and we don't want to miss the train.'

'Where are we going?'

'Birmingham.'

'Father will be travelling there and back today.'

'Then he might even be driving the engine,' said Colbeck. 'And he can't complain that I'm abducting his daughter. He did give me his permission to take you on the LNWR.'

Madeleine was flustered. 'This is all rather sudden, Robert.'

'That's in the nature of police work, I'm afraid.'

'Is this connected with your investigation?'

'It's very closely connected.'

'Why are we going to Birmingham?'

'It has a Jewellery Quarter,' he said.

While Hugh Kellow busied himself in the shop, Effie walked from room to room in wonder. The novelty of owning a home had still not worn off. Instead of cleaning someone else's house, she would soon be hiring a servant to do all the mundane chores. In time, as the business expanded, Kellow would take on an assistant and perhaps even an apprentice. Mr and Mrs Hugh Vernon would be able to live in comfort and respectability, their crimes buried deep in the past. She was in the main bedroom when Kellow joined her.

'What are you doing up here, Effie?' he asked.

'I was thinking that we needed some new curtains,' she said, fingering the drapes. 'The ones that they left are rather drab.'

'You'll have anything you want in here, my love.'

'We could do with a painting over the bed, Hugh – something with animals on, a country scene. What about an ottoman under the window? That's what Mrs Dalrymple had and I always sat on it for a few minutes when I was supposed to be cleaning their bedroom.'

'Your cleaning days are over, Effie.'

'And it's all thanks to you,' she said, taking his hands and looking up at him. 'You're the cleverest husband in the world, Hugh Vernon, do you know that?'

'It took a lot of planning to get here.'

'I could never have worked everything out like that.'

'It all started when Mr Voke sent me here to deliver something,' he recalled. 'As soon as I stepped into the Jewellery Quarter, I knew it was where I wanted to be. It's like a whole village devoted to precious metal. Whenever I had time off, I'd jump on a train and come to Birmingham just to walk around these streets.'

'We were so lucky to find this place.'

'I had to move fast, Effie. Property is snapped up around here. You'll find people working in the jewellery trade in most of the houses as well as in the factories. What made the difference,' he said, 'was that I was able to pay in cash and outbid everyone else.' He laughed. 'That was partly due to Mr Voke, of course. The old fool didn't realise that I'd been stealing money from his safe for months.'

'You'd earned it, Hugh. You were doing all the work there.'

'I'd hoped to have my name over the shop but it was not to be. I saw a copy of his will in the safe. He'd left everything to his sister in Kent and she'd have no reason to keep the place open. The stock would have been sold off and I'd have been looking for work elsewhere. I felt betrayed. So I decided to go at a time of my own choosing,' he said, 'and to teach Mr Voke a lesson in the process.'

'Between us, we outwitted everyone,' she said, giggling.

He was complacent. 'Yes, Effie – and that includes the police.'

Colbeck had been to Birmingham before while investigating the train robbery that had resulted indirectly in his friendship with Madeleine Andrews. He knew what to expect. It was a big, thriving, major city with a continuous din, smoking chimneys, bustling thoroughfares, shops, offices and factories galore, and with the abiding smell of heavy industry in the air. When they arrived at the station, they took a cab to the police station near the Jewellery Quarter. While Colbeck went in, Madeleine and Leeming were left outside to look around. What seized their attention at once was the tall spire of St Paul's Church.

'It's like the spire of St Martin's-in-the-Fields,' said Leeming. 'I'll be interested to see what the rest of the church looks like – if we get the chance, that is. The trouble with being a policeman is that we never have time to enjoy the sights of places we've been to. We're always on duty.'

'Tell me about Effie Kellow.'

'The inspector did that on the train journey.'

'Robert only talked about the crimes she helped to commit. He didn't really describe her appearance.'

'She's a very pretty young woman, Miss Andrews,' he told her. 'She's quite short and slight but with lovely big eyes. Her real name is Bridget Haggs but she'll be calling herself something else now – and so will Mr Kellow.'

'Why is that?'

'It would be too big a risk to keep it. If he puts the name of Kellow above a shop, there's always the danger that someone might recognise it. He and Mr Voke were well-known in jewellery circles in London. Kellow is a name you'd remember.'

They chatted amiably together. Leeming did not know how close Madeleine and Colbeck really were and he did not try to find out. He simply accepted that they were good friends and he was aware of how much help she had given them on some investigations. He found her extremely companionable. For her part, Madeleine was very fond of the sergeant, always asking after his family and keenly interested to hear how he reconciled married life with the time-consuming job of being a detective. She was still hearing about his children when Colbeck came out of the police station, holding a street map. He spread it out on a low wall.

'Now,' he said, jabbing with his finger, 'we are here at the moment. That's Caroline Street over there, leading to St Paul's Square. It's one place we can eliminate straight away.'

'Why is that, sir?' asked Leeming.

'According to the desk sergeant, no property has been sold there recently. It used to be a residential area though he remembers that merchants, factors, solicitors, an auctioneer and a surgeon also lived there. Many of those fine big houses have now been converted into workshops.' He pointed to the map again. 'The sergeant suggested that we look here in Vittoria Street.'

Leeming grinned. 'It's a funny way to spell the Queen's name.'

'The street commemorates a battle we won against Napoleon's army,' said Colbeck. 'I suggest that we split up, Victor. If you go down Warstone Lane and on to Frederick Street, Madeleine and I will stroll down Vittoria Street. We'll meet up here,' he tapped the map, 'at this point on Graham Street.'

'What am I looking for, sir?'

'Keep your eyes peeled for houses or shops with new owners. I'm told there are some. In fact, the sergeant offered to show me some of them but I said we'd find our own way. The sight of a police uniform would warn them.'

'Very good, Inspector,' said Leeming, moving away. 'I'll be off.'

'I still don't know why you brought me, Robert,' said Madeleine.

'You're much nicer to look at than Victor,' he joked, folding up the map. 'No, Madeleine, I'm hoping to use you as cover. Effie knows what I look like. If she looks out of a shop window and spots me, she'll be on the defensive at once. With you beside me,' he explained, offering his arm, 'I won't get a second glance.'

'Are you convinced that they're here?'

'Not at all – this is something of a gamble.'

'Then it could be a wasted journey?'

'No journey in your company is wasted, Madeleine,' he said with a grin. 'In any case, I did take advice before we left London. I called on Solomon Stern, the jeweller for whom Stephen Voke once worked. I asked him the most likely place where a young silversmith might want to set up shop – especially if he had unlimited funds. Mr Stern had no hesitation in suggesting Birmingham.'

'I do hope that he's right.'

'There's only one way to find out.'

They set off down Warstone Lane, passing narrow alleys and row upon row of small workshops. Madeleine had never seen so many people crammed into a relatively compact area. There seemed to be thousands of them, men and women, all engaged in some aspect of the jewellery trade, their workplaces ranging from a tiny back room to a factory. There was constant traffic in the streets and a sense of urgency in the pedestrians who darted past. Fascinated by the Jewellery Quarter, Madeleine tried to ignore its stench.

'It's almost like being in a foreign country,' she observed.

'Then it's a very rich one,' said Colbeck. 'We're in the middle of a miniature empire of gold, silver and precious stones.'

'I'll keep my fingers crossed that Mr Kellow is here.'

'He must be, Madeleine. It's where *I'd* be in his shoes.'

Strolling arm in arm, they turned into Vittoria Street. Colbeck's eyes missed nothing. He spoke to people standing outside their premises, making casual enquiries that made him sound like a man in search of friends rather than a detective on the trail of criminals. It took them some time to work their way to the end of the street but they were assured of one thing. Under whatever names they were now using, Kellow and Effie were definitely not there. Turning right into Graham Street, they walked on until Leeming hurried towards them.

'Did you have any luck, sir?' he asked.

'No, Victor – what about you?'

'There's one possibility. It's a small shop halfway down the street. I spoke to an engraver who works almost opposite and he told me that a young man and his wife had just moved in.'

'Did he know their names?'

'Mr and Mrs Vernon,' said Leeming. 'They've only been there two minutes. There are shutters on the shop window with a notice pinned to them.'

'What sort of notice?' said Colbeck.

'They're advertising for a servant.'

'That's interesting. They're settling in.'

Madeleine could see what was running through Colbeck's mind. When he turned inquisitively to her, she responded with a smile.

'You want me to apply for the job, don't you?' she said.

'I'm not sure that you could pass for a servant,' he replied. 'You look far too smart and well-bred.'

'I don't feel smart, Robert. I'm happy to do it.'

'Some servants are very well-dressed,' said Leeming. 'Look at the one we met at Mr Dalrymple's house. If you saw her in the street, you'd take her for a member of the family.'

'Besides,' said Madeleine, 'it's not as if I'm really after the job. I simply want to see who is on the other side of the door.'

Colbeck made the decision. 'Thank you,' he said, touching her arm in gratitude. 'It's very good of you to volunteer. With the best will in the world, neither Victor nor I could pass as domestics. But please be careful, Madeleine. Hugh Kellow and Effie may not be there, of course, and the trail will go dead. But if by chance he is, remember that he's a ruthless criminal. Just talk on the doorstep. Don't go inside. If you get invited into the shop and they start to probe, you could be in danger.'

'What do I say?'

'Simply that you've seen the advertisement and would like to know what the job involves and what sort of wage is being offered.'

'I think I can manage that.'

Madeleine was thrilled to be part of the investigation at last. Having been kept on the outside for so long, she had now been brought into action. It showed how much faith Colbeck had in her. Though she knew that she might be confronting someone who had committed heinous crimes, she was not afraid. Colbeck and Leeming would not be far away and there were plenty of other people about. That gave her confidence.

The three of them walked to the end of Frederick Street.

'It's on the left,' said Leeming, pointing a finger. 'Go past that big house with the columns outside and you'll find smaller properties. One of them is a plating workshop. Next to it is a place with the shutters closed. I didn't get the number, I'm afraid.'

'I'll find it,' she said.

'Let's be prepared,' said Colbeck. 'We may be barking up

the wrong tree, I know, but let's assume we're not. We need to cut off every means of escape.'

'Do you want me to guard the rear of the premises, sir?' said Leeming. 'You'll have to give me time to get in position.'

'Off you go, then, Victor.' As Leeming hurried away, he took Madeleine by the shoulders. 'I hope your father will forgive me.'

'There's nothing to forgive, Robert.'

'Isn't there? I take you off as his daughter and return you as a domestic servant.'

She laughed. 'Father won't turn a hair,' she said. 'We do have a servant who comes in to help but otherwise I do the household chores. Father sometimes treats me more or less as a domestic servant so I know what it feels like.' Her eyes widened earnestly. 'Besides, I'd do *anything* to help you, Robert. You must know that.'

She spoke with such affection and looked at him so longingly that he wanted to wrap her in his arms and hold her tight. Colbeck had never loved her more than at that moment. Madeleine Andrews had willingly assisted him in an investigation a number of times, never questioning his decisions and always achieving valuable results on his behalf. Her involvement in his work had brought them closer and closer. Colbeck had to suppress an urge to tell her how much she meant to him and how important she was in his life. But it was not the moment for such confidences. Duty called. There was a strong possibility that they had finally caught up with a killer and his accomplice. Colbeck needed to direct all of his energies at them.

Madeleine had watched him carefully.

'Were you going to say something?' she asked.

'It will have to wait.'

'Why?'

'Never mind that – just trust me.'

'I always do, Robert.'

He nodded in gratitude. 'Let me give you your instructions.'

Colbeck told her exactly what to look for when the door was opened to her. Madeleine was to find out where the newcomers had come from and why they had moved to Birmingham. She had a clear description of Effie and of Hugh Kellow in her head. If neither of them was there, she was to make a polite excuse and withdraw. If, on the other hand, her suspicions were aroused in any way, Madeleine was told to adjust her hat. That was the signal for Colbeck to move in.

'Remember that your safety is paramount,' said Colbeck.

'Yes, Robert.'

'Mr Kellow has a pistol. He won't need much encouragement to use it. At the slightest hint of trouble, walk quickly away.'

'I will.'

He held her hands. 'How do you feel?'

'I'm quite excited.'

'Try to look more deferential. Nobody is excited by housework.'

She grinned. 'That's one thing you *don't* need to tell me.'

They waited for five minutes before moving off. When they reached the big house that Leeming had mentioned, they paused. It was one of the most striking buildings in the Quarter. Colbeck pretended to admire its Doric columns and simple architraves while Madeleine continued on down the street.

Hugh Kellow was having his first taste of work in his new abode. Crouched over a table in the little room next to the parlour, he examined the items he had stolen from Leonard Voke and wrote down their estimated value in his new account book. All of them would bring in a tidy profit and help to establish his reputation even though he had not actually made every piece in the collection. When he heard the doorbell ring, he looked up.

'I'll answer it!' called Effie from the parlour.

'Thank you,' he replied, continuing his inventory.

As with all properties in the Quarter, attention had been paid to its security. Effie had to draw back two large bolts and turn the key in the lock before she could open the door. When she did so, she saw an attractive young woman standing at the doorstep.

'Can I help you?' asked Effie.

'I saw that notice on the shutters,' said Madeleine, injecting a note of humility into her voice. 'You want a servant.'

'Yes, that's right.'

'Could I have the details, please?'

'We're not offering accommodation,' said Effie, enjoying the feeling of superiority she now had as an employer. 'We simply need someone to come in each day to clean and help with the cooking.'

'That would suit me, Mrs…'

'Mrs Vernon. My husband is a silversmith. I should warn you that he hates being disturbed when he's working. Whoever we employ would have to bear that in mind.'

'I'll do whatever I'm told, Mrs Vernon.'

'You don't sound as if you come from Birmingham.'

'No,' said Madeleine, inventing the details. 'I was born in London but, when my father died, Mother and I moved here. We live with my aunt not far away so I've been looking for some time for work in the area.' She glanced at the shutters. 'The shop is not yet open, I see.'

'No, we've only just moved in.'

'Have you come far, Mrs Vernon?'

'Far enough,' replied Effie, guardedly. 'What's your name?'

'Madeleine Andrews.'

'Have you been in service before, Miss Andrews?'

'I worked as a parlour maid in London.'

'Which part of London?'

'How well do you know the city, Mrs Vernon?'

'I know it well enough.'

'I worked in a house near Piccadilly for some years,' said Madeleine, sensing that she might well be talking to Effie. 'I only left there when Father died and we had to move. My mother was born in Birmingham and she'd always wanted to come back here one day.'

'I see.'

'My parents had a little house in Camden but it had too many sad memories for Mother. She had to leave so I gave in my notice. I'm not afraid of hard work, I can tell you that.'

'Good.'

'Which part of London did you live in, Mrs Vernon?'

'It doesn't matter.'

'Do you know Camden at all?'

Effie was abrupt. 'I'll have to discuss this with my husband.'

'Is he at home at the moment?'

'Yes, but he's very busy. I can't bother him now.' She looked Madeleine up and down. 'Can you give me an address where we can reach you?'

'I can always come back tomorrow, if you like,' Madeleine offered. 'You'll have had time to talk to your husband by then.'

Effie's manner changed. 'There's no need for that, Miss Andrews,' she said, dismissively. 'I can see that you're not really suitable for us. Good day to you.'

Giving her a cold smile, Effie closed the door and locked it before Madeleine had time to give any signal. Effie ran along the passageway to the workroom and burst in.

'I'm worried, Hugh,' she said, glancing over her shoulder.

'Why – who was it?'

'It was a young woman called Miss Andrews. She said that she's come about the advertisement but she didn't look like a servant to me. Then there was the other thing.'

He got to his feet. 'What other thing?'

'She asked too many questions. She wanted to know where I'd lived in London and if you were at home. There was something odd about her, Hugh.'

'Which way did she go?'

'I didn't see – I shut the door in her face.'

'There's nothing to be alarmed about,' he told her, putting

297

a hand under her chin and brushing her lips with his own. 'Nobody knows we're here and they never will.'

'I'd feel a lot safer if you take a look at her.'

'Very well – but she's probably gone by now!'

Going to the door, he unlocked it and stepped out into the street. Effie went after him. Several people were walking past in both directions but it was the man and the woman conversing a little distance away who interested him.

'Is that her, Effie?' he asked, pointing.

'Yes,' she said, starting to panic. 'And I know the man's she's talking to – it's Inspector Colbeck. They've found us, Hugh!'

He was horrified. 'How *could* they?'

'What do we do?'

'Get back inside quickly.'

They darted back into the house as Colbeck started to run towards them. Pushing home the bolts, Kellow locked the door then ran up the stairs to retrieve his pistol. He thrust it into his belt. Effie, meanwhile, was grabbing her coat and hat. Kellow pounded down the stairs, unlocked the safe and reached in to take out large wads of banknotes. He stuffed some into his pockets and handed the rest to Effie. They could hear Colbeck ringing the bell and banging on the door. There was no time to waste. Kellow opened the back door and led Effie into the little garden. When they reached the fence, he bent down and hoisted her up without ceremony, hoping that she would climb over to the lane beyond. Instead she let out a loud screech. Waiting for her on the other side of the fence was Victor Leeming.

'Hello, Effie,' he said, raising his hat, 'remember me?'

* * *

After failing to break open the door with his shoulder, Colbeck turned his attention to the shutters. There was a small gap between them that allowed him to take a firm grip on the timber with both hands. Putting one foot against the wall, he pulled hard. The shutters began to creak and splinter then, as he gave one final heave, the lock burst and they flapped open like the wings of some gigantic bird. Colbeck did not hesitate. Whisking off his hat, he used it to protect his face from the shards that flew everywhere when he kicked in the shop window. The noise brought people running. Madeleine was part of a gathering crowd that watched him clamber into the property.

Colbeck cut his hand in the process but ignored the pain and the trickle of blood. He looked into the empty workroom then went on into the parlour. Through the window, he could see into the back garden. Victor Leeming had climbed over the fence and was being held at gunpoint by Hugh Kellow who had one arm around Effie. The couple were backing towards the house. Colbeck was unarmed but he saw something that might offer him some protection. It was the silver coffee pot, gleaming proudly on the sideboard. He picked it up, went into the kitchen and out into the garden.

'Good afternoon, Mr Vernon,' he said smoothly, causing both Kellow and Effie to swing round in alarm. 'I've just been admiring the locomotive you made when your name was Hugh Kellow.'

'Put that down!' snarled Kellow, waving the pistol at him.

'You wouldn't dare fire at me, sir, surely? There's a good chance you might hit this coffee pot and damage the silver.

You don't want that to happen, do you? Consider something else. The bullet could ricochet off anywhere. It might even kill one of you.'

'Stay back!' ordered Kellow, then he turned to face Leeming who had been creeping forward. 'That goes for you as well.'

Leeming held his ground. 'You can't shoot both of us with a single bullet, sir, and you'd never have time to reload.'

'Besides,' said Colbeck, 'there's been enough killing already. Mr Henley was not your only victim.'

Effie was aghast. 'How do you know about Martin?'

'We know far more than you think, Miss Haggs,' he told her. 'We know, for instance, that when you'd been to London with Constable Roberts, you didn't take a cab to Mayfair. You went straight back to Cardiff to act as an accomplice. But there's something that *you* ought to know as well. Indirectly, Mr Kellow caused another death. Leonard Voke committed suicide.'

'Is that true?' asked Kellow with a half-smile.

'The sergeant and I found him earlier today. He shot himself with an old musket. Mr Voke had nothing to live for without his son and his former assistant.'

'Well, don't expect *me* to feel sorry for him!'

'I don't, sir,' said Colbeck with aplomb. 'You'll be too busy feeling sorry for yourself in a condemned cell. Now why don't you put that pistol aside before someone gets hurt?'

'It will be one of you,' warned Kellow, aiming the pistol at each of them in turn. 'Move out of the way, Inspector.'

'I'm sorry but I can't allow you to do that, sir.'

'Move out of the way or I'll shoot. I *mean* it,' said Kellow with desperation. 'We're leaving by the front door.'

'Then you might want to take this with you,' said Colbeck.

He tossed the coffee pot to Kellow who instinctively caught it. Colbeck dived forward to grab the pistol and turn its barrel away so that the bullet went harmlessly up into the air when the gun went off. Leeming, meanwhile, grappled with Effie. Though she screamed, struggled and tried to bite his hand, she was soon overpowered and handcuffed. Hugh Kellow put up more of a fight. Pushing Colbeck away, he dropped the coffee pot and tried to use the butt of the pistol on the detective's head. Colbeck ducked out of the way and flung himself at the man's legs. Kellow was brought crashing to the ground.

The two men rolled over on the grass with Effie yelling at the top of her voice and trying to kick out at Colbeck as he finished up on top. Lifting her up, Leeming carried her yards away from the brawl. Kellow did not give in easily. Driven into frenzy by the thought of execution, he fought like a demon. Colbeck managed to knock the pistol out of his grasp but he had to take several punches to his face and body. With a supreme effort, Kellow flung him sideways then rolled over on top of him, spitting into his eyes then trying to gouge them with his fingers. Colbeck responded with a solid punch to the nose and felt Kellow's blood dribbling over his face. The two men flailed around on the grass, neither of them giving any quarter. They grappled, twisted, pushed, pulled, squeezed and traded punches.

There was a point when Leeming thought he might have to intervene but it quickly passed. Colbeck was far too strong and experienced. In the course of his career as a detective, he had had to make many arrests of violent men. It had built up his stamina. Though the silversmith was fighting to save his life, he was no match for Colbeck. His strength at last began to fade. In a last bid to escape, he tried to get up and run away but his legs were scythed from beneath him by Colbeck's foot. Kellow fell headfirst on to the grass. Before he could move, he felt a knee in his back and a pair of handcuffs being snapped on to his wrists. Bruised, dishevelled and with his frock coat torn, Colbeck stood up and hauled his prisoner to his feet. Kellow was breathless and exhausted. Effie was weeping.

Colbeck bent down to pick up the silver coffee pot and brush away some specks of dirt. He inspected it carefully all over.

'It's in perfect condition,' he said, approvingly. 'It will go to its proper home at long last.'

The two prisoners were given a temporary home in the police station nearby. While Effie and Kellow had their first experience of being locked up, Colbeck cleaned the blood from his face and brushed some of the dirt from his coat. Two policemen were sent off to secure the property bought by Kellow so that nothing could be stolen. Leeming had the coffee pot locomotive in a leather bag. He was puzzled when Colbeck asked him to wait at the police station.

'But we have to take the prisoners back to London, sir,' argued Leeming, eager to relay word of their triumph to Edward Tallis.

'All in good time,' said Colbeck.

'Where are you going?'

'I have some business to take care of, Victor.'

'Shall I come with you?'

'I think not. This is an expedition that can only ever involve two people. You'd be highly embarrassed and feel that you were in the way. We'll not be long.'

'As you wish, sir,' said Leeming, wondering what he meant.

Colbeck went through into the outer office where Madeleine was talking to the desk sergeant. She was surprised that he was alone.

'What about your prisoners?' she asked.

'They can wait.'

'Why the delay?'

'Let's step outside,' he suggested, 'and I'll explain.'

Colbeck took her out and surveyed the streets facing them. He was irritated by the tear in his coat but, since it was under his arm, it was not very noticeable. It certainly would not prevent him from taking what would be an extremely important walk. Madeleine was still bewildered.

'What about the sergeant?'

'Victor can cool his heels while we take a stroll.'

'Where are we going, Robert?'

'We're going to take advantage of a unique opportunity,' he said, holding her hands. 'It seems perverse to come to a Jewellery Quarter without buying some jewellery. I thought that we might look in a few windows.'

'Why?'

He smiled at her. 'Why else?'

Madeleine could not believe what she was hearing. It

made her head spin. As his smile broadened into a grin, her heart began to pound and she felt unsteady on her feet. Standing outside a police station in Birmingham seemed the most unlikely place for her to receive a proposal of marriage. Yet, in another sense, it was highly appropriate. She knew that Colbeck was wholly committed to his work as a detective and that any wife of his would have to accept that. Madeleine was happy to do so. She loved him enough to take him on any terms. Yet she was still troubled by uncertainty.

'Do you mean what I hope you mean, Robert?' she asked.

'I think it's high time we put your father's mind at rest,' he replied, taking her hands. 'I know that he thinks I'm trying to lead his lovely daughter astray. I need to show him that my intentions are honourable.'

'Everything you do is honourable.'

'When you have a ring on your finger, he may finally learn to trust me. You won't have to put up with his badgering any more. If, that is,' he went on, 'you accept me.'

Madeleine was overjoyed. Her mind was filled with dozens of things she wished to say but her lips refused to open. All that she could do was to luxuriate in the moment. Something she had dreamt about for years had finally become a reality. It was intoxicating.

'Well?' he pressed. She nodded her head vigorously. 'Thank heaven for that. I had a horrible feeling that you'd reject me.'

'There was never any danger of that, Robert,' she said, finding her voice at last. 'The answer is yes – yes – yes!'

Colbeck removed his hat so that he could kiss her on the lips. Then he embraced her warmly. They stood there in silence for some while, savouring the moment. Eventually, she looked up at him.

'What made you decide to ask me here?' she asked. 'It's hardly the most romantic place. You caught me completely off guard.'

'Is that a complaint?''

She laughed with pleasure. 'No, no, I'm delighted.'

'And I'm thrilled, Madeleine. Fate must have brought us here for a purpose and it wasn't simply to arrest two people. I'm sorry it wasn't quite how you might have hoped it would be but I just couldn't help myself. When we were waiting for Victor to get into position at the rear of the house, I had this sudden impulse. I knew that I wanted to spend the rest of my life with you and not simply be an occasional visitor to your house. I love you, Madeleine.'

'I love *you*, Robert – even with those bruises on your face.'

He put a hand to his cheek. 'When your father sees the state I'm in, he'll think that you've beaten me into submission.'

'I don't care what he thinks.'

Neither do I.' He offered his arm and she took it. 'Let's see what Birmingham has to offer us in the way of rings, shall we?'

Edward Tallis was so pleased to hear of the arrests that he produced a bottle of brandy from a drawer and poured a generous amount into two glasses. Handing one to Victor Leeming, he raised the other one in a silent toast before taking a long sip.

'I think we deserved that, Sergeant,' he said. 'Congratulations!'

'Thank you, sir,' said Leeming, taking a more tentative sip. 'Though the person you ought to be congratulating is the inspector.'

'Were the fellow here, I'd happily do so. Where is he?'

'He'll be here before too long. He wanted to make sure that the prisoners were in safe custody.'

Leeming knew full well that Colbeck was taking Madeleine Andrews back home before returning to Scotland Yard but he did not tell that to his superior. Nor did he let him in on the secret that the inspector was now engaged to marry. Madeleine had returned from Birmingham with an expensive ring on her finger. Leeming was touched to be the first person who knew about the betrothal and he had wished the couple health and happiness.

'Mind you,' said Tallis on reflection, 'any praise I give to the inspector must be tempered with criticism. He did make a mistake.'

'He'll be the first to admit it.'

'The pair of you went chasing after Stephen Voke in the certainty that he was the villain – so much for Inspector Colbeck's reputation for infallibility!'

'Even the best horse stumbles, sir.'

'Quite so, quite so,' confessed Tallis. 'I myself am not free from blame here. I stumbled badly in Wood Street. In telling Mr Voke that he'd alienated his son by his behaviour and created a desire for revenge in his assistant, I fear that I may have pushed him another step towards the frightful decision to take his own life.'

'That was hardly your fault, sir,' said Leeming, surprised by the frank admission. 'Leonard Voke was a fine silversmith but he was a poor father and a miserly employer. The wonder is that he got *anyone* to work for him. I'm sorry for what happened to him but I fancy that he brought it all on himself.'

'My conscience is still troubled.'

'I don't see that it should be.'

'My manner can be too forthright at times.'

Leeming was about to agree with him wholeheartedly but chose to sip his brandy instead. He did not wish to imperil such a unique occasion. As a rule, the superintendent's office was a place of great discomfort for him. Yet the sergeant was actually enjoying a visit there for once. Nothing must be allowed to spoil that. As the brandy coursed through him, Leeming remembered someone else who merited praise.

'If I might make a suggestion, sir,' he began.

'Go on.'

'Superintendent Stockdale of the Cardiff Borough Police has been extremely helpful to us at every stage. I believe that he deserves a letter of thanks from you – if not from the commissioner.'

'I'll be glad to write it,' said Tallis.

'Then the inspector can deliver it by hand tomorrow.'

'Oh?'

'He's going back to Cardiff so that he can return the stolen property to Mrs Tomkins. After all this time, she'll be so relieved to get her hands on that silver coffee pot. Inspector Colbeck is looking forward to the moment when he can at last give it to her.'

* * *

There was no performance of *Macbeth* on Sunday but Madeleine Andrews nevertheless enjoyed the visit to Cardiff. After a train journey together, she and Colbeck had the pleasure of delivering the coffee pot locomotive to Winifred Tomkins and of repaying her husband the money that was stolen. Elated beyond measure, Winifred pressed for details.

'Where did you find it, Inspector?' she asked, caressing it.

'It was in Birmingham, Mrs Tomkins.'

'Whatever was it doing there?'

'Mr Kellow had bought a shop in the Jewellery Quarter and intended to work there under a false name. He had no intention of ever parting with your locomotive but,' he said, modestly, 'I persuaded him to do so.'

'I feel ashamed that I ever doubted you.'

'Yes,' said Tomkins. 'I shall be writing to your superior to tell him how grateful we are for what you and Sergeant Leeming did for us. Having this coffee pot at last changes everything.'

'I'm glad to hear it, sir,' said Colbeck.

Winifred sniggered. 'Lady Pryde will be so put out.'

'I assume that you won't be inviting her in for coffee.'

Tomkins guffawed. 'Not blooming likely!'

The visitors stayed long enough for an exchange of pleasantries then they withdrew. When they left the Tomkins residence, Madeleine was still dazed. She looked back at the mansion.

'I've never been in a house that big,' she said. 'It was like a small castle. How can two people need somewhere so palatial?'

'They're making a statement to the world, Madeleine.'

'Then it's a very loud one.'

'Loud and altogether too ornate for my liking,' said Colbeck. 'I hope you're not expecting us to have a home like that.'

'I'll be happy *anywhere* with you, Robert.'

'That's reassuring.'

Driven back into the city, they went in search of Jeremiah Stockdale, who had just returned from a service at St John's Church. They met at the police station. The superintendent was very interested to meet Madeleine and – when told of it – he congratulated them on their betrothal. He could not, however, keep his eyes off the bruises on Colbeck's face.

'Do I take it that Mr Kellow resisted arrest?' he said.

'Very briefly,' replied Colbeck.

'Where is he now?'

'He and Effie are safely locked up behind bars. They had hoped to open a jeweller's shop in Birmingham but they were not welcome there. Some ruffian actually kicked their shop window to pieces.'

He gave an attenuated account of what had happened, drawing attention to the part played by Madeleine. Stockdale was impressed.

'Effie was no mean actress herself,' he said, 'but you seem to have been her equal, Miss Andrews.'

'Thank you,' she replied.

'Acting skills have been at the heart of this whole business,' remarked Colbeck. 'We had Effie playing the role of a bereaved sister, Kate Linnane appearing as Lady Macbeth and as a kidnap victim, and Madeleine taking on the mantle of a servant.'

'Miss Andrews gave the most effective performance,' decided Stockdale, 'because it helped to catch two killers. I don't have the slightest pity for them. If I lived in London,' he added, 'I might be tempted to see what sort of a performance they give on the scaffold.'

'I'll be too busy working on the next case to do that.'

'So will I, Inspector. Cardiff throws up new problems each day.'

'But it's not without its charms,' said Colbeck.

'Oh, it's a fine town,' agreed Stockdale, chuckling. 'That's why I settled down here. Clifford Tomkins and Archelaus Pugh keep telling me that Merthyr is bigger and better but this is the place for me. I hope to see out my three score years and ten here. Merthyr may have a glorious past but it's Cardiff that will have a glorious future.'

Colbeck offered his hand. 'Thank you for all that you did, Superintendent,' he said, feeling Stockdale's firm grip. 'You had much more than an honourable mention in my report on the investigation.'

'I was glad to work beside the Railway Detective,' said Stockdale. 'You and Sergeant Leeming once helped me with a case that took me to London. It was good to be able to return the favour.'

'I sincerely hope that we work together again.'

After a round of farewells, Colbeck and Madeleine left the police station and stepped out into the wide thoroughfare of St Mary Street. It was a fine day and the town was bathed in bright sunshine. People drove past in traps or open carriages. Shop windows shimmered, pavements had been swept clean and pedestrians were wearing their Sunday best. It was a good day to visit the town.

'Superintendent Stockdale is not the only man who deserves thanks,' said Colbeck. 'People like your father are the real heroes.'

'Why is that, Robert?'

'They drive the trains that helped us to move about the country so easily. That was a godsend. Without them, we'd have struggled to bring this investigation to an end.'

'What happens now?' she asked.

'I'm going to show you the sights of Cardiff,' he replied. 'When we've found a restaurant and had a meal, we'll see all the things that the superintendent has been telling me about.'

Madeleine issued a warning. 'We mustn't be too late back.'

'Why is that?'

'Father will be expecting me.'

'There's no hurry. Let him wait. It will give him more time to read *Dombey and Son.*'

'What train will we catch this evening?'

Colbeck grinned. 'The slowest one,' he said.

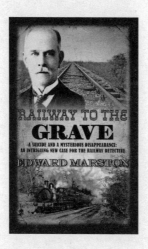